PRAISE FOR PAMELA CH
ARABELLA BEAUMON

Death Among the Ruins

"Diverting . . . fluid prose speeds the plot along . . . this romp will appeal to those who don't take their historicals too seriously."
—*Publishers Weekly*

"Arabella Beaumont returns for another zany adventure . . . a diverting caper which turns many of the Regency stereotypes upside down."
—*Booklist*

"Intriguing and well-plotted." —*RT Book Reviews*

Death and the Courtesan

"What a delicious and delightful tale! The Regency world is turned upside down—and much refreshed—by a decidedly unorthodox heroine. Pamela Christie writes with wit and verve, gifting readers with a vision of the period at once marvelously scandalous and oh-so tempting. I adore clever, spunky Arabella and look forward to her future adventures."
—Sara Poole, author of *The Borgia Mistress*

"A clever, funny, engaging read reminiscent of Fidelis Morgan's *Unnatural Fire*. Pamela Christie deftly combines the conventions of the Regency-era novel with the fast pace and careful attention to characterization found in the best modern historical mysteries."
—Kate Emerson, author of *The King's Damsel*

"A smart, witty and thoroughly entertaining read! It reminds me of some of my favorite series on *Masterpiece Theatre*."
—Diane Haeger, author of *I, Jane*

Books by Pamela Christie

DEATH AND THE COURTESAN

DEATH AMONG THE RUINS

DEATH AND THE CYPRIAN SOCIETY

Published by Kensington Publishing Corporation

DEATH *and the* CYPRIAN SOCIETY

PAMELA CHRISTIE

KENSINGTON BOOKS
www.kensingtonbooks.com

KENSINGTON BOOKS are published by

Kensington Publishing Corp.
119 West 40th Street
New York, NY 10018

All Kensington titles, imprints, and distributed lines are available at special quantity discounts for bulk purchases for sales promotion, premiums, fund-raising, educational, or institutional use.

Special book excerpts or customized printings can also be created to fit specific needs. For details, write or phone the office of the Kensington Special Sales Manager: Kensington Publishing Corp., 119 West 40th Street, New York, NY 10018. Attn. Special Sales Department. Phone: 1-800-221-2647.

Kensington and the K logo Reg. U.S. Pat. & TM Off.

eISBN-13: 978-0-7582-8645-1
eISBN-10: 0-7582-8645-7
First Kensington Electronic Edition: January 2015

ISBN-13: 978-0-7582-8644-4
ISBN-10: 0-7582-8644-9
First Kensington Trade Paperback Printing: January 2015

10 9 8 7 6 5 4 3 2 1

Printed in the United States of America

To Tom Biddison, MED,* DDD;**

For three decades of
hilarious friendship and
faithful adventures.

*Mean, Elderly Doctor
**Darling, Darling Doctor

Disclaimer: English history buffs are bound to note that there was no pier extant at Brighton in 1813. The one that appears between these covers is, like the rest of this book and novels in general, a figment of the author's imagination.

Chapter 1

Imagine, reader, a small, secret room, hidden away from the world; a room so private as to be without windows, its only illumination provided by a few candles and a dirty skylight. A room—well, more of a closet, really—with nothing in it but a bed. And what more would one need? A decanter of plum cordial and two glasses, perhaps? But those are extra!

Now picture an amorous couple in this chamber. Young and comely, the partners murmur softly as they assist one another to undress: White Alençon lace and velvet livery whisper over smooth, young limbs and drop to the floor. Shifting light from passing clouds filters through the skylight, and in the patterns that dance upon the wall, the heads of this couple, close together, form the shadow of a single heart.

Passionate moans. A rustling of sheets. The mingled scents of candle grease and vanilla toilet water, carried aloft by the flaming wicks, rise toward the ceiling, where a row of human eyes peers down at our lovers from behind the loose weave of the burlap wall covering.

Only the occasional lewd gleam of an eyeball betrays the presence of these silent watchers, each of whom has paid half as much again as the pair utilizing the bed—this couple who, all unknowing, has provided an afternoon's entertainment for a collection of dissipated degenerates.

"Well . . . ? How do I look?" Constance demanded, bursting into the pergola and thrusting her homely face at the younger Beaumont sister. "Am I not beautiful?"

"Of course," said Belinda kindly. "I have always thought so."

Constance flung her hideous reticule toward the opposite bench, causing Belinda's little greyhound to leap aside with a terrified yelp.

"No," she said, "but I mean, *especially*. Now. Am I not beautiful *now?*"

To be frank, she was not. With her thin lips and powerful jaw, Miss Worthington bore an unsettling resemblance to men in pantomimes who pretend to be women for comic effect. That her breasts were unusually large only served to heighten the impression, for males invariably exaggerate this attribute when they cross-dress, even when they are not trying to be funny.

"She's had something done," murmured Arabella, making an entry in her stud book.* "Something to her face or hair or something."

"Yes, I have," said Constance defensively. "I've spent the entire morning at La Palais de Beautay!"

"Oh! Have you really?" cried Belinda, and she began to chant from the advertisements:

---

*This was not the traditional type of registry in which thoroughbred bloodlines are documented, but a catalogue of London's most attractive men, complete with measurements and other personal details. Such directories pertaining to the city's *women* had long been available, but, so far as Arabella knew, there had never before been any kind of book for women about the men by whom they were surrounded. Her compendium, nearly finished now, was all-inclusive, and the making of it had afforded the author great personal satisfaction. She had enjoyed the research, particularly.

"'Eyes will brighten, skin will soften.
Men will smile, and glance your way often.
Eternally Fair'"

"—From cotillion to coffin!" muttered Arabella, under her breath.

"Bell says their claims are preposterous," Belinda explained, "and she is a very clever woman, but the rest of us do so want to believe in miracles, don't we? Well . . . ?" she asked. "Is it true, then? Are their methods efficacious?"

"Apparently not," replied Constance bitterly. "I have just spent thirty-eight pounds for a series of skin enhancifiers, and no one can tell the difference!"

She plumped down on the bench next to Belinda, heedless of the number of little violet and lavender cushions she squashed or displaced.

"I can see a difference," said Arabella, without looking up.

"You *can?*"

"Yes. Your sprint through the upper garden has pinkened your cheeks."

"'Pinkened'? Is that even a word?"

"It is now," Arabella grumbled resentfully. Belinda was on the point of leaving for Scotland. The sisters had brought their small occupations with them from the house in order to spend as much of their remaining time together as possible— Arabella, as has been seen, had brought her stud book, and Belinda was knitting an athletic supporter for a gentleman of whom she was fond—and the advent of Constance to their poignant garden idyll had not been welcome.

"Now, Bell," chided Belinda, who was more polite than Arabella was, "La Palais de Beautay is being touted all over town, by some of London's most famous beauties."

"*I* am one of London's most famous beauties, and I am no tout!"

"*Some* of them, I said. Perhaps, Constance, as it's a series of treatments, the effects won't be noticeable till your fourth or fifth session."

"This was my *fourteenth!*" wailed the visitor. "And anyhow, you are not to call me 'Constance' anymore. It's 'Costanze' now."

Belinda blinked. "'Costanze'? Whatever for? The name scarcely suits you!"

"That is what *you* think!" replied Costanze with withering scorn.* "Madame Zhenay, La Palais's proprietor—'la' stands for 'the' by the way did you know that I didn't—thinks otherwise for 'twas she herself gave it me along with *this!*"

She thrust her jingling red glove at Belinda, as though to punch her.

"Dear God!" exclaimed Arabella, looking up at last and leaning across the table for a closer inspection. "What is that?"

"My new-pink-and-blue-enamel-flowers-and-birds-and-crystals-charm-bracelet-on-a-gilt-chain-with-silver-coin-pendant-clasp. Don't you wish that you had one?"

"Not particularly," said Arabella. "I have just donated all my useless and ugly things to the Effing jumble sale."

"It is exceeding pretty," Belinda lied. "Did Madame Zhenay give it you for being such a faithful customer?"

"Well, in a way. She sold me this new-pink-and-blue-enamel-flowers-and-birds-and-crystals-charm-bracelet-on-a-gilt-chain-with-silver-coin-pendant-clasp for a very reasonable price."

"Bracelets are usually sold in pairs," observed Arabella. "Don't tell me you actually possess *two* of those monstrosities!"

"No," replied Costanze defensively, "Madame Zhenay says single bracelets are all the rage just now!"

---

*Whenever this young woman spoke more than a single sentence, her words tended to come tumbling out like storm water from a sewer pipe, heedless of punctuation other than full stops, exclamations, and the occasional question mark. It was a style of speaking that found favor in certain masculine circles, where it was fondly and condescendingly referred to as "women's chatter."

"So she has doubled her profit by selling one to you, and the mate to some other booby," said Arabella. "How much were you charged for this?"

"Twenty-seven pounds. But it is worth a great deal more."

"Oh? I suppose Madame told you that, too, did she?"

"Naturally! Otherwise I should have had no idea what a new-pink-and-blue-enamel—"

"Costanze, dear," said Belinda, fingering the hideous dangly bits. "What do you call this thing *for short?*"

"There is no short," Costanze replied. "It's simply my new-pink-and—"

"Whilst you are here," said Arabella, "I should prefer that you refer to it—if refer to it you must—as a bracelet."

Costanze sniffed. "Madame Zhenay believes in calling things by their true names and so do I! 'Tis the fashion these days."

"If Madame Zhenay believed in calling things by their true names," said Arabella, "she wouldn't be calling herself 'Madame Zhenay'! The woman's probably as common as come-ask-it! I'll hazard she wanted a French-sounding appellation, but not speaking the language and fearing to be found out by the many who do, she has opted instead for an Assyrian spelling. Nobody round here speaks *that.*"

Costanze's intrusion had unsettled everyone, and now that she had apparently run out of things to talk about, an awkward silence fell over the little company. Fortunately, the parlor maid appeared a moment later carrying a tea tray piled with delicate lavender cups and saucers. For it was a Lustings custom to offer tea to any visitors who stopped by, regardless of the hour, and even if it were only Constance.

"Look at this, Fielding," said Arabella, holding out her visitor's arm to display the gaudy bauble. "What do you think? I'll let you have it for two and six."

The arm's owner squawked in protest.

"No, thank you, miss," said the parlor maid, expertly lay-ing the cloth and setting out the sweet and savory dishes and the little, golden teaspoons. "I don't hold wi' trash such as that."

Her mistress raised an eyebrow. "I think you must be mistaken, Fielding. This bibelot cost Miss Worthington twenty-seven pounds! It is a rare and costly piece!"

"Your friend was rooked then, wasn't she, miss? If you'll excuse me, I'll go and fetch the teapot now."

Arabella gave Costanze her arm back.

"Madame *Zhenay!*" she sneered to herself.

"Well," said Belinda, not unreasonably, "La Palais de Beautay has made pots of money, so I cannot see that it signifies how the proprietor chuses to spell her name."

"Oh!" cried Costanze. "Pots of money! That reminds me of something I was going to say! Do you remember that forty-six thousand pounds I owe you, Bell?"

"Do I remember it?" Arabella asked. "Do I *remember* it? Constance, I cannot see your face or hear your voice without being somehow reminded of it. I cannot read the words 'constant' or 'worthy' or 'ton' without speculating on how soon you will be able to repay me."

And then, because this person always had to have things explained in a particular way, she added, "Yes, Constance, I do remember that forty-six thousand pounds you owe me. What about them? Do you recall what I taught you?"

"I . . . uh. I am to tell Pigeon everything, and then ask him to write me . . ."

"No," said Arabella.

"Write *you* a checque for that amount. Only it's to say 'pay to bearer' instead of your name. And you are to come and collect . . ."

"No . . ."

"That is, *he* is to collect . . ."

"Constance . . ."

"I told you, Bell; it's *Costanze* now."

"What is to happen to the checque, Miss Worthington?"

"Pigeon will post it to you."

Pigeon Pollard was Costanze's wealthy new protector, who was going to be recompensing Arabella for all the money his mistress had scrounged from her over the years. Mr. Pollard did not know he was going to do this, but Arabella, who had kept meticulous records of every penny Constance had ever borrowed from her, felt certain that he would. The payments were to be disguised as his inamorata's monthly allowances, and Mr. Pollard was going to be told that Arabella would be keeping the money in trust for her. After all, if Pigeon was so mad about Constance, how bright could he be?

"Very good, Constance," said Arabella. "Because . . . ?"

"Because, if I were to bring it here, I should either lose it or spend it on the way over!"

"*Très bien,*" said Arabella, passing her a plate of confections. "That 'stands for' very good. Would you care for a coconut biscuit?"

"Oh, yes! Might I have two?"

"Just this once. Remember, though, you don't want to lose your figure, or you might lose Pigeon, and then where should we be?"

"I hate to think."

"Yes, dear; I know you do."

Fielding returned with the teapot, and Arabella distributed the fragrant libation with a practiced hand.

"Pigeon is such an odd nickname!" Belinda mused, tipping a little scalding tea into her saucer to cool it. "Where does it come from?"

"Oh, from his friends, I expect," replied Costanze.

"No, we know that," said Arabella. "Bunny meant, why? Does he breed pigeons? Or race them? Is he excessively fond of hunting them or eating them? Does he look like a pigeon?

Is he an easy mark? Did he return from some exotic locale, speaking 'pidgin'? Or was his wife overheard to have called him that, once?"

" 'Speaking Pigeon'?" asked Costanze. "Do you mean to tell me that they have their own language? How interesting! I must ask him!"

"Constance. You will do no such thing."

"No I shall. Indeed I shall! If Mr. Pollard can speak to pigeons he must be able to understand what they answer back mustn't he? And there is a particular question that I have always wanted to ask them!"

"Oh, Lord!" murmured Arabella. "If she asks him whether he can speak to birds, he will certainly drop her, and then I may just go and sing for my money!"

"Not necessarily," said Belinda. "I'm told he loves it when she talks nonsense."

"Well, he would have to, wouldn't he? Even so, there are limits to how much a man can stand, despite his predilections."

Here the reader might well wonder at the Beaumont sisters conversing in this open fashion before the very person they were disparaging, but they knew their friend of old; knew everything there was to know about her, which was not a great deal, and one of those things was the fact that she never marked what people said unless they addressed her directly. Hence, you could sit next to Constance and talk about her in a normal tone of voice to a third party or a roomful of third parties, with full confidence that she would fail to heed you. This was especially likely if she had something else upon which to focus her attention meanwhile, and in this case, like the coconut biscuits absorbing her tea, the process of dunking and eating them had completely absorbed Miss Worthington's powers of concentration.

"For instance," said Arabella, spearing a lemon slice with

an exquisite little fork, "what do you suppose it is that Constance has always wanted to ask of pigeons?"

"Why they keep defiling Charles the First?"

"That would be the obvious thing, wouldn't it? No; it has to be something much sillier, even, than that. Something so stupid that neither you nor I could possibly anticipate it. Let us see, shall we? Constance," said Arabella, "what question have you always wanted to ask of pigeons?"

Her guest looked up, a few moist crumbs adhering to her chin. "How they fly," she said, around a mouthful of biscuit and tea.

"How they fly," Arabella repeated slowly. "And why should you want to ask them that?"

"Well so that I may learn to fly too of course! I should have thought that was obvious! Really Arabella you should try to use your head a little more."

Belinda choked on her tea, and had to be thumped on the back for a bit. When she had recovered, Arabella addressed herself to Costanze once again.

"Do you really think I should use my head?" she asked. "Why is that?"

"Because," replied Miss Worthington gravely, "our brains are like hedgehogs. Without regular exercise they simply go to sleep."

Arabella and Belinda exchanged glances.

"Oh!" said Costanze "That is what I was going to tell you! Last night . . . I saw a hedgehog! No. No, I didn't. Last night as my brain was going to sleep . . . Yes! That's it! Last night as I was going to sleep I couldn't. Not for the longest time. Because I was upset over that letter that came under the door but I'm all right now; I just had to get used to the idea."

"What idea, Constance?"

"Well, someone knows a secret of mine that I never told anybody and *they* won't tell anybody either as long as I pay them . . . pay them . . . I forget how much. It's in the letter. So I won't be able to pay you that forty-six thousand pounds because you see I need to pay it to this other person whoever he is because if I don't pay him he will tell Pigeon what I've been getting up to lately with Lady Ribbonhat's footman and then Pigeon will cast me off and I shall be a pauper again."

"What . . . did you . . . say?"

"Don't look at me like that, Bell! It isn't *my* fault!"

"Not your *fault?* You've been having it off with Ribbonhat's footman! How is that not your fault?"

"Oh!" Costanze squawked. "*You* know my secret, too! That must mean that *you* wrote that letter! You . . . you . . ."

"Shut your cock pocket*!" said Arabella sternly. "Here it is: Either you find a way to pay me back the entire forty-six thousand pounds by this time next year, and make me a substantial payment six weeks from today, or I will take you to court, and instruct the bailiffs to seize all your convertible property whatsoever. That means all your gowns, all your jewels—excepting that bracelet—the house Pigeon has made over to you, your carriage, and your horses. Do you understand? I have just bought an hotel, and I need that money. I need it soon, or I shall go to debtor's prison. That is where you will be. And if I am there because of you, I will make it my business to pinch, scratch, slap, and cuff you every day, Constance. And when I cannot sleep at night, owing to the fleas, I will come over to your pile of straw and kick you all over, till you are as tender as a veal cutlet!"

Costanze was wailing by this time, and her persecutor suffered a momentary qualm, for society abhors the mistreatment of mental defectives, and regards such behavior as cruel and uncivilized. But Arabella was able to reassure herself that

---

*Both Beaumont sisters disliked indecorous language and, after a few early experiments, had dispensed with it nearly altogether, except when "exceeding vexed," as Arabella now was. But being broad-minded, they were not offended when to coarse invective others had recourse, of course.

insofar as Constance was concerned, extreme measures were often necessary, in order to make the poor little moron understand that she had erred.

"I want my handkerchief!" sniffled the moron, fumbling amongst the bench cushions. "Where is it?"

"In that ridicule reticule, I expect," grumbled Arabella.

"But where's that?"

"You flung it through the moon window* when you barged in here."

"*What?* Why ever didn't you tell me?! It will have landed in the brook and gone all the way to sea by now!"

And in the blink of an eye, Costanze had scrambled down the little hill and run off along the stream bank, shrieking as she went, as if the purse might hear her, answer her, and so be pulled out again.

Arabella, seething all to herself, plucked a lavender-tinted flower from one of the stems twined round a pergola column and proceeded, methodically, to tear it to fragments. A veritable study in anger, she might have sat for a portrait of Alecto, and Belinda almost fancied she could see the giant wings of vengeance sprouting from her sister's shoulder blades.

"Do not think about this now, Bell," she said quietly. "Let it settle for a bit. We can decide what is to be done after Costanze leaves."

"*If* she leaves," growled her sister.

In the distance they could see Miss Worthington returning, in her green striped frock, bright red gloves, and blue bonnet with brown flowers.

"Why on Earth does she dress like that?" asked Arabella, in

---

*The pergola did not have walls, of course, but its two benches were elegantly backed with wooden slats, in Japanese patterns. The bench facing away from the stream had a large, round opening cut into its back, so that persons seated opposite might have a frame from which to view the water.

an effort to distract her thoughts. "Has she no maid to guide her sartorial choices? Does she never look into a mirror?"

"You know how Costanze is," said Belinda, as she buttered a muffin. "Stubborn as an ox, and equally as intelligent."

Cara followed the buttering activity with melting eyes. Her tail barely moved, and the rest of her stayed as still as a statue until at last her mistress fed her half.

"Hmm," said Arabella. "That is interesting."

"What is?"

"Your experiment. I presume you are trying to discover whether a miniature greyhound, grown fat enough, will snap its legs off with its own weight."

"Cara will have plenty of opportunities for exercise once we get to Scotland. The park at Redwelts is said to be enormous."

"So I have heard. I shall miss you sorely, Bunny."

"And I you! We must promise to write one another every—"

"Oh!" wailed Costanze, bursting into the pergola for the second time that morning and practically running into Fielding, who had just arrived to clear away the tea things, "it's gone, it's gone! I shall never see it more!"

"See *what* more?" asked Arabella testily.

"My reticule! My favorite one! Such a gay yellow silk! Such a profusion of maroon beads and gray rosettes! I'll never find another like it! Never! Never!"

"Was there something important inside it?" asked Belinda.

"How should I know? You don't suppose I go around remembering the contents of my reticule all day, do you? I shall simply have to stay here until the tide turns and brings it back in again which won't be for some hours I suppose. Fledgling or whatever your name is," said Costanze, addressing herself to the maid, "go and tell Cook that I am staying to supper."

"Do no such thing, Fledgling!" Arabella commanded.

With a crisp nod to her mistress, Fielding gathered up the loaded tray and returned to the house.

"It isn't a tidal creek, Costanze," said Belinda, who had collected her knitting and was carrying on with the athletic supporter. "And even if it were, you could scarcely expect the return to bring your property back to you! The reticule will have been waterlogged and sunk long ago."

Costanze looked blank, so Belinda tried again.

"It is a freshwater stream, you see."

Still, nothing.

"In other words," explained Arabella, "it flows in only one direction."

"That is what *you* think," said Costanze.

Arabella suddenly found that she had reached the end of her patience.

"No!" she cried. "That is what I *know!* Here!" Whereupon she withdrew the repulsive accessory from under the cushion where she'd hidden it, and hurled it at the owner. "Now, go home!"

"I'll thank you not to speak to me in that tone!" said Costanze coldly.

"Consider yourself fortunate that I am speaking to you at all!" cried Arabella. "A person less able to govern her impulses would have kicked you! I am going for a walk, Bunny, because if I remain here any longer, I shall end by throttling this prittle-prattling numbskull!"

Whereupon, Arabella strode off to the house without taking leave of the company, determined to collect her hat and gloves and be gone.

Costanze leaned back against a pillar, smiling with satisfaction.

"Well," she said, dangling her recovered reticule by the strings and holding it out to Belinda. "Here it is, if you wish to see what I keep in it."

"Oh, don't be silly, Costanze! Why should I care what you keep in your reticule? Can't you see how you've upset Arabella?"

"*I've* upset *Arabella!?* When she tried to steal this bag? Surely, Belinda, it is I who should be upset and did you mark the harsh manner in which your sister spoke to me I am certain that you must have for how could you have missed it?"

Here Costanze paused to open the bag and ponder its innards, releasing, as she did so, the scent of vanilla toilet water in an aggressively concentrated form. She began to recite the contents aloud, whether her listener would hear her or no:

"A large pin in case I am ever accosted by someone I don't fancy; a handkerchief with half a sandwich wrapped in it—it is hard as stone now but that is scarce to be wondered at as I placed it in here more than a week since; another handkerchief without a sandwich; the blackmailer's letter; a throat lozenge that I barely sucked on as I did not fancy the taste . . ."

"What?" said Belinda, dropping a stitch.

"A throat lozenge. It is stuck to the handkerchief-without-a-sandwich-in-it now but I had to spit it out because it tasted of horehound which I simply cannot—"

"Have you got the blackmailer's letter there?"

"Yes, that's what I *said* Belinda I wish you would heed me when I—"

"May I have it, please?"

The letter was handed over.

"I need to borrow this," said Belinda, tucking it into her bosom.

"You may keep it if you like; I was going to burn the horrid thing but I brought it over here to show to Arabella so that she could see for herself that I was telling the truth only I forgot that I had it about me. She is always accusing me of falsehoods and today she was especially abusive I thought; didn't you think she was? What have I ever done to her that she should use me thus?"

"I'll tell you what you have done," said Belinda. "You have been indiscreet, and your foolish behavior has jeopardized Arabella's financial standing." She saw that this was not getting through. "By indulging in dangerous practices," she said, "you have risked other people's livelihoods for your own selfish pleasures."

Costanze blinked, and goggled at her hostess with blank, widened eyes. Like one in a trance, she plucked the lozenge from the handkerchief it was stuck to, popped it into her mouth, spat it into the handkerchief again, and dropped it back into her reticule.

Belinda was nearing the end of her patience. "You got laid by a servant," she said crossly, "when you should have been faithful to Mr. Pollard. Now you are being blackmailed for it. The cash you are giving the blackmailer was supposed to have gone to Arabella, to repay her for all the loans she has made you over the years. She requires that money in order to pay the costs of her new club, and now that she may not get it, my sister stands to lose everything for which she has worked so hard: her home, her bank account, everything! She may even go to debtor's prison! All because of you!"

"Oh," replied Costanze vaguely. And after a moment, she said, "You know it's a funny thing but I cannot abide the taste of horehound though I am told that many other people like it and it is supposed to be good for sore throats. Do you want this lozenge, Belinda? I have barely sucked upon it and I should welcome the excuse to give it to someone else for it is making the inside of my reticule sticky."

Chapter 2

Ordinarily, Arabella took one of the carriages when embarking upon her daily constitutional, in order to confine her exercise to one of the attractive public parks and avoid the filth of the streets. Today was not an ordinary day, however, and she felt much too agitated to sit still for the length of time it would take to drive there. So she stalked all the way to town, in order to dissipate, somewhat, her deep sense of outrage, mulling the problem over as she walked.

Just who was this blackmailer, and what proofs did he have? There was obviously no point in questioning Constance; Arabella would have to *stay* with her, in order to be on hand when the demands came in, or the payments went out, and so see who it was that delivered the former and collected the latter. But what should she do, then? Shoot him? What if he did not come himself? Supposing he sent a child? Arabella was not overly fond of children as a rule, but she didn't think she could bring herself to shoot one.

This was probably the sort of situation where she would need to enlist the services of a man, and she immediately thought of Reverend Kendrick, who was always so useful. She would write and ask him to come see her. But then she realized that she had not heard from him for some time, and resolved to call on him in person, once she had seen Belinda off.

Springtime in the West End, before the summer stinks have a chance to really get going, is the pleasantest of seasons. The massive new mansions and public buildings quite overpower the delicate saplings recently planted in front of them, but these will one day grow large enough to shade the pavements *and* the buildings, or so we have been told. Meanwhile, the vast Portland stone façades sparkle in the sunlight like the sort of wedding cakes one sees in bakery windows: pretty enough to eat, but not actually real. Here and there, deep green parks rustle with the promise of shadowy glades and refreshing pools, and everywhere, in their light-colored summer finery, one sees the upper classes nodding and waving to one another, like field poppies in a light breeze.

Through the center of all this splendor, Lady Ribbonhat, dowager duchess of Glen*deen*, was on her way to perform some pompous little social errand when she was hailed by an acquaintance in a yellow dress with pale blue facings.

"And a good day to *you*, Mrs. Drain!" said the duchess, in response to this lady's halloo. "I am pleased to see that God has once again delivered you safely home from the heathen lands."

(Mr. Drain was a missionary, and his wife had once confided that she fully expected to die abroad.)

"Only just," replied the other. "We nearly capsized coming across in a dreadful storm! Though I should never say so in Mr. Drain's hearing, I find it a vast relief to be back amongst civilized persons!"

"Quite, my dear," said Lady Ribbonhat. "And did your husband manage to convert those godless savages to the true path?"

"Alas, no! Not as many as we had hoped! The stubborn natives have their own god, you see, and being by nature a congenitally stupid race, they are not able to see that their beliefs are wrong."

"I sympathize," said the duchess, who in fact did nothing of the kind. "Communication must have been extremely difficult, and naturally I am speaking not only of language, but of spiritual conceptions."

"Oh, my goodness," replied Mrs. Drain, fanning herself for all she was worth. "You can have no idea of the primitive superstitions, the backward viewpoints, with which we have had to contend!"

"Where were you posted, again?" asked the duchess. "Raritonga, was it?"

"Boston."

"Ah! Well, at least the Almighty has spared you long enough to bring you home. So many missionaries are taken unto death's eternal embrace without seeing England more, Mrs. Drain! You must treat every return as though it were your last, because it very well might be!"

"Yes," nodded the other, "and speaking of eternal embraces, whatever became of that hussy who ensnared your boy just before we left? I hope by now she has given way to someone more suitable."

"No," sighed Lady Ribbonhat, with genuine regret. "I am afraid there is nothing new under the son."

And she started thinking, rancorously, of Arabella. Of the insufferable injustice of it, the outrageous effrontery, and the very real danger that the "hussy" might one day become the next duchess of Glen*deen*. Probably things would never go that far, but it scarcely mattered, for however close they might remain, Lady Ribbonhat should nevermore have Lustings for her own. The duke had effectively ceded the place to Arabella for all time.

Mrs. Drain pretended to commiserate, but found a secret satisfaction in the other's distress. According to *her* lights, Lady Ribbonhat was a godless, worldly woman whom the

Almighty in His wisdom had punished in accordance with her deserts. And so, having heard the doleful tale with immense satisfaction, Mrs. Drain wished her acquaintance a brisk good morning, and went her way with a spring in her step and a glint in her eye.

But Lady Ribbonhat was working up to a state of perfect rage, which required that she remain stationary for a few moments whilst the fury spread itself through her veins, like sap through a leaf when the sun falls upon it. Once the process was complete, she went storming off in the opposite direction. As the dowager walked, her jowls trembled with passion, and her old-fashioned crinoline (a style affectation to which she stubbornly clung, whatever current fashion might dictate) bobbed in time with each angry step.

That thorn! That damned thorn, forever pricking her in the side! Something would have to be done about Arabella!

Deep in furious thought, Lady Ribbonhat went fuming round the corner, heedless of either her speed or direction, and collided headlong with the very thorn itself.

"God's teeth, madam!" cried Arabella, who, as we know, was seething also. "Mind what you are about!"

The fault had been all the dowager's, but she did not apologize, as it was not in her nature to own her mistakes. "How dare you, you . . . damned hedge whore!" she cried. "May your entrails be roasted like sausages in the flaming bowels of hell!"

The realization that her adversary was also caught in the throes of emotional turmoil, and therefore ripe for exploitation by a cooler head, broke upon Arabella like the dawn, and her own raging heart was soothed at once.

"I daresay they will be," she said, smiling. "And I suppose that you will be the one to greet me and show me the way to the disemboweling salon upon my arrival there."

"Not I!" cried the dowager. "*My* rightful place is in paradise!"

"Is it?" asked Arabella mildly. "That is somewhat problematical, then, for I should call anyplace without you in it heaven, Lady Ribbonhat. Therefore, if I am bound for hell, you must come there, too, and we are almost certain to run into one another. Don't you see? If God intends to punish *me*, He will have to send us *both* to Hades. I can only suppose that I deserve to go there on account of my pride and evil temper. But you merit admission just as much."

"Nonsense," spluttered her adversary. "*I* don't belong in hell!"

"Oh yes, you *do*, Lady Ribbonhat! Surely you realize that your selfish arrogance, bull-headed inflexibility, and, above all, your cruelty, are guaranteed to earn you a seat of honor at Satan's right hand? You doubtless have other qualities also, just as disagreeable, which it has not been my privilege to discover. In the meanwhile, may I suggest we spend no more time in one another's company than we can help? *Vita brevis*, Lady R.! Let us both enjoy life whilst we can. Especially you, who have so little of it left."

At this, the dowager duchess actually tried to strike Arabella with her faux-ruby-and-genuine-topaz-headed-vermeil-plated-coronation-walking-stick-with-concealed-perfume-vial, and that adroit young woman, leaping back, barely avoided being smacked across the shins with it. Then, affecting complete disdain, the grand dame swept off with her nose in the air, whilst our heroine, lighter of heart than heretofore, continued to make her way toward her latest money pit—and the reason she so urgently required that forty-six thousand pounds.

If we are to understand why this typically cautious courtesan decided to purchase an hotel before she received her money from Costanze, we must hearken back to the previous winter, when, virtually housebound by bad weather since her return from Italy, Arabella had fairly burst from her house upon seeing the sun for the first time in a week and had directly taken herself off to milk a cow.

This was not as odd as it sounds, for there was a farmyard at Green Park, "got up special" for the benefit of urban dwellers with rustic yearnings. And *that*, reader, is every *bit* as odd as it sounds, for the gatekeeper was none other than Beau Brummell's own aunt. The *haute ton* were welcome to stroll over, six days in the week, to see her brandishing a Bo Peep crook whilst tottering round the barnyard on pattens and trailing the hem of her crinoline-bolstered gown in the mud. Perhaps for this reason, the place was often referred to as an English Petit Trianon, and London's high society loved it just as much as the Parisian aristocracy had once loved the original. Here, for little more than double what one might expect to pay elsewhere, the wealthy shopper could buy fresh roses and plums, as well as butter, duck eggs, and cream. If she were so inclined, she might even milk the beast herself, whilst enjoying bucolic views of a thatched cottage and a picturesque pond, complete with waterfowl. It was a neat little place, and people called it "a country idyll in the very heart of the city!" But they will generally say that of any open space in London where there is grass.

As the farm proved equally popular with exalted great ladies and notorious courtesans, the management had proclaimed alternate "doxie" and "dame" days, in order to avoid any impropriety. The two types were not permitted to mix socially. After all, many of them were sharing the same man, and you may imagine the disgraceful scenes *that* would have caused! On second thought, I pray that you will not imagine it, because that is precisely the sort of thing the owners of the farm are trying to avoid. The separation of good women from bad can be devilish tricky.

Fortunately, there is no parallel to be found in the world of men, for these creatures have extra bits, which, in addition to their natural purpose, function as universal passkeys to the sort of situations that women find socially inconvenient. The masculine sex might attend the farm any day in the week, regardless of the type of female company congregating in the cow byre. Hence, men did not attend the farm very often, because, for them, the place lacked the allure of exclusivity.

Fortunately for Arabella, that first sunny day was a Friday, one of the designated "doxie" days. There were only three cows, however, and many other would-be milkmaids ahead of her, so she passed the time in exchanging witty remarks with her fellow courtesans.

These ladies were naturally quite clever, because that is one of the requirements of the profession, and somewhere in the midst of it all, it suddenly dawned upon our heroine how much she missed the regular society of other women. Her domestic staff was composed of females, of course, and they were wonderfully loyal and supportive, but they shared few of Arabella's interests. There was also Belinda, long accustomed to taking her lead from her older sister, and Constance, who was thick as a cow pat. It would be nice, Arabella thought, if she might mingle freely with women like herself; if there were someplace where demi-reps could gather without worrying what day of the week it was. Preferably some very pleasant indoor place that was permanently off-limits to respectable ladies, so that one should not have to worry about mud, weather, or having to clear out in order to make way for the socially unstained.

She dismissed the idea before fully considering it. But then, on her way home, Arabella had received an unmistakable sign—in this case, an *actual* sign—advertising a property for sale in St. James's Place. Here was a chance not to be missed, for St. James's Place is just off St. James's Street, where gentlemen of wealth and renown have their social clubs. And what could be more practical than to open a courtesans' club mere steps away from the clubs of the gentlemen who most admire courtesans?

Even thus was the seed of the Cyprian Society planted in Arabella's imagination. And within a fortnight it had sprouted, blossomed, and borne fruit, when our heroine, possessed of a deed and a shiny brass key to the front door, had found herself the new owner of an old hotel.

That had been nearly six months ago. Now construction was well under way, and there was little for Arabella to do except pay the bills. The scope and grandeur of the plans were already in evidence: There was to be a picture gallery, a ballroom, a hall for concerts and lectures, several private meeting rooms, and a great restaurant, with space for a gift shop. Up on the skeletal stage of the club's unfinished Bird o' Paradise theater, Richard Brinsley Sheridan was already rehearsing his latest play, and the Great Sarah Siddons herself would be coming out of retirement to deliver the opening-night dedication. It was vital that the money to pay for all this be recovered, and sooner rather than later.

As Arabella turned off Piccadilly onto St. James's Street, bucks and beaus of every description emerged from doorways, rushing out to the street to admire her. Because, as previously noted, this was club row, and the fashionable gentlemen who belonged to those clubs were a troop of roués on the rampage, a reprobate gang of rogering rogues. One of their establishments even had a sign in an upstairs window proclaiming to all and sundry that trespassers would be violated!

No respectable woman ever walked down St. James's Street unescorted, nor would Arabella have dreamt of doing so without a goodly supply of calling cards listing the address of her new social club. But the cards were not yet printed, and the club was not yet ready. So, whilst the gentlemen chased after her, doffing their hats, applying their quizzing glasses to their eyes, and jostling one another as they tried to catch up with and speak to her, Arabella smiled at them without slacking her pace. For she knew that greatness must always maintain a certain distance from the herd, or risk losing its luster through over-familiarity. And with head held high, she turned from St. James's Street onto St. James's Place, where the welcoming façade of the future Cyprian Society seemed to wink a welcome as she mounted the steps.

Few, if any, historical periods have produced such classic, elegant interiors as those of the English Regency, with its polished woods; clear, pale colors; graceful furniture; and large, sunny windows. The Cyprian Society was to be the epitome of Regency refinement, because Arabella would rather not have had a club at all than possess one which failed in its attempt to gratify the most sophisticated expectations. To this purpose, she had retained the services of John Soane, the great architect who had designed the Bank of England and so wonderfully remodeled Lustings. But Arabella's own house was modest in comparison to this project, which was expected to generate more income. Besides, Mr. Soane had professed himself forever in her debt, and was donating his services free of charge. She would still have to pay for everything else, though.

Soane had been watching out for her, and the moment Arabella entered, the great man darted out like a trapdoor spider, bundling her into the small glass booth he was using as an office.

"I have had a most remarkable inspiration, Miss Beaumont!" he cried. "What would you say if I told you that your public rooms might be accessed from the next street over, through the rear of the club?"

Arabella was shocked.

"From the rear entrance? From *Little* St. James's Place, d'you mean? Oh, surely, Mr. Soane, that would never do! The public rooms must have a grand and sumptuous entrance, to satisfy the most exacting tastes!"

"Naturally! That is why I propose to make the rear entrance look like another front entrance, with columns, marble steps . . . the lot!"

"Just like the other?"

"No," he replied, rubbing his hands with glee. "As fine, certainly, but altogether different! The Cyprian Society shall have *two* front entrances, and *no* rear portal! Deliveries can be made via the side doors!"

She was not at once convinced of the necessity for this, but Arabella had complete faith in her architect.

"I am listening, Mr. Soane."

He took up a blueprint and unrolled it upon the table, using his pencil like a magic wand to guide her eye along the enchanted paths of his imagination.

"Once the public enters through here, they will walk along this corridor, which runs the length of the structure, to the public rooms, completely bypassing the private club quarters. We can construct the passage so as to absorb all sound; members who are reading or napping on the other side of the wall will not be disturbed in the least."

"Oh!" breathed Arabella. "This is absolute perfection!"

He smiled at her as he rolled up the blueprint. "All in a day's work, madam. And the very least I could do, after the kindness you have shewn to me."

Arabella nodded her acknowledgment of his thanks. During the previous autumn, she had sailed to Italy and achieved the near-impossible feat of discovering and then recovering a group of bronze and marble artifacts, which had been "stolen" after she and Mr. Soane had already paid for them. The marbles were currently the pride of his collection: a frieze of ducks; a pair of lizards; and the statue of a young girl, absorbed in the act of pinning her gown.

"I thought this might interest you, as well," said Soane, unrolling another chart. Arabella saw an elevation of the hotel, depicting what looked like giant ant tunnels excavated beneath it.

"Yes," he cried, scarcely able to contain his enthusiasm, "it *is* a series of tunnels, leading off in a variety of directions! Your new club was once the site of an ancient monastery! But I have not yet given orders for the tunnels' exploration, pending your approval: If you wish, I could simply have the entrance closed off, which would save you money. Or, we could see where the tunnels lead, install sign posts and a directory, and I could design you a secret ingress panel. Because one never knows when one is going to need a sudden escape route."

Arabella approved the panel, but the exuberance which she should ordinarily have felt was checked by the realization that without the money from Constance, she would not be able to pay for it.

Chapter 3

Following her street encounter with Arabella, Lady Ribbonhat had spent a restless night. It had never before
occurred to her that she might *not* be destined for a comfortable after-existence: The dowager duchess had never been
denied admission to anything in her life, and she found the
prospect of damnation extremely unpalatable.

She had been good enough, hadn't she? It wasn't as though
she had killed anyone! Admittedly, Lady Ribbonhat did feel a
certain kinship with the Roman empress Livia, who became a
goddess after murdering most of her family, but that was not
the reason for the affinity. The dowager admired Livia's in-
flexible will; her determination to succeed, whatever the odds.
Added to this was the fact that Livia had gone to heaven despite her nefarious doings, through the intercession of her
grandson, the emperor Claudius.

Lady Ribbonhat's son was not an emperor and, so far as
she knew, he had no particular celestial connections. Still, she
saw no reason why Henry should not relieve her mind on one
or two points, and after eyeing him morosely for a time
across the breakfast table, she asked him outright whether he
thought her cruel.

"With reference to what?" asked the duke, somewhat absently, for he was attempting to challenge himself by trying to read a letter and eat toast at the same time, and the unexpected addition of a question that required an answer was on the verge of overtaxing him.

"Oh!" cried his mother. "Then I suppose you *do* think me cruel, sometimes?"

Her tone warned him that he had better stop his other two activities and attend to this new one, so Henry put down the letter and swallowed his toast. Yet he was still uncertain how to respond, for all he had retained of his mother's question was the word "sometimes."

"When?" he asked cautiously.

"The time you brought home that mongrel, for instance, and I had the coachman dispose of it without telling you."

"A mongrel?"

"Well . . . an Alsatian."

"How old was I?"

"Twenty-six."

"I don't recall ever bringing home a dog, Mama."

"Not a dog, dear . . . a bitch. I told you at the time that she'd run off with the postman."

"Oh . . ." said the duke. "So, *that's* what happened to little Jeanette! You know, I never quite believed your story, Mama; our postman was nigh on eighty at the time, and he continued to deliver the post, the same as usual. But, hang it all, I was deuced fond of that girl!"

"I was fully aware of your feelings, Henry; that's why I had the creature removed. We cannot have Miss No-bodies from No-where aspiring to the peerage. If we admitted everyone, there would be no room left for us! You can hardly call it cruel; the girl wasn't worthy of you."

Glen*deen*, who was chewing his toast again, made no immediate response.

"Henry? It *wasn't* cruel. Was it?"

"I suppose not," he said, swallowing. "Cruelty would imply that you took pleasure in it, and acted on purpose to hurt me. No, I think you are merely self-centered to the extent that you are unwilling to acknowledge the effects of your actions upon those around you."

"Oh," said his mother, somewhat mollified. "Well, that's not a sin, is it?"

Henry had resumed reading his letter.

"What?"

"Self-centeredness is not a sin?"

"Um," he said, picking his teeth. "I rather think it is, Mama. Remember the time you came into the schoolroom when I was supposed to be studying Euclidean algorithms, and caught me reading *The Governess, or The Little Female Academy,* instead? Do you recall what you did?"

"Oh, Henry, of course not! That was thirty-four years ago!"

"Was it?" he asked mildly.

Their eyes briefly met in a moment of naked comprehension.

"Anyway," he said briskly, "you had my library torched. All my books whatsoever: the illustrated French fairy tales, the studies of insects, the books full of puzzles and brain teasers . . . everything."

"I don't remember that," said Lady Ribbonhat, dabbing her lips with a napkin and dropping her eyes to the tabletop. But at the word "torched," two hot red spots had appeared on her sallow cheeks.

"No?" he pursued. "You don't remember the big bonfire you had made beneath my nursery window, and how the gardeners had to scramble to keep it from consuming the house when the wind changed?"

Lady Ribbonhat said nothing, and the duke returned his attention to his letter and his toast, to which he had now added a third complication: coffee.

After a few moments, she said, "That was a terrible thing, Henry, and I am sorry it happened to you."

"Hmm? Oh, don't give it another thought, Mama; I only mention it because you asked." After a moment, he added, "I never had much use for books anyhow, and was only reading *The Governess, or The Little Female Academy* because I thought the title suggestive. I was disappointed. But, hang it all, I'm no expert in these matters; why not ask that new rector chap? Whatshisname? Appaloosa? Percheron?"

"I can't trust Reverend Clydesdale! He has indiscreet eyes!" she said, and sighed. "You know, Henry, things have come to a pretty pass when a member of the peerage is not even permitted the solace of religion!"

But Henry's mind had turned to other matters. Rising from the table with a carefully cultivated air of distraction, he bent to kiss his mother on the cheek and quitted the house. Glen*deen* was famous for his complacency. He held a rank of considerable distinction in His Majesty's Navy because of it, and it would scarcely have done to have a row with his mother. People would blame him, as the man.

And so they should! Men are the sensible sex. They excel at problem solving, are magnanimous to a fault, and scorn to nitpick. At least, most of the time they are and do. Well, perhaps we had better amend that to "some of the time." Because when a man is focused upon a certain subject, all his common sense flies out through the window. Or, more accurately, out through his flies.

"That one, also," said Belinda, indicating a particularly pretty branch of apple blossom.

The gardener severed it for her with his long-handled secateurs.

"There be some pretty lilac bloomin' by the footbridge, miss. Mayhap 'ee might like some a thay'm, as weel?"

"No, thank you, Searle. These are all I want. They're for

the little wall vases in the landau, you know, and my sister holds that lilac cloys in confined spaces."

Belinda was leaving for Scotland today, and the sisters, soothed by the scent of apple blossom, were to travel together as far as St. Albans. There they would stay the night at Ye Olde Fighting Cocks, an inn of which they were fond, that looked like nothing so much as a cake that has collapsed on one side. This trip would be a way of prolonging their time together, because Scotland was so far away, and the date of Bunny's return as yet indefinite.

On the morrow, Arabella would see her sister safely off in a post chaise, an expedient that was not only desirable, but necessary. Thieves would often lurk in the inn yards, offering to carry one's luggage from doorway to carriage. Then they would steal it, generally after their unsuspecting victim had paid them.

A lady traveling alone, especially a tender innocent like Belinda, would be an easy mark. Once she was settled in the post chaise, though, she would be safe enough, for the driver would look after her. Besides, at Coventry, she would be joined by Peter Gentry, a gentleman of her acquaintance who was also going to Redwelts, and in whose company and care she would make the rest of her journey.

But Belinda was loathe to leave. Her sister had been anxious and angry by turns ever since receiving the bad news from Coutanrc, and Bunny was heartsick at the thought of Arabella, rattling round the house all alone in a foul temper. Just now she was calm enough, though. Belinda found her sitting at the long, mahogany dining table that often doubled as a crafts center during the daylight hours, bending over a thin copper sheet with great concentration, and employing an engraving tool.

"How does the calling card progress?" Belinda asked.

The plate was shewn to her.

"Oh!" she cried, clasping her hands in ecstasy. "How beautiful! It is the most exquisite design since . . . since . . ."

She was unable to think of a suitable comparison. This may have been because there really was nothing in all the world to compare with Arabella's engraving. But it is equally possible that Belinda was exaggerating her approval in order to flatter her sister into a better humor. We shall probably never know.

"I am glad you like it, Bunny," said Arabella, "because this illustration is going to serve as the crest for our new club. Birds of paradise* shall be carved in wood and plaster over the interior doorways, woven into the public room carpets, painted and glazed upon the club china service, and wrought in iron at the center of the window grilles. I am having stained-glass bird of paradise motifs inset in the upstairs windows, bird of paradise–embroidered napkins stocked in the linen cupboards, and bird of paradise bookends placed in the club library. The fireplace andirons shall be topped with them, as well!"

"But . . ." said Belinda.

"Yes?"

"Crests are created by the College of Arms, you know, and only people with titles may apply for them. You have thought this up yourself!"

"It is not my fault that Father failed to complete the application process," said Arabella huffily. "Besides," she added, "this isn't for *me,* or for *us;* it is for the club. And once that becomes famous, it won't matter whether the emblem is registered or not." She smiled and gazed upon her handiwork. "Centuries hence, this clever device—two birds of paradise, perched aspectant on an azure field with tails braced and bent sinister—will be more instantly recognizable than the royal coat of arms, for *all* its harps and lions!"

---

*Which, in addition to referring to a family of birds of the order Passeriformes, is another term for courtesans.

"Will it have a motto?" asked Belinda.

"Of course it will have a motto! I have taken one from Epicurus, the wisest person to have lived so far: *'Effugiat dolorem. Voluptatem!'* "

Belinda was never very good at Latin, having been educated by a governess who had seen no reason to teach it to her. Still, she had managed to pick up a smattering, from books and from Arabella.

" 'Take pleasure in sadness . . . thou strumpet thou?' " she ventured.

"What? No! It means, 'Avoid pain. Pursue pleasure.' Where do you get 'strumpet' from?"

"*Voluptatem.* I supposed it to mean 'voluptuary'."

"Well," said her sister. "That's not bad reasoning, actually. But you should have guessed from the ending that it was a verb, rather than a noun."

. . . And Arabella's good humor was restored. Just like that.

Wait! cries the skeptical reader, how can this be? The funding problems are long-term ones, with potentially serious consequences! Shewing off her knowledge and having the last word will not compensate our heroine for *that,* surely!

No, reader; you are right enough there. But Arabella recognized that gratification in the short term is better than none at all. And she was an expert on the subject.

"How are you proposing to *pay* for all these window grilles and napkins and bookends and fire irons?" Belinda ventured. "Have you spoken with Costanze? Perhaps you should arrange to stay with her for a while, and see who—"

"I have anticipated you, Bunny," said Arabella. "But Constance will not answer my notes, except to say that she is 'furrius,' and does not wish to hear from me 'evir, evir agian.' Of course, she will forget all about it in a week or two, but in the meantime, I must find some other means of divining the blackmailer's identity."

"What other means can there be?"

"I . . . do not know."

"That settles it," said Belinda. "There can be no question of my leaving you when you have such need of my help! Have Trotter remove my trunks from the landau whilst I write to Sir Birdwood-Fizzer, tendering my regrets."

Belinda had been engaged by the earl to replicate Red-welts, Scottish family seat of the Birdwood-Fizzers since 1574, in miniature. And though she could not afford to decline the absurdly generous fee he was offering, Belinda had never been really keen on the idea. As for Arabella, she could not imagine solving a case without Bunny's assistance and, in her heart of hearts, did not know how she would bear her sister's absence. So, with both of them dead-set against the journey, there was only one possible course to take.

"Of *course* you will go!" cried Arabella, throwing her arm round Belinda's shoulders and walking her into the morning room. "All is in readiness, and we have much need of the money. Besides, I am looking forward to our night at the Cocks. Press on, Bunny dearest! Never doubt that that which you have engaged to do is well worth the doing!"

They took their seats at the breakfast table, and Arabella picked up the post beside her plate. "Oh dear," she said, automatically placing all the "requests for payments due" to one side. "Here's one from Frank Dysart!"

"That is odd," said Belinda, unfolding her napkin. "Frank is not in the habit of writing letters to us."

"I have a dreadful sense of foreboding," said Arabella, handing it over. "Read it to me quickly, Bunny; I do hope it is not bad news!"

It was, and it wasn't.

> *Dear Miss Beaumont. I hope you will pardon the liberty of my writing to you, but it seems I've no one else to turn to.*

"There!" cried Arabella. "What did I tell you?"

"Would you like me to stop?" Belinda asked.

"Yes, I should! And I should like even more for that letter to never have reached me! But as it has, I suppose we may as well know the worst. Pray, continue."

> *Like many another child in our neighborhood, Edwardina caught the measles and her mother as you know, cannot bear to be round any type of illness so Sarah Jane has left us to stay with her sister in Wiyylesex.*

"I did not know Sarah Jane had a sister," said Belinda.

"She doesn't. Frank writes rather well, for a constable, don't you think? Run-on sentences notwithstanding, of course."

"Which would you rather do," asked Belinda crossly. "Sit there and pick apart his writing style, or listen to what the man has to say?"

Arabella huffed. "Get on with it, then."

> *I found myself obliged to take time off from work in order to stay home with Eddie who was improving for a while, but the disease took an alarming turn for the worse and we almost lost him. Doctor says she is out of danger now, but still very weak and cannot remain at home unattended and I must return to Bow Street or face dismissal. And so I ask, no, I implore you to take Eddie into your home miss until she is well enough to get about and come back again to look after her doting papa.*

"Goodness," said Belinda, letting her hand, with the pages still in it, fall to her lap. "How noble of him! Think of that wonderful man, caring by himself for a child that is not even his!"

"Yes," replied Arabella, reaching for the egg scissors. "It makes me so terribly ashamed of Charles!"

Their brother, Edwardina's real father, had been somewhat remiss. In fact, he had never, to their knowledge, so much as set eyes upon his daughter, who had attained the age of eleven years.

"Imagine that brainless Sarah Jane," Belinda continued, "running away because she is afraid of illness! I never thought very highly of her character anyway, but I am surprised to find her such a coward!"

Arabella snipt the top off her soft-boiled egg and stuck her spoon into the cheerful white and yellow depths. "D'you know what Charles calls these, Bunny?"

"What?"

"Cackle farts. That's rather good, don't you think?"

Belinda did not appear to think it was.

"Well, anyway," said Arabella, "I expect Sarah Jane simply got tired of being a wife and mother, and has run off with an actor or something. Never mind. Frank and Eddie will both be better off without her."

"Not if poor Mr. Dysart loses his job."

"There is no question of that. Eddie will come to us until she is better."

"Oh, Bell!" cried Belinda. "I am so glad! You know, you really are a very kind person!"

"I am a very selfish person. If I don't agree to take Eddie now, then, as you say, Constable Dysart will lose his job, and I shall be responsible for the child for the next six or seven years! An ounce of prevention today is worth hundreds of pounds in upkeep down the line."

She scraped the last of her egg from its shell and pushed the egg cup away from her.

"You enjoy playing the cynic," said Belinda, smiling, "but your heart is really as soft as that egg was. After all, you are the one responsible for bringing Sarah Jane and Mr. Dysart together. I think he only married her because he was so fond of Eddie."

"Pure self-interest again," said Arabella. "I was hoping that by providing stable home lives for Eddie and Neddy, *I* should be seeing a lot less of them. But I am not very good at matchmaking, apparently."

Neddy was another of Charles's by-blows, fathered on a woman named Polly, whom Arabella had introduced to Constable Hacker, another Bow Street Runner. That marriage was not a happy one, either. Nor did Neddy and his stepfather get along.

"Come, dearest," said Arabella, rising. "It's time we were on our way."

Belinda put down her napkin and pushed back her chair.

"Regardless of your motives," she said, "Frank Dysart has been the saving of our Eddie. You have made a world of difference to her life, Bell."

The ladies donned their hats and gloves, bid good-bye to the servants, and headed for the porte cochere, where the loaded landau awaited them.

"I am certain that you will find Sir Birdwood-Fizzer to be a perfectly amiable host," said Arabella. "But he does have one or two harmless vices, and indulging him will make the visit far more pleasant for both of you."

Belinda had already ascended the carriage via the foldout steps, and was busy settling her little dog upon the seat. "Vices?" she asked. "What vices?"

"Toe sucking," said Arabella as the driver helped her in. "*His* toes, not yours. (Thank you, Trotter.) Also being told that he is a bad, naughty boy. It is nothing, Bunny; I am confident that you will handle it."

Trotter shut the door and hoisted himself up to his seat.

"Oh, yes," said Belinda faintly. "I daresay I shall."

Unlike Arabella, Bunny was accustomed to bestow her favors only upon gentlemen whom she found attractive, and was consequently disinclined to charge them for the honor. This was a pity, since she was blessed with great personal charm, and might have made a splendid fortune for herself. But Belinda was predisposed toward fidelity and marriage, and that was all there was to that.

"Yes, I am quite certain I shall," she said again, attempting to harden her voice. "I shall be fine. Won't I?"

"Brace yourself," said Arabella.

The carriage started off with a violent jolt, and the passengers were thrown forward. But they were not jostled too badly, having prepared for this ahead of time.

"All right," Belinda said, raising her voice so as to be heard over the carriage wheels, and the horses' hooves, and the coachman's directives to the horses. "Birdwood-Fizzer is a naughty boy. Is there anything else I should know about him?"

"Well," said Arabella thoughtfully, "he *may* want you to dress like his old wet nurse, and speak to him as though you have no teeth. But probably not. After all, he barely knows you."

Arrived at last at the Lustings front door, Glen*deen* wondered, idly . . . no, he did not, he wondered *feverishly* whether Arabella were at home. For his mother's reference to his first love had caused an abrupt resurgence of manly energies, which badly wanted releasing now. He shifted from foot to foot and vigorously applied the rhinoceros-headed knocker,* but this only served to increase his agitation, for it

---

*The silver rhino head had been a gift from Mungo Park, sent to Arabella from the Gambia, during the great explorer's tragic final trip there. She had owned it for some years, but had just lately had the idea to fashion it into a knocker.

"Why a rhinoceros?" the duke had asked her. "Why not a lion?"

"Because I like rhinos," Arabella had replied. "Besides, their heads

made him think of pounding, and horns. In point of fact, his ship would be sailing soon, and it might be *months* before—

Ah! Here was Fielding, come to the door at last! But after handing her his hat and preparing to enter the house, Glendeen heard with disagreeable surprise that Miss Beaumont and Miss Belinda had left not ten minutes earlier.

"Your Grace may catch them up if you hurry," said the maid.

But he did not want to do that. Arabella, busy with family matters, would hardly be in a mood to oblige him just now. The duke whirled about and headed for his gig, savagely kicking a stone along the way that had deliberately placed itself in his path.

"Sir!" cried Fielding, running after him. "Your hat!"

He leaned down from his seat to take it from her. "What day is today?" he asked.

"Friday, your grace."

"Is it?" said the duke, brightening. "Oh! Then I shall go to Green Park Farm!"

For it was doxie day.

> *I got yer love letters to that fart catcher an I knows what I knows but Pidjin Pollard don't know do he? Wat do yeu think he'll do when he finds out? drop yeu most like! If yeu wish me to keep your secret, yeu will*

make better door knockers. They are heavy, massive, fairly indestructible, and the longer of the horns is a convenient handle."

It wasn't until later that the duke remembered "rhino's" *other* meaning, and his noble heart had recoiled from the commercial sentiment implicit in such a device. But he was also wise enough to see that Arabella was entitled to have her little joke.

have to pay me £150,000 an I want
£500 on account. I shall send
another letter advising you where to
leave it.

                                        A friend

"There is nothing else for it," said Arabella, raising her voice over the commotion of the carriage wheels as she folded the letter and re-inserted it into the envelope. "I shall have to track down Constance's blackmailer myself, and turn him over to the police."

"Can you deduce anything from the letter?" Belinda asked.

"Oh, yes. Any number of things."

Arabella had read it over a dozen times since Belinda had given it to her the previous evening, but now she studied it once again, using her traveling magnifier, in order to elicit the appropriate sense of awe from her sister.

"The paper on which it was written is middling good; not the best but certainly not the cheapest available. As for the writer, I should say he was a ruthless man; intelligent, greedy, and dangerous."

"Naturally, one might assume as much," said Belinda, "given the fact that he is engaging in blackmail."

"I am not assuming, Bunny—I *know*. I have established these things based upon the manner in which the fellow forms his letters. You see, a man's handwriting reveals his character in unexpected ways. For instance," said Arabella, pointing to the name "Worthington" on the envelope, "the rounded loop on this lowercase G resembles a money bag, which means the writer is greedy."

"That sounds like something you made up," said Belinda, stroking the head of her little dog.

"I have not made it up. It is a science. Mr. Leland has been giving me lessons."

"Who?"

"The bookseller at Hatchard's."

"Well, it is an interesting idea," said Belinda. "But how accurate is it, really?"

"Naturally, I tested the concept, before committing myself to lessons. Mr. Leland agreed to analyze a variety of script samples, which I presented to him, and spotted mine at once. He said I was witty, charming, quick-tempered, and resourceful. Then he evaluated the others, and described the writers to a T." She took the letter out again.

"Really?" asked Belinda eagerly. "What did he say about mine?"

"That you were loyal, sweet-tempered, and fond of animals."

"Remarkable!"

"In the present case," said Arabella, striking her magnifier against the page to recall Bunny's attention back from self-contemplation, "I have deduced that our blackmailer has made a deliberate attempt to sound more ignorant than he is. Anyone who does not know how to spell 'you' or 'did' would most likely not know how to spell 'friend,' 'account,' or 'advising,' either. Then, at the end, you will note that he forgets himself, and accidentally spells 'you' correctly."

"That is brilliant, Bell!"

"Thank you, dear. One thing puzzles me, though. The hand is definitely a forceful, masculine one, and yet there is an oddly feminine component which I cannot account for.

She pulled a wicker hamper from under the seat and removed a glass from it, along with a decanter of French brandy. The stuff was illegal in England, but Arabella had her sources. She took a sip from the glass, and gazed out the open window at the lush summer landscape.

"Bunny," she said, "do you know what I want, more than anything?"

"To get your money back from Costanze."

"Yes, but do you know why?"

"To avoid debtor's prison."

"Of course, but I meant, what do I want the money *for* in the long term? You will never guess, so I shall tell you: I wish to live in England, as though it were France!"

"You can't," said Belinda. "There's not enough sunshine."

Arabella seemed, on a sudden, to be possessed by an over-whelming exuberance. "I want a sparkling life!" she cried. "One that is beautiful and sad, with a wicked vein of humor running just below the surface like a comic opera, with wonderful costumes and a deliberate, sensual musical score, dropping note by note into the pool of a star-filled marble fountain!"

She fell back against the carriage upholstery, like a puppet from which the animator has withdrawn his hand.

"I see," said Belinda. "And how are you now? All right?"

"Somewhat faint," Arabella replied. "But I shall be better presently." She drank off her liquid restorative, right down to the bottom of the glass. "Poor Bunny," she observed. "It must be so difficult for you, having to live with an artistic temperament!"

"No, not really. I'm told I am rather good-natured."

"No, you goose! I was referring to *me!* I get these inspirations from French fare, you know—there is a type of small biscuit which affects me in a similar manner—and sometimes I am quite swept away!"

"If only you *would* be!" Belinda grumbled. How was it, she wondered, that despite her own creative inventions—her billy-boxes and dish gardens, her crocheted dog outfits and the Birdwood-Fizzer commission—that Arabella always got to be "the artistic one"? Thereafter, Belinda maintained an implacable silence for some minutes, and her older sister assumed she was sulking.

Arabella was wrong, though. For over a week, Belinda had

been searching for a way to acquaint her sibling with a shocking piece of news, but the proper occasion had not as yet presented itself. First there was all the flurry over the club construction, and then this terrible financial setback had arisen. But time was growing short, and Arabella simply *had* to be told before the sisters parted company. Otherwise she would hear it from some other source, and accuse Bunny of deliberate duplicity.

"Well," said Belinda at last, "as distressing as the situation is, in a way it is good this has happened. Mysteries are the very thing to keep your mind off missing me. And you're always so clever at solving them!"

"*Twice,*" Arabella replied, replacing the decanter in its basket. "I have been presented with *two* mysteries to date, and have succeeded in solving them *twice*. With, I might add, massive amounts of assistance from other people."

"Right," Belinda said. "Like Reverend Kendrick."

Arabella did not respond at once, as she had begun to study the blackmailer's letter once again.

"I'll own that the rector has proven not unhelpful," she said slowly.

"Well, it's odd that you should mention Mr. Kendrick," said Belinda, "for I have recently had a letter from him." There! It was out, at last!

"Hum!" said Arabella. "If he is seeking a donation for his Effing parish church, I am afraid he will have to wait at the end of the queue, behind all the creditors who will shortly be gathering outside my door."

"No," said Belinda. "This is something different. I am afraid . . . that is, I am sorry to tell you, that the Reverend Kendrick is . . . no longer with us."

"Do you know, Bunny, between you and Constance, I sometimes think I shall go mad? Constance always tells more than she means to, whereas *you* seldom come to the point without prodding! What, exactly, are you trying to say?"

"Only that you should bid Mr. Kendrick adieu in whatever organ passes for your heart," replied her sister grimly, "for he is gone."

"But, you had a letter from him, you said."

Belinda nodded. "Once he had made up his mind to leave this world for another, he thoughtfully found the time to write me before he . . . before he departed. I have been looking all this week for a way to break it to you."

"Break what? If Kendrick had the time to write, why didn't he write to *me?*"

"His heart was too full, he said."

Arabella snorted. "What is *that* supposed to mean?"

"I think you know what it means," said Belinda, glaring at her, rather.

"Well . . . what did he want you to tell me?"

"That he has accepted a mission to . . . I don't remember exactly. Pago Pago? Bora Bora? Some place like that, with a double name."

"Nonsense!" said Arabella. And reaching for the carriage vase, she plucked an apple blossom. "When is he leaving?" she asked, beginning to pull the petals off.

"But I have just been telling you!" cried Belinda. "He has already gone!"

"He . . . what?" The rest of the flower fell from Arabella's hand. "He has gone? And you don't know where? Think, Bunny, think!"

Belinda bit her cuticle. "Well, it definitely wasn't Baden-Baden," she said. "It might have been Dum Dum. . . . Or was it Budge Budge? No, I don't think so. Wagga Wagga, perhaps. Ngorongoro? Possibly Sing Sing?"

"Oh, stop," groaned Arabella, "before I Puka-Puka!"

"That's the one!" cried Belinda.

"The Disappointment Islands? But we don't even own those!"

"Well, *I* don't know the first thing about it! Mr. Kendrick did not supply particulars. He just said he was going there, and asked me to inform you of it."

"Silly man!" said Arabella half-angrily. "What did he want to go and do a thing like that for? It was rude of him not to inform me that he was contemplating such a rash act! I shall not even write to him!"

"Well, just as you like," said Belinda. "He has left a parcel for you at the rectory, though."

"A parcel?"

"Yes. But he asked me to make it clear that you are under no obligation to collect it. He only left it in case you should be interested."

"Did he say what it was?"

"No."

"Then how could I *know* whether I would be interested? I cannot imagine why he . . . no. No, I am *not* interested! Reverend Kendrick could not possibly have left me anything I could actually want!"

"I see," said Belinda, firmly. "It is all for the best, then, isn't it? This affords the perfect opportunity to sever that irksome tie for good."

"What do you mean?"

"I mean that it must have been troubling your conscience, the way Mr. Kendrick always cared so deeply for you, while you never gave a fig for him."

The fig grudger mulled this over. But Arabella could never be happy until she'd had the last word.

"Quite," she said finally. "I was on the point of making that very observation!"

And oddly enough, she still was not happy.

Chapter 4

The sisters slept but fitfully that night, despite the deep comfort of their bed at the Cocks. At their final parting the next morning, Arabella had a sudden presentiment, but she kept quiet about it, and upbraided herself all the way home for being so daft. Of *course* Bunny would be all right! She would be fine!

And in a few days, Arabella's stern self-discipline was rewarded with a letter.

> *Dear Bell,*
>
> *Cara and I are safely arrived. Mr. Gentry kept me entertained with wonderful stories for the whole of the journey, so that I scarcely noticed the time passing. Did you know that the Gentrys claim direct descent from Lady Godiva's husband, Leofric? Mr. Gentry says that all the while Godiva was riding through the streets wearing nothing but her own skin and hair, her infamous husband was pleasuring one of the servants, upon*

whom he begat Mr. Gentry's many-times great-
grandfather. In fact, that was the reason Leofric
made his wife take her naked ride in the first
place: He wanted her out of the way, as she appears
to have been of the same disposition as Mrs.
Pepys, and used to watch her husband "like a
hawk that has nothing else to do but watch, and is
concentrating." (That is a quote from Mr.
Gentry, not from Pepys.)

Speaking of hawks, Sir Birdwood-Fizzor keeps a
number of trained ones, and has promised to get
up a hunting party for his guests next week. I am
glad, for though I do not approve of blood sports,
and plan to remain in the house, it will be a relief
to be quit of Sir Birdwood's guests, who are very
queer indeed!

My work here proceeds apace. I have not yet
made up my mind whether to stay indoors and
devote myself to the model today, or to take Cara
for a walk in the park. Actually, if I take Cara, I
shall wind up alone, for she runs right away as
soon as I let her off the lead, returning hours
later, all muddy, with her pads torn and bleeding.
I think I shall go out, though. It is so quiet here
in the highlands, and so very beautiful. I have
been told that I must not wander the woods alone,
but no one will tell me <u>why</u> I mustn't.

How does your mystery progress? Have you
found out the blackmailer's identity? You know,
you might ask the Cyprian Society for assistance

with your sleuthing. I am certain that your sister
courtesans would be delighted to help you, and
they all seem so clever! I shall be extremely sorry
to miss the first officers' meeting at the new club,
but perhaps I shall dream about it.

Ever your
Bunny

As a matter of fact, the first CS meeting could *not* be held at the club, owing to the construction chaos which reigned there. Moreover, the noise served as a reminder that the fellows responsible for making it had not yet been paid, so Arabella decided to hold the initial conclave at Lustings.

Here, the Cyprians might loll about on her comfy chairs as much as they liked, laughing aloud, saying rude things, stretching out their legs, and even shouting or talking with their mouths full if they liked, for courtesans are inclined to be more informal in one another's company than proper ladies are. Of course, they might have done all these things at the club, too, but there is something about grand architecture, with its lofty ceilings, which acts as a natural damper on relaxed social behavior. Besides, here at Lustings there were only three of them.

The secretary, Feben Desta, was an enchanting creature of Abyssinian parentage and exquisite deportment. She was famous for her sumptuous parties and was always exquisitely turned out. The *netela* Feben wore today—a kind of Abyssinian shawl—was of finest voile, edged with a ribbon of shining silver and cobalt-blue embroidery. Though she often dressed in African garb, and loved regency turbans, nothing Feben wore ever looked like itself. To English Empire fashions she added such foreign touches as cowry shells and iridescent beetles' wings, whilst her African robes frequently sounded such non-African notes as sable collars, or gold sailor buttons. On most people, such fanciful details would have seemed outlandish, but on Feben they always looked stunning.

"I was blessed, at my christening, by my fairy godmother," she explained, "who gave me the gift of good taste."

Feben not only dressed in a variety of different ways, but also spoke and acted according to her mood. She could easily slip from the beautifully modulated Abyssinian accent of her parents to vulgar London street vernacular, veering from delicate to crude in the blink of an eye. These quicksilver changes unnerved some of her friends, and she was frequently asked why she found it necessary to affect so many different disguises.

"They are not *dis*guises," Feben explained. "They are *pan*guises. None of us is really a single entity; every individual is a thousand different people. A mob can overthrow a king, repulse an invasion, or celebrate a holiday with universal abandon. Human beings may act as one, because we *are* one; we are all of us interchangeable with everybody else. So why do we limit ourselves to the same look, the same personality, day after day? If I dress like an aristocrat, it is because I am an aristocrat. When I talk like a fishwife, nothing could be more natural, for that is what I am. The truly strange thing for a human being, the real disguise, would be to suddenly start behaving like a canary, or a tomato worm."

There was something about Feben that implied that she dwelt on a higher plane than you did, in a place where the standards were much stricter than you could possibly imagine or live up to, and Arabella found her slightly intimidating. At finishing school, Feben had been elected the girl most likely to marry an ambassador.

The treasurer, on the other hand, was a loafer and a sloucher, who, in repose, liked to prop her feet up on tables. But once Amy Golder-Green came out of doors, she was grace personified. Amy was an all-round athlete, who, with her lion's mane of golden hair, rather put one in mind of the goddess Diana, except for the chastity part. Amy preferred to dress like a man, but could never be mistaken for one. In any event, it scarcely mattered, for this in no way diminished her attraction for the opposite sex. In some cases, it even enhanced it.

"I would like to propose Lady Caroline Lamb for membership," said Amy, resting one tasseled Hessian boot on the opposite buckskinned knee.

"She isn't a courtesan," Arabella replied.

"Well, not technically, perhaps, but she certainly behaves like one of us. So, what shall it be, ladies? Yea or nay?"

"Oh, I don't think so," said Arabella. "She shares our glamour, but incurs none of our risks or disadvantages. Besides, the woman is tediously unstable. If we admit her, we shall be obliged to spend all our time in trying to soothe her frequent bouts of hysteria."

"Why not put it to a vote?" asked Feben diplomatically.

"Why should we?" countered Arabella. "This is a courtesans' club, and she is not a courtesan. Let us proceed to the next item."

Arabella was the CS president. No surprises there. But the secretary and treasurer glanced at one another sidelong: If she persisted with this high-handed, dictatorial attitude, the club was destined for failure. Arabella may have been queen of her own establishment, but she needed to realize that the other members were also monarchs in their own right.

"I have here," said the president, unrolling a print-sized version of her Birds of Paradise etching, "my design for the Cyprian Society's calling cards. Subject to your approval, each of our members will initially receive a packet of three hundred."

The officers inspected and approved the design, but voted

two to one against Arabella's motto, which Feben felt was too obscure. Instead, the secretary proposed *Ut nos simus* ("We are as we are") and when she and Amy both elected to use it, Arabella gave in with good grace.

"That concludes today's agenda," she said, smiling. "And now I beg your indulgence upon an unofficial matter. If either of you read *Bell's Weekly Messenger*—(ahem!) whose title in no way implies that it is all about me, though it does, on occasion, print articles about my life—you know that I occasionally dabble in what, for want of a better term, I shall call 'mysterious adventures.' "

"Right you are!" Amy enthused. "It sounds ever so much fun!"

"Though, of course, not everyone could do it," said Feben. "I think one must have an inborn talent for detection, as Arabella does."

"Nonsense," replied Arabella modestly. "It is a skill, like any other. I scarcely know what I am doing most of the time. But the fact is, I am working on a sort of case just now, and am curious as to whether you think anyone at the club should like to assist me with it."

Feben's eyes sparkled with pleasure. "Speaking for myself, I should love to!"

"Huzzah!" shouted Amy, leaping up from the sopha and tossing her beaver hat into the air. "A detectives' club!"

"Oh, no! Hardly that!" cried Arabella. "I merely wondered whether I might ask occasionally for your assistance, and whether . . ." She was interrupted by the sound of a carriage pulling into the drive. "Goodness!" she cried. "That will be my niece, Edwardina. But I was not expecting her till tomorrow!"

"Perhaps it is somebody else, then," said Amy.

"No. It is Eddie and her stepfather. I would stake my life upon it."

Fielding settled the matter by putting her head through the doorway and saying, "Mr. Dysart has arrived with Miss Edwardina, miss."

Arabella's fellow officers were thrilled.

"How did you know who it was?" asked Feben.

"Because carriages go round to the porte cochere, as a rule," Arabella replied. "Edwardina, being an invalid, must be brought as close to the front door as possible."

Feben nodded at Amy as if to say, There! *That* is the mark of a great detective! Then they arose, for they were tactful, and understood that their hostess needed to attend to her family matters.

"It's really quite wonderful," said Amy, picking up her hat again and wiping its crown with a circular motion of her forearm, like a gentleman would, "how keenly perceptive you are, Arabella!"

She placed the hat upon her head and rapped the crown smartly, to affix it more securely about her ears.

"I thank you," said the hostess, "but there's really no secret to it, you know. In fact, it's quite elementary."

She was all aglow from their compliments as she escorted her sister Cyprians to a side door. It was awfully good to have other women about, even though they would probably tear her character to pieces once they were out of earshot. After all, one can always ignore what one does not hear. Then she returned to welcome Constable Dysart as he came through the front door, hatless and distracted, with the fragile Edwardina in his arms.

"Hello, Frank," said Arabella. "Come this way, if you please." She preceded him up the spiral stairwell, along the passage, and into the bedroom next her own. "You'll have lots of sunshine in this room, Eddie," she said, pulling back the bedcovers, "and a lovely view of the garden. The spires of the city are just visible beyond the trees."

The child slumped weakly against her stepfather's chest, as though there were no bones to her body.

"Thank you, Aunt Bell," she whispered. "I am ever so grateful that you have let me come!"

As Frank tucked her in, Eddie's head fell back against the pillow and she was instantly asleep.

"I'm afraid the journey has exhausted her," said Dysart. "Poor little poppet."

"Well, she needs quiet, fresh air, and gentle amusements, I expect," said Arabella. "She'll get plenty of those things with me. Feel free to visit whenever you like, Frank, and tell Sarah Jane, when she returns, that she is welcome, also."

Frank shifted his gaze to the wall. "Eddie's mother is gone to Canada," he said.

"To *Canada*? Surely she needn't have gone as far away as that!"

Frank persisted in not looking at her.

"Well, at any rate," said Arabella, "*you* will come to see Eddie. And I promise to take the very best care of her."

Frank opened his jacket and produced a black glass bottle from an interior pocket.

"Please give her this, if you would—three drops in a tumbler of water, thrice daily, after meals."

"Meals? Is she even eating?"

"Well, the odd cup of beef tea is all I've been able to get down her for the past two days. But she must take this, afterward," he said, handing the bottle to Arabella

"What is it?"

"A restorative and strengthener."

"What's it made of?"

"Lead, mercury, and other healthful things. It's all right, you know; the doctor prescribed it. You will see that she takes it, won't you?"

Arabella patted his arm. "You may rest assured. So long as

Edwardina remains under my care, I shall always act in her best interests."

"God bless you, Miss Beaumont!" said Frank. (He could never bring himself to call her "Arabella," although she had invited him, on several occasions, to do so.) "I don't know what I should have done, but for you! You are a . . . an angel!"

"Well, not quite," she said, smiling. "Nevertheless, I shall do what I can."

Frank bent and kissed his slumbering stepchild on the forehead.

"I am sorry to have to leave you so abruptly," he said, straightening, "but I must return to Bow Street with all haste."

The dubious angel followed him downstairs and watched from her door as the hackney pulled away from the house.

At least Eddie has *him*, poor motherless kitten, she thought.

In the drawing room, the dishes had not yet been cleared away from the officers' meeting, and Arabella poured a last cup of tepid tea for herself. But before drinking it, she mentally asked, Is this worthy of me? She decided that it wasn't, and set the cup down again.

The day had progressed to that hour of the afternoon when one should either find employment at some useful task or take a nap if one is not to feel the sadness that settles briefly over everything when one is alone. In her quiet drawing room, Arabella was seized on a sudden by the notion that the world had abandoned her. Feben and Amy had gone home, Frank Dysart had returned to work, Belinda was in Scotland, and Mr. Kendrick had fled from her to the other side of the world. Arabella was a woman rich in friends, but most of these were males. The London season was in full swing, and men of rank were currently in high demand at a never-ending round of parties, fetes, balls, and regattas. Additionally, the part of her brain that found solutions to problems like this one seemed to have gone numb; she could only think of a single person whom she could call on to relieve her loneliness, and he was gone.

But what was she doing? If there was one thing Arabella despised . . . well, there was not; there were any number of things. Self-pity was certainly among them, though. So she squared her shoulders, helped herself to a cigar from the humidor on the mantel, fetched a bottle and a glass from the dining room, and went downstairs to retrieve her fishing pole from behind the kitchen door.

Out in the garden, surrounded by restful greenery and serenaded by the brook, Arabella sat upon the grass and poured herself some claret. Then, with a sigh, she cast her line upon the waters.

Nature is the best smoother of ruffled human feathers, and it seemed to be working on birds' feathers, too, if their cheerful songs were any indication. But Arabella recalled that avian songs, which sound so joyful to the human ear, weren't really happy at all; were, in fact, hostile territorial challenges.

She wondered what the bird calls were like on Puka-Puka, and memories of Reverend Kendrick played through her mind as she leaned against a tree, smoking and considering. If he were here now, Mr. Kendrick would find a hundred ways to help her with the case: running errands, following up leads, offering suggestions. But Kendrick had renounced her. Once, he had spoken to Arabella of marriage, in a roundabout way. Now she was left to discover her fate alone. But she could not have accepted his proposal, even if she had wanted to: Kendrick belonged to the church, and she was a glittering courtesan in the world's most glamorous city, with many good earning years still ahead of her. So she had toyed with him. She needn't have done that, but she had—taking his devotion for granted, and even finding it irritating at times. In Italy, for instance, she had . . . she had been monstrous. Obliging him to fetch and carry for her, and making him stay behind to look after Charles, whilst she and Belinda had feasted, and . . . and . . . enjoyed themselves with . . . others. Once Arabella had even tried to send Kendrick away on a frivolous errand so that she might be alone with Lord Byron. And he had seen through her.

This brief session of introspection acted upon Arabella like a mirror, reflecting her despicable behavior in all its dreadful colors. She was heartily ashamed of herself. John Kendrick would have died for her, and nearly had done, once. Yet she had been . . . not oblivious, for then she should not have been at fault. No, Arabella had been arrogant, vain; heedless to the point of brutishness.

Then had come the regent's party, where he had approached her in disguise, and, ignorant of his true identity, she had looked into his eyes and felt her heart turn over. Why had she only been able to really *see* him when she completely failed to recognize him? Was she put off by his ecclesiastical garb? But he did not wear that all the time. Was she too frightened to face her own feelings? No, she decided, it wasn't that, but Mr. Kendrick possessed one of those romantic natures that becomes quiet and moon-eyed in the presence of the beloved. And Arabella, who preferred ardent, assertive men, had consequently considered him to be . . . well, insufficiently stimulating.

And she had been wrong. Though confounded by his emotions, he was actually—she saw now—dashing, considerate, supportive, and kind. He was also well read, and had a sense of humor . . . not a highly developed one, it was true, but no one was perfect. Arabella recalled how he had fought with a sword to rescue her from her abductors, how he had saved her fortune from annihilation at the regent's gaming table, and how he had read aloud to her from Suetonius and Herodotus when she was peevish, calling her attention to their wonderfully detailed stylings. Mr. Kendrick had invented the fascinating pastime of composing farewell letters from doomed persons in early historical periods, writing as though he were truly of the time. And then, when the idea created a sensation at her salons, he had allowed Arabella to take the credit for it. Mr. Kendrick, she now recalled, had even risked his chastity, consenting to a tête-à-tête with a madwoman bent on seduction, just to obtain information that Arabella wanted.

Once again she recalled that sublime moment, when she had looked deep into his eyes without knowing who he was, and had felt stirred to the roots of her being. But Kendrick had given her up as a bad job at last, and had moved on with his life. Perhaps *that* was why Arabella felt as though she had missed her happiness by inches: No one had ever walked away from her before.

She ground her cigar butt angrily into the grass, gathered up the bottle, the wineglass, and the fishing pole and stumped off back to the house.

There would be no need to dress for dinner, of course, because she would be dining alone. Alone . . . alone . . . the word ran through her mind like a dirge. But actually it was just as well that she had no engagements, because Eddie was here now.

Arabella filled a fresh water carafe and took it upstairs to the sickroom. She placed it on the nightstand, and had just tiptoed out again when Fielding came puffing up the stairs.

"Mr. Charles is here, ma'am! I asked him to wait in the liberry, but I'm afraid he's gone an' went into the dining room!"

"Really? How extraordinary!"

Arabella went to see for herself, because, as far as she knew, her brother had never clapped eyes on Eddie. But here he was now, come to meet his little child at last, and no doubt made wretched with remorse over his callous dereliction, even as Arabella was made over her treatment of Mr. Kendrick. Wasn't it wonderful the way people could change? How they could suddenly see their past conduct and vow, henceforth, to atone for a lifetime of neglect?

"Hello, Charles," she said. "It was good of you to come. Eddie is asleep just now, but I think if she knew you were here, she would want you to wake her."

"Who?" asked Charles. His voice sounded hollow with indifference, but then Arabella saw that he was on his knees in front of her liquor cabinet, and had answered her with his head buried inside it.

Reassured, she ventured again. "I assume you have come to visit Edwardina. She is out of danger, I am happy to say, and you may go up to see her, if you like."

"See her?" said Charles, standing up with a bottle in each hand. "Oh, I don't think I will, you know; there is still apt to be some danger of contagion."

Now Arabella perceived that he had a pal with him, who stood in the shadows holding a large box, to which Charles added the latest two bottles.

"What are you doing?" she asked.

"What does it look like? I'm weeding your liquor cabinet. The boys and me have decided to have ourselves a reg'lar smash-up tonight, and I'm providin' the smash!"

"With *my* liquor?"

"Why not? It's a cinch we haven't got any ourselves! There, Bumpy; that'll do us for starters. Now, morris off to Benson's, and I'll look in around ten."

"Right-ho!" said Bumpy, who was, in fact, the disinherited son of Arabella's architect. "Pleasure to see you, Miss Beaumont!"

And he awkwardly tried to tip his hat, but with his hands full of liquor box, it just wasn't possible.

"I wish I could say the same, Mr. Soane," Arabella replied coldly. "But as I have made it clear that you are not welcome in this house, you would hardly believe me. Fielding, please escort this person to the door at once."

"Yes, miss. Sorry, miss; I couldn't see who it was, with his face hid behind them box flaps."

"That's all right, Fielding. Just get him out now, if you please."

"She doesn't have to," said Charles, bending down to brush off the knees of his breeches. "Bumpy was leaving anyway."

He regarded his sister warily for a few moments, and she glared back at him, ready for anything. "Well," he said at last, slapping his chest with open palms. "I don't hold much with fancy French cooking, as you know. But since I'm here, I suppose I may as well stay to supper."

Over their meal, Arabella acquainted Charles with the circumstances of her pecuniary predicament. Not that she expected any help or sympathy from that quarter; her brother always gambled away any money he himself could manage to get hold of, and was not interested in helping other people. But he was a living, breathing dining companion, and Arabella felt that she either had to complain to someone or go mad.

"So!" he said, when she had finished her tale of woe. " 'Cunny' Worthington's being blackmailed, is she? I am not surprised."

"You are not supposed to know that, Charles, so please don't go bruiting it about at your club, or wherever you go to bruit these days. Anyway, what do you mean, you're 'not surprised'? Why aren't you?"

"Why aren't I? Didn't I apprehend Miss Round Heels with my own goggles, dancing the mattress jig with Lady Ribbonhat's footman?"

"You mean, you *saw* her?"

"Me and half-half a dozen other coves!" (Arabella mentally did the arithmetic for this and decided that he meant "three.")

"Where were you?"

"Haven't the foggiest. All of us were very much the worse for wear. I just remember Snoodles gathering everybody together at the club and herding us somewhere like so many goats." Charles wiped the sauce from his mouth. "Turned out to be a peep shew! A cove and a mort going at it in a back room, and we looking down on them from above, through peepholes! Ha! I nearly laughed out loud when I realized I'd seen Cunny's cunny! It was a most instructive quarter of an hour, I must say—her enthusiasm more than compensates for her want of decorum."

Arabella was livid.

"Do you mean to say you *watched* Constance do the four-legged frolic?"

"Yes. Isn't that what I've just been—"

"You *stood* there, with your chums, and watched her play hide the bone, *without paying her?!*"

"I expect Snoodles paid something to somebody. Cunny probably got her cut, all right. Besides," he added, "I didn't even realize it *was* her, till it was all over."

"And why was that?"

"Well, she hadn't any clothes on during the performance, and all naked women look alike, you know, more or less. Besides, the light was dim." He paused to take a sip from his glass. "But when she was halfway dressed again, she started complaining that her partner'd stained her green-and-purple-peau-de-soie-slipper-with-silver-ribbons-and-charming-gold-embroidered-fleur-de-lis-toe-decoration. She spoke in a particular sort of gobbling fashion, the way a turkey would, were it suddenly granted the gift of human speech. 'Hello,' says I to meself. 'I know that moon-eyed hen! Either that's Cunny Worthington, or I'm a nanny house gnarler!' Then when they'd finished dressing and I saw the cove in his livery, I recognized him as well! What a lark! 'Twas Lady Ribbon-hat's fart catcher!"

"Well, well!" said Arabella. "What a sad pack of cads! I am certain poor Constance had no idea you idiots were up there, and now one of your number seems to be blackmailing her!"

"What makes you think it was one of us?"

"The blackmailer makes reference to Constance's tryst with the footman."

"Good luck to him, then, if he has no other proof than his own eyes!"

"He claims to have their love letters, also."

"Bell," said Charles, spearing a potato, "how could one of *us* have got hold of her love letters?"

"That remains to be seen," said Arabella. "I want you to give me the names of everyone who attended that performance!"

"Sorry; no can do. Clubmen don't rat on one another!"

"Oh, don't they? Well, you had better think again, Mr. Rat! You have already told more than you ought, and there is cheese all over your whiskers! If you are not forthcoming with those names, I shall go round to your 'gentlemen only' club, force my way in, and announce your betrayal to one and all before they can gather their feeble wits together to eject me!"

Charles paled. "You wouldn't do that!"

"No? Would you care to test that hypothesis?"

"Oh, very well, then: Snoodles, Bumpy, and Arsy-Varsey."

"Thank you," said Arabella.

"Don't mention it. You know," he said, spooning up a second liberal helping from the serving dish, "these little nobbly things in here are awful good! What are they?"

"Snails," said Arabella.

Charles grabbed his dinner and returned, before stumbling to his feet and knocking over his chair. Fielding stepped adroitly aside from the doorway as he lunged out of the dining room, and both she and Arabella subsequently heard the unlovely sounds of him being sick out the library window.

"Waste of a good dinner, that," Arabella remarked.

"Yes, miss," replied Fielding. "Cook will be furious!"

"Let's not tell her, then."

* * *

Two days later, the Duke of Glen*deen* stood once more upon Arabella's doorstep. Outwardly imposing in his gold-braided, brass-buttoned, medal-bestrewn naval officer's uniform, he was inwardly wondering how soon he might get through the tedious preliminaries with Arabella, and so proceed to the main event: There wasn't much time left before he had to catch his ship. But as he was lifting the rhinoceros-headed knocker, the front door swung open and the lady herself appeared, obviously on the point of departure.

"Why, Puddles!" she cried in astonishment. "Had I been informed of your coming, I should not have made plans to be elsewhere!"

This was meant as a not-so-subtle hint that he had breached decorum in failing to fix the time and date of his visit in advance. But the duke was too incensed to take it.

"I say, Arabella," he said, frowning and removing his gold-braided bicorn. "You might have waited till I'd sailed before keeping assignations with other men!"

Now it was Arabella's turn to bristle. "And *you* ought to know me well enough by now, Henry, to realize that I would never do such a thing! As a matter of fact, I was on the way to my club, to quiz some witnesses."

"Witnesses? To what?"

She sighed and opened the door wider. "You had better come in and sit down," she said. "This will take some time to explain."

All the while she was describing what had happened with Constance, the blackmailer, and the witless witnesses, the duke roared with laughter till he got a stitch in his side, and Arabella began to hope that Glen*deen* might volunteer to provide her with the funds she so desperately needed. She was not broke, exactly, but at the rate the construction and other costs were mounting, she soon would be. However, after Arabella had finished her story, as the duke sat wiping his eyes and sipping from a tumbler of water, he made it quite clear that she was on her own.

"I told you not to start this club, Bell," he said, rising from the couch and reaching for his hat. "I won't pay for it, you know; makes me look like a whoremonger."

The duke was the sort of man who can only entertain one idea at a time, and it wasn't till he was driving away that he realized he had forgotten to press for his farewell frolic. By that time he was halfway to the dock, and it was too late to go back again.

Directly after he left, Arabella went upstairs to take leave of her niece.

"Where are you going, Aunt Bell?" asked the child weakly.

"I must talk with some people, dearest—but I promise to be back soon." She smoothed the bedclothes and tucked them under Eddie's chin. "Doyle and Mrs. Janks will look after you whilst I'm gone. Cook is poaching a lovely chicken for your luncheon, and I want you to eat every bite."

"I shall try. Will you come back in time to sit with me?"

"Probably not, dearest."

"But I shall be lonely!"

"No, you won't. You will be sleeping. And if you are better by this evening, I shall read to you."

"Oh! Shall you? What from?" cried Eddie.

"A new collection of old German stories that I think you will like—they're full of witches and wolves. In one of them, a lady is popped naked into a barrel with nails driven through it, and dragged along the street by horses till she dies."

"Is she a bad lady, then?"

"Yes; a terrible, wicked lady!"

"Oh," said Eddie. "I like it better when such things happen to *good* ladies."

Arabella was shocked. "Why ever do you say that?"

"Because when awful things happen to the wicked, we

cannot help but feel glad, and it is not right to take joy in the suffering of others. But when mishaps befall the virtuous, we get to feel sorry for them. Sympathy is a lovely virtue, and it gives us an excuse to cry. You must admit that it feels good to cry sometimes."

Arabella looked at her niece with doubtful regard: Was the girl turning into a Catholic? It was possible. Though barely eleven, she frequently came out with mature pronouncements and shrewd observations, and Edwardina behaved more like a wife toward Frank than her mother ever had: mending his stockings, boiling his eggs, and seeing that he wrapped up warmly before going out in the cold. Now that Sarah Jane had left, it would not surprise Arabella very much if the pair were to marry when the girl came of age. But there was very little that *would* surprise her, insofar as Eddie was concerned. The child might grow up to be a saint, or a scientist, or the Northwest Passage's discoverer. And, if she did decide to become a Catholic, she might conceivably become the second female pope.

"I thought I heard a gentleman's voice just before you came in," Eddie said.

"Yes, I expect it was Glen*deen*."

"Had he come to see me?"

"Why . . . no, dear. You've never met the duke, have you?"

"No," she replied drowsily. "But I thought he might have come to see me, all the same."

"You old silly!" said Arabella affectionately. "Why should a complete stranger come here especially to see you?"

"From curiosity," said Eddie. "Because I am your niece, and I am a virgin. Soon I shall be old enough to do what you do." She sighed and smiled. "I should think they *will* be coming to see me, you know," she said, "sooner or later."

Well, perhaps Eddie would not be ascending to heaven after all. But the idea that Arabella's admirers might start coming to her house in order to visit her niece was not an agreeable one. The old making way for the new was one of Arabella's least favorite themes, *especially* where it concerned her personally, and *particularly* especially when she herself was relegated to the role of "the old."

She opened the drawer in the bedside table and removed Frank's little black bottle. Eddie watched her pull the stopper and sniff the contents.

"Faugh!" cried Arabella. "How say you, niece? Do you feel restored after taking this?"

The child shook her head feebly but emphatically on the pillow.

"I thought not," said Arabella. "Let's leave it up to Mrs. Moly to bring you round with nourishing food. I always prefer meals to medicines, don't you? Besides," she said as she emptied the bottle's contents into the bedpan, "pot liquor and beef tea are much better restoratives than mercury."

"But Frank and the doctor want me to take it," whispered Eddie.

"They want you to get well," said Arabella. "And I rather think, my dear, that the proof is in the pudding."

Chapter 5

The din was unbearable. Plasterers, carpenters, and pipe fitters overran the place, all sawing away, hammering, shouting, and dropping things from heights. Only the Cyprian Society's tiny reception room, located just inside the front door and designed for a single occupant, was sufficiently removed from the chaos to allow for anything approaching normal conversation. But it was not very comfortable. The yellow chamber was intended as a holding area, where outsiders (preferably one at a time) were kept until they could be properly vetted and/or met by the member they had come to see. It wasn't really large enough for two persons, but the alternative was unacceptable: Arabella was not about to entertain Charles's disreputable friends at her house.

Owing to Glen*deen*'s unexpected visit and the prolonged leave she had subsequently taken of Eddie, Arabella arrived late to find that her first witness had disappeared. The idea of a drunken sot wandering around loose did not sit well. Mr. Tilbury was supposed to prevent this kind of thing from happening. But the porter had been obliged to vacate his booth in order to rescue a plasterer who'd slipped from a scaffold.

The poor fellow had been dangling by one arm, high above the floor, and the porter had gone to fetch one of the state tablecloths, which he instructed the others to use as a net. In the meantime, "Snoodles" had escaped.

The plasterer's dilemma had been concluded without injuries; Arabella forgave Mr. Tilbury for leaving his post, and commended him upon his quick thinking. But by the time she found Penderel Skeen, he was fairly well snockered on club wine.

Arabella guided him back to the little waiting room, whilst Mr. Tilbury went off to arrange for a pot of black coffee. She did not expect to get much helpful information from this fellow, but she had to try, for her leads were few.

"Mr. Skeen," said she, "can you tell me, please, about your activities on the night you went with your friends to spy upon a pair of lovers?"

She opened the pale pink notebook she had brought with her and took a short pencil from behind her ear, wetting the tip of it with her tongue.

"Call me 'Snoodles,' " he said. "Ev'ryone does."

"I'd rather not, if you don't mind. What can you tell me about that night?"

"When?"

"When you watched a couple having sex in a back room."

"Wasn't night. Sun was still up. 'S late afternoon."

"Yes?" said Arabella, making a note. "What else do you remember?"

"Charley wanned t' go t' Drury Lane. Tha's where the girls are, 'f you ever wanna girl, which I don' expect you ever do. Charley did, though, an' he's frens with the chap who runs one o' the muffin shops there. There's . . . there's a song about it; how does it go . . . ?" he trailed off, and his narrative came to a halt.

"Do get on with it!" said Arabella impatiently.

"Sorry. Well, it sounded like a fine idea to the res' of us.

We thought, you know, we'd get some hot 'muffins,' fresh from this fellow's 'bakery.' But then we lost our way . . . that tune. You know the one I mean. We sang it as we were . . . were going along . . ."

And to Arabella's annoyance, he began to sing:

> *Oh, do you know the muffin man,*
> *the muffin man, the muffin man.*
> *Oh, do you know the muffin man*
> *who lives in Drury Lane?*

"That one."

The coffeepot arrived, and Arabella poured a cup for her witless witness, just as he was starting on the next verse:

"*Oh, yes I know the muffin man, the muffin man, the—*"

"But that's not where you went," she said, cutting him off.

"No. Wouldn' have done us any good. B'cause we were too inc . . . incap . . . incupabble. Y'know . . . y' gotta be able to get it up, I mean . . ."

"I know," said Arabella.

"It was Arsy-Varsey's," he said suddenly, and gulped down the contents of his cup in a single swig. Then he spluttered an obscenity and grabbed his throat as the coffee scalded his trachea.

"*What* was Arsy-Varsey's?" asked Arabella, giving him a moment to recover.

"The idea. Arsy thought of it first. B'cause he knew where it was. An' he was taking us there when Charley decided we should go to Drury Lane instead. . . . '*Then, both of us know the muffin man, the muff—*'"

"That's enough singing, if you don't mind."

Snoodles shook his head, as if to clear it, and regarded his coffee cup with dislike. "You know, I don't much care for this wine," he said in an undertone. "The other vintage was much better. Let's have some more of that one."

"Not just now," said Arabella, scribbling fiercely in her notebook. "You were saying that Mr. Savory-Pratt originally planned to take you to the live performance, but Charley wanted to go to Drury Lane?"

"Yeah. But Drury Lane wasn' open. Too early, y'see. An' besides, we were too drunk to . . . to be able to . . ."

"Yes. So Mr. Savory-Pratt took you to the other place, like he'd originally planned. Do you remember where it was that he took you?"

Snoodles frowned with the strain of remembering. "Shop of some kind. We went in through the rear. Ha! 'Went in through the rear!' Mus' remember to tell that one to Bumpy!"

"Do you recall what street you were in, Mr. Skeen?"

"No. I jus' followed the other chaps. In fact, *I brought up the rear!* Haw!"

Arabella noted with relief that despite the man's frequent, idiotic asides, he was beginning to show signs of sobering up.

"All right," she said. "And then what happened?"

"Well, this bloke met us at the door, an' took us upstairs."

She straightened. "What sort of bloke? Do you remember what he looked like? Did you catch his name?"

"No idea. Shortish. Darkish. Thick-settish."

"Did he have any scars? An unusual nose, perhaps, or a glass eye?"

"Hmm," said Snoodles, considering. "A ring in his ear. I think. With an oddly-colored stone like your notebook: all sort-of pinkish. I took rather a fancy to it, and offered to give him my sister in exchange, but he wasn't having any of that."

"A pink earring," said Arabella, and she jotted down: "pink sapphire?" and "pink quartz?" "Good!" she said. "Did you notice anything else?"

"No. It wasn't him I'd come to look at, if you know what I mean. He took us into a room and shewed us the peepholes we were to use. They were all at about eye level for us, but when we looked through 'em, they were actchully up near the ceiling of the other room, the one on the other side of the wall, so that we were looking down at the couple on the bed. It wasn't really all that easy to see 'em, though, because we were looking through the wall covering."

"Through the wallpaper?"

"Not paper; Hessian cloth, I think."

"And whom did you pay?"

"Bumpy paid. Because Charley an' me were skinned, as usual."

"Thank you, Mr. Skeen," said Arabella, rising and dismissing him with a curt nod. She almost said, "You've been very helpful," out of habit, but she didn't.

"Bumpy" was the selfsame George Soane whom Arabella had ordered from her house on the night that Charles had disagreed so violently with the escargot. She'd had good cause for her inhospitality, as he had come out to Lustings once with her brother when Arabella was away and, sometime during the ensuing rout, had vomited into Belinda's work basket. Afterward, Bumpy claimed to have no memory of the incident, which in his opinion should have made everything all right again, and he could not understand why Arabella should go on holding a grudge against him for so long. It had been nearly three weeks ago, now.

Although the day had turned chilly, Arabella insisted on meeting Bumpy out of doors, as he was known to possess "the most appalling-bad cleanliness habits," and having just insulted her ears with Penderel Skeen's brainless "muffin" refrain, she was loathe to do as badly by her nose.

Readers will recall that the Cyprian Society was going to have one front door facing St. James's Place, and another facing *Little* St. James's Place. Ergo, there could be no rear garden, because no "rear" existed. There was, however, a small strip of land at the side, which intervened between the former hotel and the building next door to it, and here Arabella had commissioned a garden feature, formed on one she had admired in Italy. A rectangle of velvety green lawn was planted down the length of its two longer sides in golden poplar trees, and a marble bench, placed at one of the rectangle's short ends, faced a marble fountain at the other. Quiet, pretty, and private, this "meditation grove" afforded the perfect spot for quizzing a witness with a foxy reek.

Arabella had never before had occasion to observe Bumpy in daylight, where his fiery hair, dead-white skin, and scarlet pimples (the famous "bumps" for which he was named, and the sort often referred to as "grog blossoms") made an arresting impression. But at least this witness was sober.

"All I can tell you," said Bumpy, "is that we went to the back door of a shop in Jermyn Street and then climbed up some stairs."

"Jermyn Street?" asked Arabella. "Are you certain?"

"Quite certain."

"Do you remember what type of business it was? What did they sell?"

"No idea. And as I never saw the front of the place, I wouldn't be able to take you back there, or say for certain which shop it was."

"Jermyn Street," said Arabella to herself. "Well, that's something to go on, anyway. Who took you upstairs? Was it anyone you knew?"

"Chap called Tyke. Jerry Tyke."

Arabella's heart beat faster. "Can you describe him?"

"Rum customer. Short, dark, no neck."

"Was there a ring in his ear?"

"I think so. Yes. Well, there *would* be, wouldn't there?"

"Snoodles told me you paid for the entertainment. Is that whom you paid? This Mr. Tyke person?"

"No; I paid half to Arsy-Varsey up front, and then Arsy took care of it. The tickets weren't cheap, you know, which is more than I can say for the mort!"

Arabella bridled. "The woman, do you mean? What about her partner? Wouldn't you say that he was cheap, too?"

"No, I wouldn't."

"Why not?"

"Because a man doesn't mind what he does, or who sees him when he does it. He is always true to his instincts, like the noble savage that he is. A woman, on the other hand, is wrapped to the eyes in pretense and propriety. Everything must always appear proper on the surface; no one must know what she is getting up to behind that closed door. Do you see? It is always the woman who sets the tone in society matters, because she is the one who *cares* to. So, if she lets her end down, the fault is hers, not his."

"That's very neat!"

"Well, so it should be! Women are the ones who regulate sex, and insist on only having it at certain times with certain restrictions. Men would love to have more freedom with regard to these matters, but women won't let 'em. That is why, when a woman breaks the rules, she's cheap, because they're *her* rules, you see. That is also the reason we cheer on the man when he does the same thing. Because it isn't *his* code he's breaking, but that of the oppressor."

Arabella blinked. An outrageous line of cant, perhaps, but one that represented an entirely new approach to an old resentment. She would have to think about this later. Bumpy may have been unattractive, but he had a first-class reasoning machine behind his revolting visage.

He gets his wit from his sire, Arabella thought. Aloud, she asked, "How was this *particular* woman cheap, though? Since she had no idea she was being observed?"

"Come on!" said Soane. "She was doing Lady Ribbonhat's footman, behind the back of the man who cossets and adores her! Besides, she knew we were up there!"

"No, she didn't!"

"I beg to differ, Miss Beaumont. Why else would a woman

agree to a tryst in the back of a shop? She didn't just 'happen' to find herself in a strange storage room outfitted with a bed. That footman didn't just bumble in, thinking he was entering a taproom. And I'll lay you even money that the pair hadn't clapped eyes upon each other for the first time the instant we arrived. They went there on purpose for the sake of a tryst. It was all pre-arranged. Arsy was told what time we had to be there."

"Perhaps," said Arabella. "But that does not mean that some unscrupulous character didn't find out about the time of the tryst and then tell you, for his own profit."

"What about the eyeholes, then? Besides, we purchased tickets."

He had mentioned this before, but it hadn't registered until now.

"*Tickets?*" she cried.

"With a list of dates and times printed along the bottom. Your friend was not only familiar with the setup; she was getting paid from the takings!"

"But how do you *know* that?"

"Because as we were leaving, I saw Jerry Tyke headed downstairs with an envelope that had her name on it."

"You knew her name?" Arabella asked.

"Charley recognized her. Said she was a friend of yours called 'Constance.' The name on the envelope was 'Costanze,' though. Must be her stage name."

"Well! You were certainly very observant!"

"I have to be. I'm a newspaperman."

Arabella had forgotten that. Soane was not only a journalist, he was the kind that specialized in digging up dirt and spreading scandal under the guise of "telling the truth." Of course! It all made sense, now!

"And how much are you charging Constance to keep this out of your newspaper?" she asked. But Soane shook his head.

"Pigeon Pollard's a friend of mine. He'll find out what his piece is up to soon enough without my help. I may be a rotter, Miss Beaumont, and I own I occasionally get caught up in some pretty rum shenanigans, but I wouldn't stoop to blackmail, and when a friend or an innocent party stands to lose by the information I've collected, I do not feel compelled to spill my guts."

"As to that, sir," said Arabella, grimly thinking on Belinda's little work basket, "I'm afraid I have seen and smelt evidence to the contrary!"

The last witness, Arsy-Varsey, otherwise known as the Hon. Cuthbert St. Eustace Savory-Pratt, had not replied to her letter, and when Arabella called at his lodgings, no one seemed to know where he'd gone. Apparently, he owed people money. A couple of bailiffs skulking outside told her they'd been watching his place for over a week, but had seen no sign of the occupant.

"Have you questioned his servants, or neighbors, or anyone?" Arabella asked the less aggressive-looking of the two fellows.

"Yeah. 'Is valet says Mr. Savory-Pratt 'ad a visitor on the last night 'e was 'ome. A Mr. Tyke."

"Tyke!"

"You wouldn't be knowin' 'im, miss. 'E's what you'd call a shit sack, if you'll pardon my French."

"You are quite correct, sir; I *don't* know him, but I have heard of him, and I cannot imagine that Mr. Savory-Pratt would have doings with such a disreputable person!"

The other man grinned, and Arabella nearly swooned at the sight of his teeth.

"Yer quite right there, missy," said this second bailiff. "Oy'm sure Mr. Pratt wouldn't 'ave doin's wi' Tyke if he 'ad a choice like. But Jerry Tyke ain't exac'ly in the habit o' payin' social calls. If he came 'ere t' see your Mr. Savory-Pratt, you can bet 'e didn' 'ave no invite-ation!" And he laughed until he started to choke, so that the outburst ended in a coughing fit.

"'E's right, miss," the first bailiff agreed. "We're only 'ere because we're bein' paid to be 'ere. But the fact is, we don't reckon we'll ever see this partic'lar gennelmun again. Leastways, not alive. We're just waitin' for official word that 'e's been found givin' the crows a puddin' in some ditch. Then we'll enter the 'ouse an' recover what we can for our clients. I've seen this sorta thing plenty o' times before: Jerry Tyke drops in for a visit, an' then the cove 'e drops in on drops out a sight. That's what you might call a pattern, that is."

CIN Entry:

I have written to Frank about Jerry Tyke. If the fellow is a known criminal, there will surely be some sort of record of his crimes. And if there is such a record, perhaps Frank will let me read it. After all, I am looking after his stepchild.

For the reader who comes late to these adventures, and is starting with this, rather than the first volume, a brief word about CINs—criminal inquiry notebooks—is in order. Prior to acquiring her accidental avocation, Arabella had commissioned a sizable collection of these items, having originally planned to use them as diaries. Bound in different pastel shades, they took up an entire shelf in her boudoir, where she now sat, writing her latest entry. Arabella used a different notebook for each case she worked on. This time she had chosen a pink one, and was reflecting on the coincidence that pink also happened to be the color of her suspect's earring jewel, when Fielding came up the stairs with Frank's reply to her note about Jerry Tyke. Arabella read it over with satisfaction, and tucked it into the front pocket of her CIN.

"Aunt Bell?" came a weak little voice from down the passage.

"Yes, Eddie darling!" replied Arabella, rising. "I am coming directly!"

The child was looking a bit better. Not much. But a bit.

"How pretty," said Eddie, pointing at the CIN. "Is that your memoirs?"

"No, darling. These are my case notes."

"Oh! Are you working on another mystery? How exciting!"

"Now, Eddie," said her aunt, "excitement is expressly forbidden you until you are better."

"All right, then. It's *not* exciting. But do tell me about your case, *please!* I shall lie here very still all the whilst you are talking. Probably, you know, I shall even fall asleep. You would like me to sleep, wouldn't you, Aunt Bell?"

"Yes, I should. But the moment you demonstrate the least avidity, I shall take away the lamp and close the door."

"Agreed."

"Well, you see, someone owes me money—"

"How much?"

"A great deal. Which I need very badly in order to pay for my new club."

"Yes. The Cyprian Society—what a wonderful idea!"

"Thank you, dear. I shan't explain the entire case to you now, but the person who owes me this money cannot pay it to me, because she's being blackmailed—"

"I know. It's Miss Worthington, isn't it? The silly creature has had an intrigue with Lady Ribbonhat's footman."

"How on Earth . . . ?"

"I overheard Doyle and Mrs. Janks discussing it whilst they were making up your room today. Please take me into your confidence, Aunt Bell! You won't be sorry; I can be of great use to you."

Arabella could not help smiling at this. "How could you

possibly be of any use? You are not only a child, and small for your age; you are bedridden!"

"I shan't *always* be bedridden. And I don't know how I may help yet, as you have not told me the facts of the case. But Frank says I am a useful sort of person, and I do so want to learn to be a sleuth! Remember that fable you read to me once, about the lion and the mouse?* And how you quoted Aphra Ben as saying one should never despise any form of service? The fact that I am little and humble does not mean that I may not be of help to you. Think of me as your mouse."

Arabella took her niece's hand and looked her earnestly in the face.

"Girls cannot be sleuths, Eddie. *I* only do this because I have to, when circumstances intervene between me and something I want. I do not enjoy solving mysteries. This is not a career, and it will not pay you anything."

"Oh, I know; I only mean to do it as a sort of hobby. And I shall have time for hobbies when I grow up, because I am going to be a great courtesan, like you!"

Arabella was pleased. "Are you, really?" she asked. "Well! Allow me to say that I think you have made a fine choice, and I shall be only too happy to teach you the ropes when the time comes. The career of a demi-mondaine can be very satisfying—even noble, sometimes—but it does have certain drawbacks."

"I know what they are," said Eddie, "and I shan't mind them. Now, please tell me about your problem."

---

*One of Aesop's fables tells of a mouse who cleverly talks a lion out of eating her by appealing to his honor, and hinting that she might one day be able to return the favor. The amused lion takes his paw off her tail and sets her free. Some time later, he finds himself ensnared in a net of ropes so cunningly woven that he is unable to move. The mouse gnaws through the ropes to free her lordly friend, proving, once again, that you should never eat any creature with both the ability to speak your language, and the wit to beg for its life.

"Tomorrow," said Arabella.

"Why must I wait till tomorrow? Is it because you think me too weak?"

"Partly. But mostly it's because I may have more to tell you by then. Your stepfather has kindly agreed to help me. We are going to meet with the blackmailer tonight."

"You *are?*"

She withdrew Frank's note, shook it open, and read aloud from it:

> *Meet me at the Prospect of Whitby (the pub,*
> *not the ship) at ten o'clock this evening. Mr. Tyke*
> *is expected there at around eleven. We can decide*
> *upon our best approach if and when he arrives.*
> *Please come dressed in mourning.*
>
> *Your humble servant,*
> *Constable Frank Dysart*
>
> *P.S. With a veil.*

"Oh," breathed Eddie. "How I should like to be able to come along!"

"Nonsense. It is much too dangerous, even if you were well."

"Well, it's dangerous for you, too," said the child, reasonably enough, "and yet, *you* are going."

"That is different. *I* have a personal stake in the matter."

Personal stake or no, Arabella had been positively delighted by Frank's note. She had no idea what he was up to, but she loved the secrecy, the opportunity to wear a disguise, and, above all, the danger. The Prospect of Whitby may or may not have been London's oldest pub—many other establishments made the same claim—but it was certainly situated in one of the most nefarious riverside neighborhoods. Wapping's reputation was so dreadful that Arabella's coachman tried to dissuade her from making the trip.

"'Ere, you don' wanna go dere now, miss. Lemme take you tomorrer. Be much safer inna daytime."

"You'll take me now, Trotter, if you don't mind."

"But I *do* mind, miss. Drivers've been knowed t' disappear from there! Dey grabs 'em right hoff the coach!"

"Oh, I see; you're not concerned for *my* safety; you're only worried about your own!"

"'At's right, miss; it's your choice to go. It ain't mine."

"We'll compromise, Trotter. If you'll agree to take me there, you may come into the pub and have a pint at my expense whilst I transact my business."

"Oh!" he said, grinning broadly and shifting his hat farther back on his head. "Well, that do put a diff'runt complexion on things, has it were! Thank ye', miss! Get you inside an' we'll be orff di-rect!"

On arrival, Arabella lowered her veil as she alighted from the coach, and was obliged to bury her lower face in a handkerchief, as well, for the fetid mist rising from the river stank like a charnel house after a plague. The Prospect stood dead in front of her. By all accounts, a whimsical riverfront structure by day, the pub appeared even more suggestive in the moonlight, managing to look both quaint and sinister at the same time. All was quiet outside, though she had half expected to see bodies flying out the door and kegs of ale hurtling through the front windows, to the accompaniment of shattered glass and shouted oaths. So when Arabella swept into the room in her widow's weeds, she was shocked to find the place packed; it was virtually chock-a-block! And yet, all was as orderly as one might wish. The mingled aromas of warm beer, pipe tobacco, and roasting meat filled her nostrils, her mouth, lungs, head, everything—so that she felt she was ceasing to be herself and becoming, instead, the smell of the inn.

That said, the patrons did not appear friendly. As angry-looking a band of cutthroats and wharf rats as ever she had seen turned to glare at her when she entered, and the counterfeit widow froze in the entry, uncertain of her next move. One might have heard a cockroach hiccup.

"Mrs. Greely!" called Constable Dysart, beckoning to her over the sea of heads. "This way, if you please!"

Arabella steeled herself to push through that villainous company, but the crowd parted for her obligingly, almost reverently, as Frank reached her side and began to steer her toward the back of the room.

"Who is Mrs. Greely?" she asked in an undertone.

"A smuggler's widow," said Frank. And as more people began to move out of the way, Arabella could see an open coffin resting on a couple of crates.

"Is that my husband?" she whispered.

"*Was* your husband, yes. I'm sorry about this, miss," Frank murmured. "Just a quick glance, if you would. Then we can go sit down."

The corpse was a gruesome sight, with a bluish face and popped eyes. An engorged tongue seemed far too big for the open mouth from which it protruded, purple and horrible, and the man would appear to have strangled on it. But round his neck was the mark of a rope, and Arabella's calculated swoon into Frank's arms was only half-feigned. He set her on her feet again, and helped her to a table as far away from the coffin as possible.

"What happened to him?" she asked.

"Poor sod was hanged this morning. At Tyburn."

"At Tyburn! No one has been hanged there for more than twenty years!"

"I never said it was a *lawful* hanging, miss."

Wordlessly, they turned to gaze out the back window at Execution Dock. The gibbet there was still used for the occasional pirate, but just now the noose hung empty. Arabella shuddered. And as she was turning round again, a man the size of a troll came up to her, his hat clutched to his breast.

"Name's Gun Jensen, missus. I knows 'oo *you* are. Just want to say it warn't right, what happened to Tom." This voice, raised in anger, would surely have shattered ceiling beams. "But never you fear! We found the rat what done it, alright! And Tom's been avenged!"

What should she say? Arabella thought wildly of Feben, with her wardrobe of character accents. Feben would have been up to this. What was it she said? "Every individual is a thousand different people." Keeping her head down, and her face covered, Arabella replied, in a tight, tense voice, "'Oo was it, Gun? 'Oo was it killed my Tommy?"

"Nobody as you'd know t' speak to, ma'm; just a hen-hearted coward for hire. Now 'e's outta the way like, an' you can rest easy. But *we* won't. We aim t' find the bastard as *ordered* it, an' we won't stop lookin' fer 'im till 'e's found. You have my word on that!" He turned his head, spat to one side, and without waiting for Arabella's thanks, he trudged back to the bar.

"That was brilliant, miss," whispered Frank. "All the same, I think we're both a bit out of our depth here. We'll have one drink, for form's sake, and be on our way. The barmaid told me just before you arrived that Tyke won't be here."

"Actually," said Arabella, "I'd rather we left *now*, if you don't mind."

"All right. We needn't stay. Let's get outside where we can walk and talk. No one will bother us, now they think you're Greely's widow."

"But that is one of the reasons I wish to be gone; I'm worried lest the real Mrs. Greely should pop in and denounce me as an imposter!"

She signaled to her coachman, who followed them outside. It was a relief to raise her veil again, and Arabella thrilled to feel the fog's cool tendrils slither across her cheeks—most welcome after the overheated atmosphere of that hellish room.

"Follow us, please, Trotter," she said. "Not too closely."

"There was really no need to worry, miss," said Frank. "I'd never have taken such a risk, if I didn't know for certain that Mrs. Greely wouldn't be visiting the Prospect tonight."

"No?" asked Arabella. "With her dead husband lying there in state? What could possibly take precedence over that? Where is Mrs. Greely?"

"At home, miss. Having her twelfth child."

"Oh, the poor woman! How will she care for her family alone?"

"I shouldn't worry about that, either, miss," said Frank. "Greely was something of a legend in these parts. You saw the way those ruffians treated his supposed widow!"

"Yes," said Arabella. "And I am accustomed to celebrity, as you know. Usually people crowd around, vying for a chance to talk to me. But this lot didn't even dare! I felt like a queen!"

"Mrs. Greely *is* a sort of queen, down here," said Frank. "The criminal community will take good care of her family, and see to it that the kiddies all grow up to be first-class smugglers, like their pa!"

Arabella stared meditatively at the toes of her shoes as they walked toward the bridge, the carriage following at a discreet distance. This was a terrible part of town. The Ratcliff Highway murders had happened near here only two years ago: a young family, and their apprentice, slaughtered like hogs in a pen. The case was never solved. Not really. But she didn't want to think about that just now.

"Frank," said Arabella, "what would you have done if Mr. Tyke had appeared?"

"Stood him to a drink and invited him to our table," said Frank.

"No! Would you really?"

"Oh, yes. Then I'd have introduced him to Mrs. Greely, the most powerful person in that room, and told him to produce Miss Worthington's letters or face the consequences."

"Brilliant!" breathed Arabella. "Oh, damn! Why didn't he come? I could have had the case solved tonight!"

By this time, Frank and the suppositional Widow Greely had arrived at London Bridge, and they decided to walk out upon it for a little way. The clammy mist engulfed them like wet smoke.

"You see, miss," Frank was saying, "the most vicious crimes always occur near the river, because the gangs are all based here. It's the ideal setup for them: tiny, crooked little streets, derelict warehouses, ships moored so close together you can leap from one deck to another when being pursued. Your Mr. Tyke stays here when he's at home, but he's a solo operator, not a gang member; what you might call a henchman for hire."

"Not *my* Mr. Tyke!" Arabella protested. "I don't know the first thing about him!"

"Ah," said Frank. "Well, he's a man of many talents. Routinely hires himself out for 'protective services,' if you know what I mean."

"No, I'm afraid I—"

"He roughs people up, for a price. I can't say if he's ever murdered anybody, but he's certainly been in a position to do so. We're searching for him now, as a matter of fact, in connection with a little matter involving a missing person."

"Oh!" said Arabella. "You wouldn't by any chance be referring to Mr. Savory-Pratt, would you?"

"Bless my soul! How did you come to know that?" Frank pulled out a notepad and a pencil from his breast pocket. "What can you tell me about this matter, miss?"

"Nothing that the police don't already know, I'm afraid; I had it from a couple of bailiffs who were watching his house."

"Oh," said Frank, masking his disappointment and putting his notepad away again. "Yes. We've already spoken to those two."

The idea of tracking Tyke to his lair had little appeal for Arabella now. She suddenly wanted to go home, but they were halfway across the bridge, and her carriage waited behind them, at the end of it. She tried to tell herself that it was not so bad as all that. New gas fixtures had recently been installed along the parapet here, and their light was somewhat reassuring when one stood directly beneath them, but for the most part, they only served to heighten the effect of the deep shadows that gathered and pooled in the spaces between the poles: They were more eerie than cheery. Watery moonlight, fighting its way through the miasma, lit up the water in uncanny patches, as sinister personages materialized ahead of them, or brushed past them from behind, their features indistinct in the fog.

"I should have liked to see this bridge in its heyday," Arabella said, resting her arms on the parapet and affecting a heartiness that she did not feel, "when it was all covered over in shops and houses."

"I doubt you'd have liked it, miss. It was filthy, crowded, and stinking in those days, worse even than now. Imagine all those blokes up at the Prospect, brought to this bridge with cartloads more, and herded along till they completely covered it over. That's your old London Bridge."

Despite her avocation, Arabella was averse to crime as a subject for study, except for highway robbery, of course, which she and everybody else considered dashing and romantic. That profession had all but died out now, though. The other sorts of crime were generally associated with garbage, violence, and unattractive locales. Why would anyone want to go to such places voluntarily, when they might stay comfortably at home? Why should *she*? Well, there was the danger, of course. And danger had an attraction all its own, for some people.

"I wish it were possible to arrest all the criminals—every last one—and send them to Tasmania," she said.

"It *isn't* possible, I'm afraid. What we really want is a strategy to prevent the commission of crimes in the first place."

"You're right, Frank. That would make far more sense. But it would also take a long time to see any results, and something should be done immediately. Law-abiding citizens are virtual prisoners after dark, cowering in their houses, afraid to go out. It's not even safe to visit the theater or the opera, despite the presence of so many other people."

"What do they expect?" Frank asked her. "People refuse to vote for a police force, because they're afraid it'll be a government spy system like the one they have in France. Londoners don't want their liberty threatened."

"Ridiculous!" snorted Arabella.

"Not at all—it will be threatened! We have good laws here, that no one pays any attention to, at present. It's unlawful to wander about drunk and disorderly; illegal to pick up a girl on a street corner for salacious doings. Half the practical jokes the bucks and dandies play on each other should by rights earn them a pleasant holiday in the stone jug! (Newgate, miss.) Nobody wants to be nicked for those things. Particularly the nobs, and they would be, if the laws were enforced."

"Well," said Arabella, "things would definitely be different if women had the vote."

"Yes," said her escort, who had always harbored a private respect for the fair sex. "No doubt, no doubt. Life would be safer if cooler heads prevailed."

A rowboat was pulling silently along the river toward them, its red and green lights winking in the darkness.

"That'll be the River Patrol," said Frank quietly, as they watched the boat draw nearer. "I'm thinking of going over to them."

"What! You'd leave the Runners?"

"I'm considering it. They've passed me over for promotion twice now, and the River Patrol has offered me a captaincy."

"Well," said Arabella uncertainly, "that is something, isn't it? What is it these fellows do, exactly?"

"They patrol the river by night, miss."

"No, I know that, but why? What are they looking for?"

"Thieves, mostly. Because there's no effective way to lock up a boat, you see."

Arabella's mind was racing: Would Frank really leave the Runners? He was such a useful connection! A river patrol captain would not be nearly as valuable to her, but Frank was prattling on as though he'd already accepted the post:

"Just imagine what it would be like if all the merchants on Bond Street were to leave their shop doors wide open behind them when they went home at night. That's what the Thames is like after dark."

"I should think you'd be bored, Frank, spending your nights rowing up and down, looking for thieves."

"The job also requires body retrieval, miss. Occasionally the river police are able to save suicides before they drown. Seems a waste of time, though, as they just have to hand them over to the hangman."

"How beastly! It seems to me that a person should have the right to take his own life if he wants to."

Frank was shocked. "Oh, by no means, miss! That's a crime against God!"

"Oh, well; put it out of your mind, then," said Arabella, whose views on the subject were somewhat unorthodox.

"Yes, miss; that I will!"

By now, the patrol boat was almost directly beneath them, and Frank, spotting an officer he knew, waved his arms. "Hoy!" he cried. "Up here!"

The man in the bow raised his lantern.

"Cap'n Dysart," he called, cupping his free hand around his mouth. "Something here for you, sir! Can you come down?"

"Why is he calling you 'captain' already?" Arabella asked, suspiciously. "I thought you were just thinking it over."

"Yes. Well, I *am*. But they're quite keen to bring me on board, as it were." He coughed, diffidently. "I'm just going to nip down there and see what they've found." He moved to the head of the stairs. "Come along, if you please, miss. I can't risk leaving you alone up here."

Arabella was not looking forward to whatever it was the river police had pulled out of the water, but she saw the folly in remaining on the bridge alone, and reluctantly followed Frank down the stairs.

"It's deuced hard hauling a corpse into a boat from the river," Frank was saying. "All dead weight, you see. I'm working on patenting an attachment for the stern, whereby bodies can be seized and hauled aboard more readily."

They descended the steps and stood in the ooze at the river's edge whilst the oarsmen brought the boat ashore. Inside, a sodden white corpse lay curled on the burden boards like an outsized shrimp. Its hands were tied behind it, and the throat had been slashed. There was no blood, though. It must have all drained out after the victim was dumped in the river. Arabella turned her head away, pulled down her veil, and shut her eyes.

"Where'd you find him?" Frank asked with genuine interest.

"Just here, sir; near Wapping Steps. He's been dead a few hours."

"I thought as much. Fellow up the pub as good as confessed to this. Miss Beaumont," he said, "may I present the late Mr. Jerry Tyke?"

She whipt round, and saw the beam from the lantern sparking off a pink jewel in the corpse's ear.

Arabella was something of an expert when it came to gemstones, and was capable of making instant identifications, even in poor lighting.

"Tourmaline!" she exclaimed. "Of *course!* Why didn't *I* think of that?"

Chapter 6

When she woke the next morning, the sun was streaming through her windows, as if inviting Arabella to enjoy life again, and chiding her for sleeping so late. But she ignored the summons, and sat up only to draw the pineapple bed curtains closer together.

Well, she thought, turning her face to the wall, at least I shall have my money now. And for some minutes she lay reveling in the luxury of her silken pillows, her lace-edged sheets, and the warm, rich, floral scents wafting through her window from the garden. Thus, laved in the atmosphere of a summer morning, she could almost have fancied the previous night's sinister adventure a bad dream . . . except for the corpses, of course. There could be no question that those were real—Tyke in the bottom of the patrol boat, with his slashed throat and maggot-white face. And Greely, his probable victim. Greely hadn't deserved that death, whatever he may have done, and the ghosts that haunted Tyburn Gallows would be surprised to find his shade among their number—a newcomer, after so many years. No doubt they would end by snubbing him. After all, *they* had been lawfully executed; Greely didn't belong there.

But this was not what Arabella wanted to think about on her first trouble-free day since Costanze's last visit. She should have been able to go back to sleep. She should have been happy . . . relieved . . . a lot of things. Instead, Arabella felt as if she had swallowed a heavy, chilled stone the size of her own stomach. The case, such as it was, had been too quickly solved. Now she would have nothing to do until Belinda returned.

That reminded her of Belinda's letter, which had arrived yesterday when Arabella had not had time to read it, and she rolled over to pluck the missive from her nightstand.

> *Dearest Bell,*
>
> *Following my last letter to you, I decided to take a walk in the woods by myself. The day was warm, and very still. There were no birds singing, which I found odd, if not ominous, and the only sound I could hear was that of the river. Presently, though, I became aware of another sound, a buzzing, which I took for bees until I drew closer and realized that it came from flies. Then I smelt blood. As I rounded the path, there was a great flurry of black wings and the alarmed croaking of ravens, which had been feasting upon half a stag. Just half. The poor creature, bisected at the midriff, was quite fresh, and the hind end appeared to have been dragged off into the bushes.*
>
> *I was frightened, Bell, for there is no predator in these parts large enough to do that. Then I heard something in the undergrowth, so I left, but all the way home I fancied I could hear it coming along behind me.*

*Mr. Gentry says there is a local legend about
some sort of tiger, with fangs like scimitars—
ridiculous, of course. All the same, he says the next
time I feel like a walk, I must take him with me,
and he'll bring a gun!*

Belinda's letter was a trifle unsettling, but in the company
of Peter Gentry and his gun, Arabella decided that Bunny
could be in no real danger.

At that point, the door creaked, and Rooney pushed it
open wide enough to admit his head. Then he leapt onto the
bed, where he began smiling and kneading the coverlet even
before Arabella had begun to stroke him.

"Well, I am glad that *you* don't have fangs like scimitars,"
she said, scratching his ears. "Feeding you half a stag a day
would be far too expensive!"

She reflected that even Belinda was having adventures
now, whilst her own had clearly come to an end. Of course, it
was a vast relief to be free from monetary worries, but the
case had provided a welcome distraction from loneliness, and
from those obtrusive reflections concerning Mr. Kendrick,
whose face kept popping into her mind at odd moments.
Like now.

"Oh! What am I doing?" cried Arabella, throwing back
the covers and slipping into her satin slippers. "I have the
Cyprian Society to think about!"

She floated down her spiral staircase, in the rosy glow produced from the round skylight and the softly tinted walls,
imagining herself inside a nautilus shell and at one with the
universe. She tried to tell herself that she was happy, but in
the pit of her stomach, the heavy, empty sensation persisted.

And it only oppressed her more when she saw that her
morning post contained a reply from the heretofore missing
Cuthbert Savory-Pratt. He had "concluded his business

abroad," he said, and was most eager to meet with her. This was not surprising: Arsy-Varsey was a voracious womanizer.

"Well, finally!" said Mrs. Janks, with whom Arabella was having breakfast.* "Now you can interview the last of your brother's gnat-brained friends, and have done with them, once and for all!"

"Well, this comes a bit late, I fear. The blackmailer was murdered last night."

"Murdered! There now; what did I tell you? That's what comes of you traipsin' about Putney at all hours!"

"It was Wapping, Mrs. J."

"I'm sure it was! And it might have been you that got murdered, 'stead of the blackmailer! I don't suppose you ever thought of *that,* did you?"

"Not for a moment. Because Constable Dysart was with me all evening," said Arabella, sipping her coffee. "Anyway, don't you want to hear about it? Somebody trussed the fellow like a chicken, cut his throat, and threw him into the Thames."

"You don't say so?" said the housekeeper with genuine interest. "Now, there's a to-do, if you like!"

"Quite," agreed Arabella, ripping the end off her croissant. "It seems to have been a vengeance killing: the murdered man committed a murder himself early yesterday morning, and I'm told his victim was quite popular, in certain sinister circles."

"Hmm. They done him the same way, I expect," murmured Mrs. Janks.

"No, actually they didn't. The first victim was hanged at the old Tyburn Gallows."

---

*Her decadent style of living had so corrupted Arabella, that she had fallen into the disreputable habit of occasionally sharing meals with her servants. Forgive her, reader, for she was accustomed to living on her own, and had grown a stranger to propriety.

"At Tyburn! Bless my soul! Why they don't tear that place down is beyond me, so it is! Maybe now they will, seeing as it's been christened as an official health hazard!" She paused to sprinkle pepper on her egg. "Well, leastways now you know that Mr. Savory-Pratt wasn't killed."

"Yes," said Arabella, "but as he's a friend of Charles's, that can scarcely matter to *me.*" She tore the letter in two and dropped it back onto the tray. "Between ourselves, Mrs. Janks, I am only too glad to wash my hands of this business!"

The housekeeper wiped her buttery fingers on her napkin. "Well, I think you ought to see the gentleman anyways, miss. Just to tie up all them loose ends and what have you."

"What loose ends?"

"Didn't you say this Snivelly-Pratt was the one who paid for the peep show?"

"Half of it."

"Then why not hear what he has to say? Either he'll confirm your suspicions about this Mr. Tyke or he won't. And perhaps he'll have something more to tell you. Then you'll be able to finish your CIN."

"That is sound advice, Mrs. Janks," said Arabella, retrieving the letter halves from the postal tray. "Thank you. I shall write to him and request an interview for this afternoon."

A quarter of an hour later she was dripping sealing wax upon her letter when Fielding announced the arrival of Miss Worthington and Mr. Pollard.

"So, Costanze has 'forgiven' me, has she?" asked Arabella with a grim smile. "Tell her I am not at home! . . . but stay a moment, Fielding; what is Mr. Pollard like?"

"I couldn't say, miss," replied the maid. "'E *looks* all right. But that don't mean 'e *is.*"

"Hmm, I confess I am curious to know what sort of man, with so many other options available to him, would voluntarily take up with Costanze. Very well. Shew the visitors into the morning room, if you please."

"Don't 'ave to," said the maid. "Miss Worthington's already dragged 'im in there 'erself and ordered tea, bold as you please! You'd think *she* was mistress 'ere, if you didn't know better!"

"Don't fuss, Fielding. I'd have given them tea, anyhow."

"Yes, but, seein' as 'ow she's bankrupted you, I thought you might want to make an exception in 'er case."

"That's all taken care of, now," said Arabella. "I am happy to report that we are once again 'in the chinks,' as they say."

"I'm pleased to 'ear it, miss. Oh, and Mr. Davies is come, too."

"Scrope Davies has arrived with *Costanze?*"

"No, he come on 'is own. But they was all three standing on the step together when I opened the door, and so when Miss Worthington and 'er gentleman went into the morning room, I put Mr. Davies in there with 'em."

"Oh, dear! Poor Davies!" cried Arabella. "I had better rescue him at once!"

"I think you'd better, miss."

Scrope Davies was a particular friend of Arabella's, and too rare a wit to be wasting his time with what Costanze herself referred to as "feathered brains." But when the hostess arrived at the morning room, she found to her surprise that Mr. Davies was already acquainted with Miss Worthington, through having been a longtime gambling companion of her protector's. Therefore, it was Scrope, rather than Costanze, who undertook the introductions between Arabella and Pigeon Pollard.

Mr. Pollard seemed pleasant enough. He had a fat under lip, and a good-natured, dullish sort of face, framed by a receding hairline and a small double chin. His hair, such as it was, was brown, silvered with gray, and he put Arabella in mind of an avuncular butcher. He was exactly the same height as Costanze, and did not appear to be in any way deranged or mentally deficient. Their introduction left Arabella none the wiser as to the source of his attachment to Miss Worthington.

"Bell!" Costanze burst out, once everyone had curtsied and bowed and curtsied and bowed. "What d'you think? Mr. Brinsley Sheridan has given me a part in his new comedy! I'm to play a roll!"

"Really?" asked Arabella in some surprise. "I should have thought Mr. Sheridan would know better than to tax you with a speaking part, Costanze! What sort of role is it?"

"Oh, any sort. A yeasty white one, I daresay."

"Well, he could scarcely have cast you as an African. Your eyes are too blue."

"Rolls don't have eyes!"

"No; but characters do. What part will you play? The heroine? The villainess? The village idiot?"

"Potatoes have eyes," said Pigeon helpfully.

And with that single remark, Arabella had her answer: Pigeon and Costanze were two of a kind.

"Yes, thank you, Mr. Pollard," she said dismissively. "Whatever should we do without you?"

"No, Bell; I *told* you," Costanze insisted. "I'm to play a *roll!*"

Mr. Davies, who had listened to the foregoing with amusement, now felt it time to weigh in.

"If the ladies will permit me? Mr. Sheridan's play is about a coffeehouse. Most of the parts are rolls or buns or meat pies. It's a parody, you see. Young Faraday is to be a Cornish pasty; Major Scott plays a crusty roll . . ."

"And what sort of roll is Costanze supposed to be?"

"I believe Miss Worthington is a *stale.*"

Davies and Arabella shared a knowing smile.

"There!" said Costanze, "I am glad that you are here, Mr. Davies, for *I* should never in a thousand years have been able to make Arabella understand me!"

"That is very true," said the hostess mildly. "Ignorance and the inability to make oneself understood are generally considered undesirable traits, but I cannot imagine you without them, Costanze."

Miss Worthington looked gratified, as though she had just received a compliment, and moved her chair closer to Arabella's. "Listen," she said, winking grotesquely, "I've been telling Pigeon what a splendid billiard table you have! Mayn't he go see it? And perhaps play a game or two with Mr. Davies?"

"By all means."

"Come along, Pigeon," said Scrope. "The ladies evidently wish to discuss something in private."

"They do?" Pigeon asked. "But how can they? We've only just arrived! I have not yet had time to do anything that they could possibly need to talk about!"

"Nevertheless . . ." said Scrope. And bowing to the courtesans, he made himself scarce, drawing the vaguely protesting Mr. Pollard after him.

"Costanze," said Arabella swiftly, before the other had a chance to spout any more of her absurd rigmarole. "You knew about the peepholes, didn't you?"

"Peepholes?"

"That day, when you and Lady Ribbonhat's footman were—"

Costanze put her hands over her ears. "Stop! Stop! Pigeon will hear you!"

"You should have thought of that before you decided to perform for the public!"

"What?"

"You knew that those men were up there, spying on you,

because afterwards . . . and I have this on good authority . . . afterwards, you took an envelope from Jerry Tyke, with money in it!"

"What a disgusting mind you have!" Costanze exclaimed. "Peepholes! Performing for the public! I don't know any Jerry Tyke and the only envelope I saw was the one with the blackmailer's letter inside it that I found pushed under the door after I got home from . . . after I got home!"

Arabella considered this. Could the envelope that Bumpy had seen—the one with Costanze's name on it, that he assumed contained payment for her performance—actually have held the blackmail threat? Bumpy had seemed very sure of his facts, and yet, Arabella felt sure that Costanze was too stupid to lie to her. She decided to change her approach.

"Costanze, do you suppose that Mr. Pollard would actually be angry to learn of your illicit amour? He seems a very amiable, easygoing sort of man. Perhaps he would forgive you, if, God forbid, this matter should ever come to light."

"Oh, no, Pigeon would throw me out at once—he said as much only last week—because he's actually a very jealous man though you would not think so to look at him so naturally I was horolized and scandified when I read that letter and realized what might have happened!"

"Well, I hope you will never be so stupid again," said Arabella. "I mean, I know that you *will* be stupid again, but hopefully not stupid enough to risk an affair behind his back. Mr. Pollard is perfect for you, Costanze. Promise me you will do nothing further to jeopardize your standing with him."

"All right," said Costanze. "But now you have made me forget what I came over here to tell you."

"Well, it probably wasn't important."

"Oh, but it *was!* I am certain it was something to do with the blackmailer!"

"You may put your worries to rest on that score," said

Arabella. "The blackmailer was murdered last night. Just in the nick of time, too; I don't want to dip into my capital if I can avoid it."

"That is odd," said Costanze. "Because I just received another demand this morning. The butler says it was handed in around nine o'clock. . . . Oh! That must be what I was going to tell you! Yes, it was! I have had another demand this morning and I want to know when you are going to catch this person and make him stop because I am getting jolly sick of these letters as it is a great nuisance to have to keep hiding them all from Pigeon!"

"You are mistaken," said Arabella, "the man is dead."

"Mistaken or not," said Costanze, extracting a crumpled note from her reticule, "here it is. And in the very same hand as the other one, too!"

She passed it to Arabella, who took it with wonder.

"But, this makes no sense," she said.

"Yes, it does!" Costanze replied. "He is ever so clear! He wants one thousand pounds, wrapped in brown paper and marked 'to be called for,' left with the postmaster! What is nonsensical about that?"

"No, I meant it does not make sense that you should have received a note from a dead man."

"Well, perhaps his ghost wrote it for him. Or maybe this Mr. Tyke of yours wasn't really the blackmailer after all."

Arabella groaned.

"Whatever is the matter, Bell? Don't you feel well?"

"No," replied Arabella faintly. "Not very."

Cuthbert Savory-Pratt was possessed of a monocle that he did not need, a libido he made no attempt to govern, and a nose so pointy that some people called him "Cuth*bird*." Everyone else called him "Arsy-Varsey," and sometimes even "Good Old Arsy-Varsey." The nickname had originated, according to Charles, following the forfeit in a game of Reverence. Charles had recounted the story to Arabella on the night of the snail dinner, sometime before he'd discovered what he was eating.

" 'Reverence'?" his sister had asked. "I have not heard of this game."

"Well, it's not a game so much as a tradition. And I'm not surprised at your unfamiliarity with it, you being a woman."

"Oh!" cried Arabella, who delighted in finding out such things. "Do you mean it is a secret male ritual of some kind, that women aren't to know about?"

"If you like to put it that way."

"Tell me, Charles! Tell me at once!" she commanded, seizing his little finger and bending it backward.

"Ow! You needn't go to such extremes! I'll gladly share it with you, but you won't like it."

And she hadn't.

CIN Entry:

This has nothing to do with the case: I am putting it down purely for posterity. Because I do not imagine that future generations will believe that such a thing ever happened.

When, in the course of an evening, a fellow finds himself in need of a privy and unable to discover one, he goes where he can, and decency dictates that he chuse a spot not too near the road or footpath or where many people pass by. But sometimes, via bad oyster stew or too much drink, the need is so urgent that there is no time to scout out a proper location. And if, in his vulnerable position, he is discovered by persons using the footpath or road that he is befouling, the miscreant is forced to take his hat in his teeth, and, with his hands behind him, fling it up and over his noggin with a toss of his head. Usually—almost always, actually—the hat lands in the deposit he has lately made. If the fellow refuses to do this, he is pushed hard in the chest, so that he falls, arsy-varsey, into his own excrement.

"Do you mean to say," said Arabella, "that this Savory-Pratt has actually . . ."

"Taken a pratfall, yes," Charles had replied. "On several occasions."

"He sounds like quite an *un*-savory prat, if you ask me!"

She decided to conduct this interview in the Cyprian Society's grand saloon, whose space was so vast as to suggest the opposite of intimacy. Given Arsy's salacious nature, Arabella intended that their tête-à-tête should more closely resemble a chance meeting at Lord's Cricket Ground. The *former* Lord's, we should have said. For that place being currently under demolition to make way for the Regent's Canal, Scrope Davies had jokingly suggested that matches might be held at the CS grand saloon until the new field should be ready. The meeting was set for Sunday, when there would be no interruptions from construction noise.

"Thank you for agreeing to meet with me, Mr. Savory-Pratt," said Arabella conversationally. "Everybody thought you were dead."

"Did they really? How awfully funny! I wasn't, you know—merely hiding out from Tyke. Now that *he's* the one who's officially dead, I shall at last be able to sleep soundly o'nights."

"Yes, well, good for you. I wonder whether you can tell me anything about the afternoon when you and the boys went to Bond Street. You know, where you watched the, er, rumpy pumpy through peepholes?"

"Right you are! That's when all the trouble started, you know. With this Tyke fellow, I mean. I say, would you mind moving in a bit closer? I prefer not to have to shout my answers."

"Actually, I prefer it this way," said Arabella. "We can always move to a smaller room if anyone else should come in and find us too loud. Do you think the two incidents were related?"

"'Course they were related! I paid for half that night's entertainment with a rubber checque. Of course, I didn't know it would bounce at the time; I never keep track of those things. But the mort sent Tyke round to see me, and I don't mind telling you I was scared half out of me wits!"

"Just a minute, if you please, Mr. Pratt; *who* sent Tyke round to see you?"

"Well, *she* did. The mort. It was all my idea, you know," he added. "I fixed the date—or rather, she told me the date and what time to come round. Bumpy paid her half down for the tickets, and I paid the other half—this bad checque I was telling you about—to Jerry Tyke. But that was afterwards."

Arabella could not believe what she was hearing. And yet, this was the second person who had identified Constance as the mastermind behind her own public humiliation. Now Savory-Pratt was claiming that she had sent Tyke to his house to collect on a bad checque! But she *couldn't* have! Constance simply did not possess the commercial acumen that such a setup would require.

"I see," said Arabella, who didn't at all, "but weren't you planning to go to Drury Lane, originally?"

"No. That was an idea that came to Charley after we started out. But I knew where we were headed, all right."

"Of course," she said, trying to sound casual. "And so, you saw the opportunity for blackmail, and simply seized it."

Arabella had hoped to catch him off guard. He was, after all, her last hope. But this disturbing news about Costanze had thrown off her timing.

"Ha!" said Savory-Pratt without turning a hair. "Blackmail's not my style, don' chew know. Even if it were, I shouldn't be such a fool as to tangle with *that* spider!"

"Now you're being absurd!" cried Arabella. "The woman's an utter simpleton!"

"You obviously don't know her, then."

"Know her? I should think I *do* know her! We grew up together!"

"Hum! Well, I don't mean to challenge your veracity, madam, but I rather doubt that, you know. I mean, she may have been your nanny or something—though I can't say as I could picture her working with sprats—but she's nearly twice your age, surely!"

"Constance? Twice my age? Whatever can you mean?"

"Is that her Christian name? It certainly doesn't match the surname."

"Of course it does! 'Constance,' as in steadfast, and 'Worthington,' as in worthy. The names fit perfectly *together*. As to whether they fit the *subject* . . ."

"I think we may be talking about different people," said Arsy-Varsey. "Who is Constance Worthington?"

"The woman you were *spying* upon," said Arabella, rather rudely. "The woman you *paid*."

"Which one?"

"What?"

"Which one is Constance? The woman we spied upon, or the woman I paid?"

Arabella looked confused.

"There!" he cried. "You see? I knew it! Knew it all along! You've got the whole thing muddled up! Constance may be the name of the entertainer, I'm sure I don't know, but the woman I *paid* was . . . well, actually, I *don't* know her Christian name, if she has such a thing, but the old bawd styles herself 'Madame Zhenay.' "

"Madame Zhenay!"

"That's the one. She runs a swank shop for the gentry, and struts about like a jackdaw in peacock's feathers, but she's nothing more than an ordinary crack salesman, with a dash of the devil thrown in. Anyhow, that's the crone that took the money—the one who staged the show at her place—whatcha-macallit's—Palais de Beautay."

"*That's* where you went?"

"Naturally. That's where she lives and works and every-thing. Well, in the end, you know, I persuaded my old man to buy her off. Otherwise, she would have had my balls on a plate. I'm certainly not going back there in a hurry! I say, are you nearly done with the questions? I'm coming over all peckish."

"Nearly, Mr. Savory-Pratt," said Arabella, writing furi ously, "and then I shall give you a slap-up dinner. You say this back room you were peeping into was at La Palais de Beautay?"

"That's right."

"Can you remember anything else?"

"What sort of thing?"

"Anything at all?"

"I saw Zhenay hand an envelope to that henchman of hers, the one who later came round and threatened to . . . well, anyway he's dead now, so you say—she gave him this envelope, and told him to deliver it to Miss Worthington."

"Yes," said Arabella, half to herself. "I suppose that must have been Constance's share of the takings."

"No. No, it wasn't. Because then she said, 'Don't bother opening it, Tyke; it ain't money.' I say, do you think we could eat now? I'm near famished!"

"By all means," said Arabella, summoning a waiter and rising from her chair. "Order whatever you wish. The restau-rant is just behind you."

"Oh! But . . . dear lady!" he cried, grabbing her hand and trying to pull her down onto his lap. "Surely . . . you are din-ing *with* me?"

The "dear lady" pulled her hand away before he could cover it with kisses.

"Surely . . . you jest," Arabella replied. And she left him there, in order to seek more agreeable company.

Of all the wonderful rooms-to-be at the Cyprian Society, the library was Arabella's favorite. Two full stories high, with an upper-level loggia, it featured two marble fireplaces, romantic mullioned windows, and floor-to-ceiling bookcases of red elm burl, which stood empty at the moment. The books they were destined to contain lay packed away in numerous wooden crates, which were stacked in orderly towers here, collected together in careless heaps there, or simply scattered at random about the room.

As she entered, Arabella saw, to her satisfaction, half a dozen courtesans distributed about the library like so many brilliant ornaments, for it had been decided, as a cost-cutting measure, that CS members might volunteer to do as much of the *amusing* labor as they liked. This was a cataloguing party.

Marguerite Le Marchand had enjoyed a brilliant stage career before discovering that she could earn more money on her back. This tall, bold Amazon was now pulling books from a crate and calling out their titles and authors in those ringing tones that had formerly been famous for reaching not only the back row, but all the way to the street.

In breeches, neckcloth, and handsome, cutaway coat, Amy Golder-Green sat drawing up a list from Marguerite's announcements, whilst the very lovely Victorine Cobb wrote out catalogue cards, placing them in piles according to subject.

Idina Almond was diligently transferring excelsior and empty crates to an out-of-the-way corner for later disposal by somebody else. With her little, pointed chin and enormous blue eyes, she resembled nothing so much as a kitten with a plan.

Over in a corner, Dido Laithwaite, a woman of classic proportions who liked to conserve energy for activities that paid her, reclined upon a crate, reading one of the books she'd lately unpacked. And motherly May Tilden wove her way continuously through the crates and courtesans with a teapot, keeping everyone's cup filled.

"Hullo, Miss Beaumont!" shouted Amy, abandoning her list and coming over to join Arabella. "These new bookcases are absolutely top hole! Marguerite thinks they should have carved designs, but I say you were right to keep them plain—carving would detract from the patterns in the burl."

Arabella smiled with satisfaction. She was open to members' suggestions on how best to decorate the club, but all of the major decisions were to be hers. This was only right, as it was her money that was paying for everything. Or would be, once she got the blackmailer squared away. The decision to allow Samuel Johnson's "witticisms" a place in the CS library had not been her choice (Arabella could not bear him. Or Boswell, either), but the resolution to give in graciously to popular demand had.

"Ow! My sitting bone!" complained Dido, rising from her crate to rub the spot named. "I cannot wait till the day when everything's finished, and all the sophas, cushions, and comfy chairs shall have been placed in every room!"

"That day approaches," said Arabella. "Though perhaps it won't be soon."

"Soon enough, I daresay," said Idina, smiling. "And then we may come here whenever we wish, to relax and be free, without having to always be smartly dressed and made up! It will be heavenly!"

"Speaking of being made up," said Arabella. "I wonder whether any of you is in the habit of patronizing La Palais de Beautay?"

An affirmative murmur went up from the company.

"And what can you tell me of Madame Zhenay?"

"A horrible old harridan!" said Marguerite with vehemence, "though I must admit that she makes the best Disappearment Cream in town."

"Oh! Doesn't she, though?" cried Victorine. "I go there at least once a fortnight for a pot of Divine Beautificience, but I try to time it when I know Zhenay won't be there. I much prefer to deal with the shop assistant."

"She charges the earth for her beautifying bran baths," said Dido indignantly, "and then has the effrontery to make *more* money off us without our knowledge! Gentlemen pay as much as a guinea to watch us through peepholes!"

"Do they!" exclaimed Arabella.

"She tried to do that with me," said Marguerite. "But I outfoxed her! I reserved a bath, and had just begun to remove my clothing, when I noticed a dozen pair of eyes peering at me from behind the wall!"

"What did you do?" asked Victorine.

"I put my shoes and gloves back on, and returned to the sales floor, claiming to have been stricken with a sudden, violent headache. Zhenay allowed me to reschedule for the following day, and when I returned the eyes were there, just as before. This time, I pretended not to see them and began to undress, but when I got down to my shift, and reckoned that my audience was completely absorbed, I said very loudly, 'If anyone gets paid for this, it should be me!' Then I took out a bundle of paper slips bearing my address, and poked them into the eyeholes. Carefully, of course, so as not to blind anyone."

Her listeners broke into applause, and Marguerite curtsied to them, out of habit perhaps, with lowered eyes and a finger under her chin.

"In that case," said Arabella, "the news that Madame Zhenay is blackmailing one of our members probably won't surprise anyone."

"Why should it?" Dido replied. "She runs the most lucrative blackmailing business in London. Amongst other things."

"What other things?"

"Well, I couldn't say for *certain*, but I've *heard* that she goes in for baby snatching, burglary, and murder-for-hire."

"Don't forget bribery," said May.

"That goes without saying. Wherever there's an illegal penny to be made, you'll find Madame Zhenay at the front of the queue."

"She's got thugs and pickpockets working for her all over London," said Amy.

"Why is she not in prison?" Arabella asked.

"Too sharp. She's always one step ahead of the law."

"Well, I must meet with her, and stop her from blackmailing our Cyprian sister. Would one of you be so good as to accompany me to La Palais de Beautay tomorrow, and effect an introduction?"

"Why wait till tomorrow?" asked Victorine. "I can take you now."

"But it's Sunday," said Arabella.

"That makes no difference to Madame! She is open every day, including Christmas! Anyhow, I pass right by her shop, and I am almost out of Aphrodi-tease Elegant Extract Balm."

"Here's a fiver," said Dido. "Buy me a bottle of Milk of Paradise Satin Carressment Serum, there's a darling, and you may keep the change."

Arabella winced. "Other outrages aside," said she, "I think this Madame Zhenay should be hanged for what she is doing to the language!"

But nobody minded her.

"Victorine," said Marguerite, "would you mind getting me some Dewy Buttock Veneer?"

There followed an interlude of sundry verbal requests, a plethora of little notations, and the handing over of rather a lot of money. But all was accomplished in short order, and a list of who wanted what drawn up, because the library, even at this early stage, was plentifully supplied with note paper, and it will be remembered that Arabella always kept a pencil behind her ear.

"I cannot comprehend this," she remarked to Victorine as they made their way to Bond Street, "Madame Zhenay doesn't *need* to be a criminal. Her cosmeticks business is doing very well, I hear."

Victorine shrugged. "For some people," she said, "there is *never* enough."

"What's she like, then?" asked Arabella.

"What! Have you never seen her?"

"No, but I can just imagine what she must—"

"Oh! It's Miss Cobb! The very person I was hopin' to meet!" cried a young woman, coming up to them.

"I'm sorry," said Victorine. "I'm afraid you have the advantage."

"It's me!" said the young lady. "'Arriet! You know; the shop assistant what worked at Madame Zhenay's! I'm not s'prised you didn't know me. Nobody never *does* recognize shop girls outside the shops, do they?"

Victorine visibly recoiled. For a shop assistant to hail a customer in public, boldly claiming familiarity through having served her from behind the counter, was a breach of decorum meriting immediate dismissal. But the girl seemed fully aware of this, for she apologized, and explained herself at once.

"I just wanted to let you know," said she, "that I've been given the sack. So you'll 'ave to deal with the old witch 'erself from now on, 'stead of me waitin' on you. I'm sorry for coming up to you on the street like this, but I know 'ow you feel about 'er, and I wanted to spare you from a nasty shock when you went in."

Victorine made a gracious recovery.

"Why, thank you, Harriet! That is most kind of you. But why on Earth should you be sacked?"

The girl shrugged. "*She* said it's on account of the way I speak. You know, not genteel enough for 'er fancy kly-on-tell. But she knew 'ow I talked when she took me on, didn't she? The word is, Madame gets rid of all 'er girls after they been there six months. It's 'er policy like, only she won't admit it. Thinks we'll discover 'er sidelines, I shouldn't wonder. Actchully, miss, I'm that relieved not to be workin' there anymore. She's a menace in a mobcap, that's what she is; the very sight of 'er fair gives me the collywobbles."

Arabella felt a sudden coldness at the base of her spine, as she saw, in her mind's eye, a tall figure, bulky rather than willowy, with enormous, knot-knuckled hands dangling from a pair of sinewy arms, and reaching almost to her knees; a hideous face, pop-eyed, with a vast expanse of white eyeball showing all around the black irises, the way they do with mad persons. Warts surrounded the eyes, which surmounted a pendant nose and nether lip. There were also the dark beginnings of a mustache. So vivid and startling was this vision, that Arabella wondered whether it were some sort of psychic warning. But a moment's reflection yielded the source: an illustration of a female ogre, from the fairy-tale book she was reading to Eddie.

Whilst Victorine and the shop girl stood commiserating with one another, Arabella gazed across the street at La Palais de Beautay, where even now a hand was placing a HELP WANTED, ENQUIRE WITHIN sign in the window.

"Will you excuse me, Victorine?" she asked. "I have just remembered something which requires my urgent attention at home."

"Oh!" shrieked the other in sudden alarm. "Surely you cannot mean to abandon me! When you know how I feel about . . . about *her!* How can I possibly go in there alone?"

"I am sorry, my dear," Arabella replied, hastening away. "But I shall have to save you another time!"

Eddie had been taking her naps and eating her meals as instructed, and was now enjoying the promised reward: a visit to the downstairs divan, which the servants had bolstered with ten thousand cushions after wrapping their charge in a wool shawl. The day was too warm for this, and Eddie was perspiring freely, but it was better than staying upstairs with only the four walls for company. Here, at least, Doyle and Fielding were sitting nearby with their mending, though actually they were not much better than the upstairs walls, for neither had the slightest idea how to talk to children. They spoke quietly to each other as though Eddie were not present, so that she had frequently to obtrude herself.

"I wish Aunt Belinda were here," she said to the ceiling. "What did she want to go to Scotland for, anyway?"

"She was given a c'mission to work on a model of Sir Birdwood-Fizzer's family castle," said Fielding. "It's got to be perfect, down to the last detail, and Miss Belinda is decorating the little rooms."

"By herself?" asked Eddie.

"Not 'ardly, miss! There's a staff of ten for the decorations alone! And Miss Belinda's in charge! We're all ever so proud of 'er!"

"Well, now," said Doyle. "Oy'd almost fergot; yer aunt sent word that we was to give you somet'in' when ye were strong enough t' sit up. So, seein' as how yer doin' that now . . ."

"Oh, but she ain't yet," Fielding broke in. "She's only propped up wif cushions! Besides, the mistress said we wasn't supposed to excite the child."

"Fiddlesticks!" said Doyle. "Jist lookit her! We'll not be doin' the child any favor by withholdin' the gift now it's been mentioned! Besoyds, no one as Oy've heard of ever suffered no harm from receivin' a present!" And she left to fetch it.

Belinda had only learned of Eddie's arrival when she herself was on the point of departure, so there had been no time to make up one of her famous billy-boxes. But there was a "box for a little girl" amongst her general stock, which was decorated with such feminine touches as ribbons and velvet scraps, and which contained a string of beads, a tiny doll, seashells, a paper fan, some pretty stones, a little pinecone, sea glass, a silver pencil, a notebook, some foreign coins, and a child-sized spyglass.

Eddie was enchanted with her box, and joyfully exclaimed over each item as she drew it forth, holding it up for Doyle and Fielding to see and then setting it down on the table next to the divan. When she was through, she put them all carefully back again, except for the notebook, the pencil, and the telescope.

"These are my favorites," she said decisively.

"Oh, yes?" Fielding asked. "Why those, in particular?"

"Because I want to be a detective, like—"

The front door slammed, and Arabella rushed into the room. Without stopping to explain herself, she began tearing off her clothes as though they were on fire.

"Fielding, I must ask a favor, and am in a dreadful hurry. I need to borrow one of your frocks. And shoes, stockings, a hat . . . everything."

"Yes, miss. Any particular frock? I 'ave three."

"Just get me whatever you would wear to an interview with a prospective employer."

"Right you are, miss! I'll fetch you down a outfit in two shakes of a dice box!"

The faithful Fielding was still upstairs when somebody knocked at the front door, so Doyle had to answer it.

"How do you do?" said Feben Desta politely. "I shan't come in; I have just stopped by to deliver the meeting minutes to Miss Beaumont."

"Miss Desta?" said Arabella, emerging from the drawing room in her shift. "Please stop a while! I should be ever so grateful for your critical eye."

"Well," said the visitor, looking her over, "it's a good-ish sort of shift, in its way, but I know a seamstress who, despite her excellent work and lavish hand with lace, charges very reasonable rates for underclothing."

"No, I meant that I want your opinion on . . . really? Lavish with lace, yet reasonable? Remind me to ask you about her, later. Just now I am dressing myself as a humble member of the working class, and I must look absolutely convincing."

Feben followed Arabella into the drawing room, just as Fielding arrived with the clothing. The frock was fuller and the fabric coarser than Arabella was used to, but she would only be wearing it for a short while. Today, anyway.

"Wait, miss," said Doyle. "You've fergot the pockets, so ye have!"

"Damn!" said Arabella, lifting her skirts. "That's right! I cannot have a reticule, can I?"

"No, indeed," said Feben, as Doyle tied the pockets round her mistress's waist. "Not if you intend to pass for working class. People will assume you have stolen it from a lady, or out of a shop window."

"But I shall require *some* means of carrying the goods, and I may not always be in a position to hike up my skirts and search for the pocket openings!"

"These pockets'll do ye just fine, miss," said Doyle firmly. "See? There's a slit in the skirt's either side. An' if they're tied on just so, you can slip anything ye fancy straight into 'em!"

Put to rights at last, Arabella reached for her hat.

"No," said Feben, taking it from her. "Let's try a soft cap, shall we?"

"But those are only worn indoors," Arabella protested. "I have seen respectable working-class women in hats."

"Not hats like *this,*" Feben replied, holding up Arabella's expensive little watered-silk number. "Poor women cannot afford such expensive trifles. Borrow a mobcap from your maid."

"Saints alive!" said Doyle after the ladies had left in Miss Desta's carriage. "Whatever in the world is the mistress up to now?"

"I 'aven't a clue," Fielding replied.

"Well, *I* have!" said Eddie, her eyes sparkling with excitement. "Aunt Bell is back on the case!"

At a quarter past three precisely, a quiet, young woman rang the rear bell at La Palais de Beautay, and informed the shoe-faced servant who answered that she was come to apply for the position.

"Name?" asked the servant disinterestedly.

"Bella Daltry," Arabella replied. That would be easy enough to remember, she thought: "Bell Adultery."

"Wait 'ere," said Boot Face, and went off to find the mistress.

From where she stood, Arabella caught a glimpse through an open door of a small, windowless room, with walls covered in Hessian cloth and an unmade bed. She wondered again what Madame Zhenay would look like, and to her initial image, Arabella now added veritable tusks and a head scarf, tied peasant fashion under the chin. She was therefore surprised and relieved when a rather average-looking woman of middle age appeared and beckoned her through to the shop proper. She was about Arabella's height, but considerably heavier, with olive skin and very fierce eyebrows. No, Arabella decided—not average, after all. There was something frightening, and at the same time compelling, about those black eyes of hers. You didn't want to look into them, but all the same, you could not quite look away, either. They held you there, without blinking, their watchful stillness like a cobra's that has marked its prey from a distance. The former shop assistant had got it right: She was a menace in a mobcap. And yet, Madame might have been a sensation in her youth, if only she had kept her eyebrows plucked.

" 'Bella,' " she said. "That's a nickname, I take it. Your real name would be Arabella?"

The utterance of her real name was so unexpected that the

applicant blushed, and began to babble, somewhat in the manner of Constance.

"Why . . . yes! Yes, it is! So common, really—every other female in London is an Arabella—poor Mother wasn't very imaginative but she was a dear; you should have tasted her pork pies—that's how we survived after Papa drank himself to death, you know—they were the best pork pies in Holborn! At least everyone said they were . . ."

"Hmm," said Madame. "Ever worked in shop before?"

"Yes! That is, not exactly a *shop* . . . Mother and I sold our pies on the street, from a basket, and I can remember—"

"Have you any references, girl?"

"I can get some, if you'd like me to, but I thought I had better come to you directly I saw your sign in the window, lest you should hire somebody else."

"I like your initiative," said Madame. "And you know how to sell, if you're telling the truth. But do you know how to sell *to gentry?* This is a high-class shop."

Arabella detected the barest suggestion of an accent. Not foreign, though: Cheapside, perhaps.

"High class!" simpered Arabella. "Well, I should think so! One could scarcely imagine a lady like yourself selling to . . . to just anyone!"

Madame grunted again, but seemed pleased. "Tell me, how is selling to the gentry different from selling to the poor?"

"I believe the best way," Arabella replied, "is to seem *not* to be selling so much as describing the merits of a product. It should feel as though the two of you were having a quiet cup of tea together and discussing a topic of mutual interest."

Madame Zhenay raised her eyebrows in surprise. "You speak very prettily, girl! And you seem to know a lot about the gentry."

That was what she *said,* but her eyes, her gestures—everything else about her told Arabella, whose business it was to notice such things, a very different story. This woman found her attractive. In a *particular* way.

"Well, naturally I don't like to talk about it, ma'm," said Arabella, "but I used to move in higher circles than those to which I have grown accustomed of late. You see, my father was a baronet, in Durham. He speculated and lost everything, and—"

"I thought you said he drank himself to death."

"Yes. He took to drink after losing all our houses. Poor Papa was so ashamed that he couldn't face us sober. That's why Mother took to selling p-p-pork p-p—" Here Arabella broke off to bury her face in her handkerchief, overcome by the hopeless abyss into which fate had cast her.

"There, there," said Madame, stroking the applicant's cheek and squeezing her round the waist. "They say God never sends us more than we can bear."

"Yes," sniffed Arabella. "They do say that!"

"And you don't think it would upset you to wait upon ladies who might have been your friends under happier circumstances?"

"Oh, no; quite the contrary! For I shall sometimes be able to pretend, without presuming, of course, that I am back in dear old Durham House once more, holding an at-home day."

"In that case, I have made up my mind. Miss Daltry, the position is yours!"

"Mr. Tyke wasn't the blackmailer after all, was he?" Eddie asked, when Arabella came up to see her that evening. "It's someone else, isn't it?"

"Yes, I am afraid so."

"Do you know who it is, then?"

"As a matter of fact, I do. It is Madame Zhenay, proprietor of La Palais de Beautay, and I have just procured employment there as her shop assistant!"

"Oh, brilliant, Aunt Bell! Now what?"

"I shall take every opportunity to search the premises for Constance's correspondence with that blasted footman. Once I have got the letters, I shall denounce Madame to the police and have her arrested."

Arabella expected to hear more accolades upon her cleverness, but Eddie lay very still, looking pale and pensive amongst the pillows.

"Arrested? On what charge?" she asked. (For it will be remembered that her stepfather was a policeman.)

"Blackmail, of course!"

"But how will you prove it? You're not planning to show the letters to anybody, are you, Aunt Bell? That would defeat your purpose."

"I . . . no, of course not . . . but I am certain that Madame Zhenay is up to more than blackmail. I expect I shall find proof of all sorts of dark doings!"

"Well, I hope you are right. Because I fear that you will have a hard time securing her arrest, otherwise."

"One has to take these things a step at a time, Eddie," said Arabella, who was starting to feel rather cross. "First I must find the letters. Then I shall worry about how to dispose of Madame Zhenay."

Eddie smiled, but it only made her look anxious, and Arabella reminded herself that the child was ill, after all. "Just as you like, Auntie," she said. "And you will keep me informed, won't you? To tell me how you get on?"

"Naturally. You and I are partners, now."

And this time, Eddie's smile lit up her face like good health and sunshine.

Chapter 7

Over the course of the next two weeks, Arabella lost nearly all her friends. Such things often happen when one falls in love, and Arabella certainly exhibited every symptom synonymous with that giddy state: She scarcely ate or slept. Frequently she would go into a trance and not hear a word that was spoken to her. Worst of all, she became an expert on the subject of her affections, and would ramble on interminably about every slightest detail pertaining to her beloved's outstanding qualities.

For, though she had a career, Arabella had never held an actual job before, and quickly fell into the novice's manner of thinking that everything about her place of work made for exciting conversation. Hence, her subject embraced, but was not limited to, customer relations, standard procedures for opening and closing the shop, taking inventory, and quality control. She should no doubt have loved to discuss the chemical composition of the facial creams and hair dyes, as well, but fortunately for everyone else, these were trade secrets, and Arabella had taken an oath never to reveal them.

Her friends had been supportive at first. But the London season was under way, and there were those who felt they might have had more lavish entertainments from their celebrated hostess than they in fact got. At first, everyone had endured Arabella's ecstatic descriptions of shelving systems and stockroom routines in the hopes that she would soon settle in and stop talking about them so much. But she didn't, and at last even her most fervent admirers were forced to admit that she was not going to get over this anytime soon. A few friends who had gone out of town, and who were in the habit of corresponding with her from wherever they happened to be, stopped writing after receiving one or two letters full of nothing but Palais de Beautay minutiae.

It was easier for the Cyprians. They barely knew Arabella yet, and simply found things to do elsewhere. But in time, her gentleman admirers of long standing came to openly resent Arabella's fixation, and one by one, began to give excuses for non-attendance at her twice-weekly gatherings. It was a shame, really. The Lustings salons had been famous for their stimulating discussions, and the men lamented amongst themselves the unhappy change that had come over their favorite hostess.

Arabella scarcely noticed. The imposition upon her free-living lifestyle of a job with set times and daily routines imparted meaning to her days and soothed her restless spirit. Sometimes she nearly forgot what she was really going there for.

In fact, if it were not for Eddie continually asking questions and making suggestions, Arabella might have devoted herself to the shop completely, and never been heard from again. But Eddie kept her focused—responding patiently to every enraptured description of the business, and the stock, and the customers—by reminding her aunt what this was all in aid of, until the child's persistence was finally rewarded.

"Not yet," said Arabella, in reply to the usual question, "but I believe I now know the room in which Zhenay must keep them, for I have inspected every square inch of the ground floor, including the lab kitchen, where our inventory is cooked and created, and there are definitely no letters there."

"You will need to search upstairs, then," said Eddie.

"Quite. Of course, I have suspected they were up there all along; they are almost certain to be somewhere in Madame's bedroom."

"Why the bedroom, especially?"

"Isn't that where you would keep them, were you a black-mailer?"

"No," said Eddie promptly. "I should place them in the right-hand drawer of my boudoir desk."

"I am fairly certain that Madame does not have a bou-doir," said Arabella. "Besides, her desk is downstairs in the office, and I have already checked there."

"In that case, I suppose I *would* hide them in my bed-room," said Eddie thoughtfully. "Underneath the mattress."

"That might serve if there were only a few letters. But hav-ing observed the behavior of the customers who come into our shop, I feel certain that Madame Zhenay is blackmailing nearly all of them. If my guess is correct, she would have far too many letters to stuff under a mattress. Besides, that would be risky. She probably keeps them in a strongbox. The trouble is, I have no excuse to go upstairs and look for it."

Arabella would have to find one soon, however, as her debtors were growing increasingly impatient. She had to keep telling herself, I am all right now. For this moment and this day, I am all right. But when she went to the printers to collect the new CS calling cards, her supply of good moments suddenly ran out.

Mr. Weems, ordinarily the soul of cordiality, gave her the fish eye as she entered. Arabella surmised at first that he was having an off day, and that it had nothing to do with her, per-sonally.

"Ah!" she said. "Good afternoon, Mr. Weems! My calling cards, if you please!"

He drew out a box from under the counter, and lifted the lid to show her the top card: Two golden birds of paradise, facing each other with tails intertwined, against a background of imperial blue, and in the space thus framed by their necks, breasts and legs:

THE CYPRIAN SOCIETY
ST. JAMES'S PLACE
LONDON
MISS A. BEAUMONT

Arabella professed herself delighted. As arranged, in lieu of payment, she produced for the proprietor two passes to her new theater's opening-night extravaganza.

"I've changed my mind," said Weems, shoving the passes back at her. "We do this on a strictly cash basis, or we don't do it at all."

Arabella was shocked. "But . . . I thought we agreed . . ."

"Yeah. Well, it's different now; the missus said you was practically bankrupt. Besides, she's not keen to go—says she'd rather attend the Samuel Johnson review at the Haymarket."

Taking up the passes again, Arabella turned on Mr. Weems an icy, gray-green stare. "A good businessman never goes back on his word, sir." Her voice was level, low, and deadly. "I offered you free admission to what promises to be the season's greatest gala, if not the decade's, and you agreed to take passes in lieu of payment. That you have gone back on your word is an unforeseen development, as I have known you for an honest and fair-dealing tradesman in the past. But the fact that you and your . . . 'missus' . . . have decided instead upon the Samuel Johnson revue does not surprise me in the least. Simple minds are unimpressed by the astounding, and simply astounded by the unimpressive!"

"It's not that," said the printer, quailing before her unassailable supremacy. "We'd just . . . rather have the money, that's all."

"You would rather have the money," said Arabella, exhaling forcefully through her nostrils, "when you might have been the envy of your circle! The number of tickets is limited, Mr. Weems. We have had a great many applications for them. Had you decided to accept the passes, and then offered them up for sale, you might have made ten times what you are charging for the calling cards. However," she said, returning the tickets to her reticule, "I am glad this has happened, for these are worth their weight in gold, and I would much prefer to bestow them upon someone who fully appreciates their value. Good day!"

A short time later, she was sitting in her carriage beneath the plane trees in Berkeley Square, consoling herself with a frozen pineapple mousse brought over from Gunter's by no less a personage than James Gunter himself. At least *he* had had the sense to accept passes in lieu of currency, although Arabella might have paid cash for this little indulgence. Indeed, she might have paid for the calling cards, too; things had not got quite so bad as all that. But she was worried, and when Arabella worried, she instinctively curtailed the outflow of all monies whatsoever, excepting her servants' wages. She was reflecting on the possibility that it might be equally unwise to squander her theater passes, when Trotter was hailed by a passing postman, who handed up a letter for his mistress.

Belinda had written again, and Arabella found herself torn between two pleasures, for she could not wait to read this latest missive from her sister, yet dared not risk setting aside the pineapple mousse on such a warm day. She therefore attempted two options simultaneously whilst the carriage was moving, with predictable results: Drops of melting mousse began to adorn the pages of the letter, but as they only fell on the margins, Arabella did not care.

Dearest Bell,

Last week I had a very queer dream, which, given your interest in such matters, I shall endeavor to relate to you as best I can. Well, then, I found myself on a rooftop in Baghdad, admiring the city at dawn. Everything was touched with gold, and one of the minarets was smothered in climbing roses. I thought it very pretty at first, although the color of the roses—a threatening scarlet—bothered me, for some reason. All at once, they began to throb and pulse with a kind of palpable evil. The next thing I knew, Baghdad had disappeared, and the roses were scarlet spots on someone's skin. My skin! When I woke up, I learned that Sir Birdwood-Fizzer had come over all spotty in the night. It is Measles, and the house is under quarantine until further notice. So I am afraid that I shall not be returning home next week, after all.

Arabella groaned aloud. Absolutely nothing seemed to be going her way these days. She had been unable to afford Bath this season. She had not found Costanze's letters yet. And now she would be denied the solace of her sister's presence until nobody knew when.

Stop this, she told herself. It's never as bad as one thinks! Look at all the things I have to be happy about: a beautiful summer; a fascinating new job, which earns me a small but regular salary; the slow but steady return of Eddie's health . . .

This last was a mixed blessing, as the child had commenced a terrific teasing campaign to be allowed to go out of doors. But although Arabella was obliged to run risks in her professional life, she was loathe to take chances when it came to her niece's health, and she stood her ground against Eddie's sorties with a determination that would have impressed General Wellesley.

Arabella looked in on her charge as soon as she got home, and discovered the little invalid with her eyes shut and an open book face-down upon the coverlet. When her aunt attempted to remove it, Eddie said, "I am not asleep, you know; I'm thinking."

"Are you? What about?"

"Murder. If a murder were discovered, how should I proceed?"

"And how should you?"

"First, I should go to the scene where the crime was committed. That is key. And I should look all over it for anything unusual or out of place which might be important. Then I should hold private conversations with each person who either saw or heard anything, or who lived nearby."

"Ah! And what should you ask them?"

"That would depend upon the circumstances. But mostly, I think, I should just let them talk, and watch their faces and gestures, to see whether they were lying or frightened, or keeping something back. Then I should write up all the details in a notebook, the way you do, so as not to forget anything, and when I had done all I could, I should take the case to my stepfather, and ask for police assistance."

"That is impressive, Eddie. Did you just think all this up whilst lying here?"

"Some of it. The rest came from this book Frank brought me whilst you were out." She held it up so that Arabella could read the title: *Proven Techniques for the Modern Detective.* "But now I'm dull, again. I am staying in bed, like you told me I should, but there is nothing to *do* here." She sighed tragically. "Probably, I shall go mad."

"I don't think there is much danger of *that,*" said Arabella, smiling.

"But there *is,* though. For instance, before you came in, I was lying here quietly, with my hands folded, thinking the things I have just told you about. When you leave the room I shall go on lying here, but now that I've told you what I was thinking, there is no reason to go on with that. So I shall simply stare and stare and stare out the window. Perhaps a bird will fly past. Or a breeze will shake that bough and cause it to bob up and down a bit. I shall observe it through my little telescope. There is a very early peach hanging from a branch out there, which is nearly ripe. Will the breeze be strong enough to shake it off? Probably it won't. And then I shall put the telescope away and use the chamber pot.

"Life is so short, Aunt Bell! I might be dead in a week or a month or thirty-five years, but however long I live, I shall always regret having spent so many precious days lying in bed and being dull, when I might have been solving a mystery!"

"Well," said Arabella, "I'll tell you what: If you will consent to lying here for the rest of the day like a good little invalid, then tomorrow I shall allow you to go out of doors. You must agree to stay in a chair, though, and there is to be no excitement; no exerting yourself. The last time I allowed you to come downstairs, you were exhausted for three days afterward!"

"I perceive your problem," said Eddie astutely. "You are on the horns of an ethical dilemma, here: Should you confine me to bed, and risk losing me to madness, or allow me to go outside, where I might be excited to death? But I promise you, the former plan incurs the greater risk."

"Where did you learn the term 'ethical dilemma'?" asked Arabella in amazement.

"From Epicurus."

"You're reading *Epicurus?*"

"There is very little else one can do in bed, at my age."

Arabella smiled. "Eddie, dear; you may be my brother's issue, but I suspect that you are actually more like me."

"Exactly," said Eddie, with a smile. "I am the daughter you never had."

The next afternoon Eddie was permitted to sit for an hour in the garden whilst her aunt read aloud to her from *Grimm's Household Tales*.

" 'Then Sana put the water on to boil, and began to sharpen the knives,' " read Arabella, " 'for she was preparing to cook the little boy that very day and serve him up for her master's supper.' Now, that's odd, wouldn't you say?"

"Yes, rather," Eddie replied. "I doubt that her master, being told he was eating his ward, would have been happy about it."

"No, I did not mean that. Well, that, *too,* of course, but I was referring principally to the fact that whilst the Grimms seldom give names to their heroes, they almost never give names to their villains, being satisfied with 'the wolf,' 'the witch,' or 'the giant.' And yet this person, the very worst of them all, the cannibal servant, is named 'Sana.' I wonder . . ."

"What, Aunt Bell?"

"Whether this story isn't based on a true incident. Not the part further on, where the children turn themselves into ducks and chandeliers; I mean this beginning bit. *Was* there a cook named Sana, who killed and cooked her master's stepchild? She might have been an ancestor of Madame Zhenay's!"

But Eddie, delighted to be out of doors again, was admiring the natural beauty that surrounded her, and giving little heed to cannibals, with or without names.

"Look, Aunt Bell! Is that not the cunningest thing you have ever seen?"

A fledgling was perched upon the uppermost erection of Arabella's double-phallused Pan statue, frantically fluttering its wings and emitting loud, insistent cheeps. As they watched, the parent bird alighted with a beakful of smashed insects, and proceeded to stuff the buggy porridge down its youngster's gullet.

"No," replied her aunt, who resented being upstaged. "I have seen any number of things more cunning than *that!*"

(Nevertheless, it was the first subject she wrote about in her next letter to Belinda: *"The weather continues glorious here, and yesterday, Eddie and I saw a pair of tits on Pan's penis . . ."*)

Arabella resumed reading aloud from where she had left off. But in glancing up a moment later, she saw that Eddie now wore a wide-eyed, fixed expression. Perhaps, Arabella reflected, the subject of pedicide was not the wisest choice for youthful convalescents.

A second later, Eddie sprang from her chair and commenced scrabbling in the dirt.

"What on Earth are you *doing?*" cried Arabella.

In point of fact, "earth" was exactly what she was doing. It flew in the air as she dug, and in short order, it covered the child's hands, lined her fingernails, stained the front of her wrapper where she was kneeling in it, and soiled the hem of her nightgown.

"Look, Aunt Bell!" Eddie cried, holding up a stone the size of a cow's heart. "It's Stupid-Looking!"

"It certainly is," said Arabella crossly. "You were supposed to remain in your chair and not move!"

"No! I mean, it's Stupid-Looking! Neddy's turtle! Remember?"

Observing the "stone" more closely, Arabella now saw that it had a face. And a pair of sleepy-looking red eyes that blinked in the sun.

Two years previously, Eddie's half-brother, Neddy, had brought a pair of turtles to Lustings, which had promptly escaped into the house. One of them, and Arabella rather thought it had been this one, had later resurfaced in Costanze's plate of cake, with spectacular, if predictable consequences.

"He is hibernating," said Arabella. "Put him back, and cover him up; he'll come out when he's ready."

"All right," said Eddie, stashing the reptile in the pocket of her wrapper.

"No, darling; I meant put him back in the *ground.*"

"I shall, Auntie. But not till he's served his purpose."

"What do you mean?"

"I have an idea about our mystery. It mightn't work, but it won't hurt the turtle, either way. Now, where could Klunk be?"

"Why? Is it a two-turtle idea?"

"No. I am just wondering what happened to him, because Klunk and Stupid-Looking were such good friends."

"Were they?"

"Well, you never saw one without the other."

"The fact of their forced proximity does not mean they liked one another," said Arabella. "They might have been enemies, who lost no time in separating once they were free to do so. One must never presume too much from surface appearances."

Eddie nodded happily. Arabella was the wonder-fullest aunt! Instead of scolding her, she had immediately accepted that her niece had made a plan, and had then respected the child's judgment enough to allow her to carry on with it, rather than demanding to know what it was.

That night, when she came downstairs for dinner, Eddie ate with a hearty appetite, and Arabella was gratified to note that the color had returned to her face. Well, actually, color was entering her face for the first time, for Eddie at her healthiest was always extremely pale.

"Oh, dear; I hope you are not getting your fever back again!"

"I'm not, Aunt Bell. I am just excited about my idea."

"The idea about the turtle?"

"Yes!"

"All right, dear," said Arabella. "But please try not to get *too* excited."

Chapter 8

"We have had to put the price of our Silky Select Creamy Pearl Night Cream for the Face up to three pounds," said Arabella. "I thought it was quite exorbitant at first, but when Madame Zhenay explained that the lar— That some of the ingredients, I mean, were imported from Morocco, I apprehended the necessity, and marked up all the jars myself."

It was Tuesday, one of Arabella's twice-weekly salon nights, and a faithful smattering of the old crowd was still in attendance. These gentlemen, who were grouped about Arabella drinking German wine, delighted to discourse on a wide variety of subjects, but ladies' face creams was not one of them.

"Do tell us about your new courtesans' club, Miss Beaumont," said Lord Uxbridge. "I have heard that you already have an extensive subscription list."

"I wouldn't call it extensive," replied Arabella, suppressing a yawn. "But at twenty-nine subscribers, we are closed to new applicants."

"So few?" asked Colonel Cooke. "My club has over two hundred members! How do you expect to keep afloat financially?"

"The subscription cost is prohibitively high," said Arabella, beginning to warm to her subject. "And with all the public events we have planned, I expect to be operating in the black within a year or two."

"Is it true," leered Mr. Lloyd, "that the Cyprian Society has actual *bedrooms?*"

"That is correct, sir," said Arabella. "It used to be an hotel, you know."

"I don't understand," said the colonel. "Is this to be a club, or a brothel?"

"A club. The bedrooms are strictly for the use of our members. Gentlemen are not allowed upstairs."

"But I still don't understand," said Lumley Skeffington. "Haven't your members all got London residences of their own?"

"Yes, my dear Lum. But one does not always wish to stay at home. One might be having one's house fumigated or renovated; there could be loud construction in the vicinity, or objectionable relatives come to stay. And sometimes," she added quietly, "through no fault of one's own, one might find oneself turned out of doors. In these and numerous other instances, a bedroom at one's club might prove invaluable."

"Hmm," said Lord Uxbridge. "That's not at all a bad idea, you know. And is it true that Isabella Entwistle has taken out a membership?"

"Oh! I can't," said Bull Hughes.

"I am not at liberty to discuss CS associates," said Arabella severely. "We are as much entitled to privacy as are the members of any gentlemen's club."

"But *we* talk about each other!" exclaimed Ball. "All the time! I mean, we wouldn't start rumors or turn a fellow member over to the law, but we are free to praise one another's horsemanship, or recount each other's jokes or gambling losses. No one is asking you to gossip about the

Cyprians, Miss Beaumont; we do enough of that on our own! For instance, d'you know what we call your new club, stocked as it is with the finest fillies in England?"

"The Stable d'Or," said Lumley. "That's rather good, isn't it?"

"Actually, it *is* rather good," Arabella conceded.

"And your new theater," said Lord Alvanley. "The Bird o' Paradise. We've shortened that to 'the Bird.' "

Arabella sniggered.

"I intend to write a piece about it for the *Morning Chronicle*: 'We are indebted to Shakespeare for giving us the Globe, and now we must thank Miss Beaumont, for giving us the Bird!' "

The company laughed heartily, and Arabella laughed loudest of all.

"You see?" said Lord Uxbridge. "There's nothing harmful in our interest! The Cyprian Society is London's most glorious achievement since the king's birthday of 1811! We just want to ascertain who the members *are*."

"Very well," replied Arabella. "Miss Entwistle is a member, but that is all I am prepared to tell you."

"And Alouette L'Etoille? Is she a member, also?"

"Yes!" said Arabella, with an irritable snap of her fan. For she was not fond of discussing other women with men, unless it was to disclose something disagreeable about them, for the men's own good.

"And Fanny Moon?" asked Captain Gronow. This time, she did not answer at all, but merely gave a curt nod. "Oh!" cried the captain rapturously. "Oh, Miss Beaumont! If you could effect an introduction to Miss Moon, I should be *very* much obliged to you!"

The insult was inadvertently issued, for it was plain to see that Rees Gronow was suffering under the influence of an overpowering infatuation, but there was a limit to what Arabella was willing to endure, and he had quite overstept it.

"No!" she said loudly. "I am not now, and never shall be, a pander for other women! You must all go home at once!"

But the gentlemen were greatly enjoying themselves now that Arabella had finally stopped talking about her adventures in retail, and they gathered tightly round her, with words of reassurance and conciliation.

"Pray, do not be vexed, dear, dear Arabella," said Lord Alvanley, whose reputation as "sayer of good things" was well-deserved. "You will get wrinkles in that heavenly face if you frown! Though I'll wager Madame Zhenay has something that will minimize their severity," he added slyly.

"Indeed she has!" said Arabella. "Several things, in fact!"

The company was far too well-bred (and too conscious of Arabella's temper) to groan, but inwardly, many a divinely gifted guest must have been plotting dire things for Alvanley, despite the fact that he had just forestalled their eviction from Lustings. Because when Arabella "talked shop," that is literally what she did. On this occasion, though, the hostess did not continue over-long, and the rest of the evening was actually quite a pleasant one for everybody. It was almost like the old days, even, except for a very few more anecdotes pertaining to a product called Face of the Infanta Youth-Tinted Visage Glaze.

But not all was hearts and flowers—or even moisturizer and gentle exfoliant—the next day at La Palais de Beautay. Arabella was still unable to find an opportunity for slipping upstairs to search for Costanze's letters. And as she perched upon her high stool behind the counter on this bright June morning, she was close to despair, for a new thought had occurred to her: Was it possible that Madame Zhenay was bluffing? It would not be at all surprising if the idiotic Costanze still retained those letters herself, and had merely mislaid them. Madame Zhenay might easily have convinced the silly creature that *she* had them, when, in fact, she did not. But if Arabella's cork-brained friend had those letters about her, Pigeon Pollard might chance upon them at any time . . . and then Arabella should either have to flee the country, or spend the rest of her life in the Marshalsea.

I won't think about this now, she said to herself. Not until I have had a look upstairs and *assured* myself that the letters are not to be found on these premises.

The shop bell rang as a customer entered.

Arabella hopped off her stool and curtsied, reflexively. "Good morning, madam, how may I . . ."

Dear God! It was Lady Ribbonhat!

"Where is your mistress, gel?" demanded the dowager, thumping her stick upon the floor.

"M-Madame Zhenay is not come down yet, my lady," stammered Arabella.

Could Lady Ribbonhat really have failed to recognize her? The enemy's pugs had certainly done so, for they immediately burst into a volley of barks and snarls.

"Quiet, Angouleme!" ordered their mistress. "Shut up, Bathsheba, you idiot!"

The pugs subsided at once, for they knew upon which side their bread was buttered, and were loathe to bite the hand that fed it to them.

"Well," said Lady Ribbonhat, glancing round at the shelves, "as long as I am here, I'll have some Corinthian Knee and Elbow Emollient, Tender Dreams of Misty Loveliness Extract, and a bottle of Sultana Roxelana's Essence of Divinely Scented Arabian White Roses." As she counted off the items on her fingers, Lady Ribbonhat never once looked Arabella in the face. And our heroine, who, in the past, had tried and failed so often to disguise herself, finally understood the secret of anonymity. Apparently, all she needed to do was impersonate a member from a lower social class, and then nobody, not even her worst enemy, would look at her long enough to see who she was.

"There you are, Sinead!" exclaimed Lady Ribbonhat, abruptly brushing past Arabella. "You have certainly made me wait long enough!"

Sinead! thought Arabella. *That's* where "Zhenay" comes from!

"Oh, keep your hat on!" growled the proprietor. "I'm not at your beck and bloody call!"

"Is the carriage waiting?" asked La Ribbonhat.

"Naturally."

"Because Lady Bessborough is dreadfully punctual, you know! If we're late, she's liable to refuse us!"

"Shuddup."

Zhenay muttered this so quietly that only Arabella heard her, and the proprietress flashed her a conspiratorial smile. "Look after things whilst I'm away, Bella," she said. "I'll only be gone a couple of hours."

Duchess and shop owner walked to the carriage, their arms companionably linked, as Arabella watched from the window. Well, well, she thought. What do you know about that?

Ever since she'd obtained employment at La Palais de Beautay, Arabella had been bringing her CIN to the shop and jotting down anything unusual having to do with Madame Zhenay. This friendship with Lady Ribbonhat, for instance, was distinctly peculiar. Whoever heard of a dowager duchess fawning over a common shopkeeper? A shopkeeper, whom she was taking with her to meet Lady Bessborough? And Madame Zhenay had told Arabella never to charge Lady Ribbonhat for any cosmeticks or beauty treatments! Well, if these two had worked out a reciprocal commercial arrangement to their mutual benefit, that was odd, certainly, but it probably had nothing to do with the case. Best note it down, though. And she added in a postscript that greed evidently predominated over snobbery with Lady Ribbonhat, which, relevant or not, was a useful thing to know.

As soon as the carriage had driven off, Arabella headed for the rear of the shop, intending to investigate the upper regions at last. But just as she was about to mount the staircase, the shop bell rang and five customers came in all at once.

"The place was thronged for the whole of the afternoon," she complained to Eddie that evening. "I never got upstairs at all! And I shall probably never have such an opportunity again."

"How frustrating for you," said Eddie. "You cannot possibly do this without an accomplice, Aunt Bell. Fortunately, you have me. I should like to accompany you to the shop tomorrow."

"I am sorry, Eddie, but that is out of the question. La Palais is no place for children. Anyway, you are not yet strong enough to go out."

"But I *am!* And the time is right to test my idea!"

"Well, tell it to me, then, and I shall test it for you."

"It won't work if you do it," said Eddie. "It has to be a child."

"Why?"

"Because people make silly assumptions about children which tend to work in our favor. We can get away with more than adults can. Please, Aunt Bell! I shall fall sick again if I am thwarted!"

Arabella eyed her speculatively.

"Do you think you can find the letters?"

"I don't know, but I can certainly search the bedroom whilst you are downstairs."

"All right, then. If you are apprehended, however, I shall be obliged to give you a severe wigging, for form's sake. I shan't mean a word of it, but I shall have to sound convincing."

"I understand. I won't mind a thing you say."

"In this instance *alone,* Edwardina!" said Arabella. "On all other occasions, you had better!"

My mind misgives me about exposing Eddie to
danger. But the child is so headstrong! When she
says she will fall sick again lest I take her with
me, I know that she means it. Perhaps it will be
all right, Bunny. After all, I shall be right down-
stairs. And if I am dismissed, it will not be the
end of the world—just a lot more difficult to get
into the bedroom when I am no longer working
there!

Arabella was in a pensive mood as she blotted her letter.
Edwardina was proving a staunch little ally, but the child's
forthright approach was perhaps too bold for the delicate
matter currently in contemplation. If only Belinda were
there! But she was not, and Arabella, with only herself for
counsel, hoped with all her might that she had made the right
decision.

"I'm very sorry, Madame," she said the next morning,
"but I could not find anyone to stay at home with our Eddie,
and the child is still too weak to be left by herself. As it is
only this once, I hope that you will not mind her being here.
Edwardina is a good girl. She won't be any bother. I'll have
her sit out of the way in the back passage."

Whereupon Eddie, as pale and silent as a Zamboangan or-
chid, settled herself near the staircase as though she never intended to move again. But as soon as the adults had busied
themselves with the daily bustle of opening the shop, she
raced upstairs and into Madame's bedroom, whose location
Arabella had described to her over breakfast that morning.

The chamber was overly furnished for its size, with bu-
reaus, chairs, a divan, a vanity, a folding screen, two imposing wardrobes, and a profusion of little tables. The bed was
enormous, with red curtains. Directly across from it was a

desk. And next to this, tucked away in the corner, stood an iron strongbox that came up to Eddie's waist. Whatever it contained was deemed of sufficient import to safeguard its discovery, for the lid was locked. But that was all right; Eddie had only wanted to ascertain the presence of a strongbox in this room, and now that she had done so, all that remained was to nip back out and down the stairs.

She was halfway to the door when the dreadful sound of footsteps coming along the passage reached her ears, but Eddie was prepared for this, too. Wheeling about, she ran back toward the bed, threw herself onto the floor, and reached one arm underneath, as though in quest of something. A split second later, Madame Zhenay entered the room.

"What are you doing here?" she thundered. And Eddie, cool though she was, trembled as a suppliant before a merciless pagan god.

"Please, ma'm," cried the child, her voice muffled by the bed skirt, "I have lost my turtle. Is that you, Stupid-Looking?" She extended her arm farther into the dusty cavern. "I can't . . . quite touch . . . have you anything that might be long enough to reach him?"

"Here," said Madame, handing her the hook-end pole with which the upper transoms were opened and closed. "Use this. How could a turtle have got up the stairs so fast?"

"He's a tricky one, ma'm," said Eddie, who had surreptitiously taken Stupid-Looking from the pocket of her pinafore and placed him under the bed whilst Madame was fetching the pole. "That's why we call him Stupid-Looking. He only looks stupid, you see. But he isn't . . . there! I've got you!"

She scrambled to her feet and held out the Testudine, now convincingly covered in dust, that the other might observe its fatuous expression.

Madame Zhenay grabbed her spectacles off the nightstand and peered at the turtle through them, without unfolding the ear pieces. She was unfamiliar with the habits of *Emys orbic-*

ularis, or she would have known that Stupid-Looking could never have got up the stairs unaided. But her ignorance upon the subject of terrapin locomotion, combined with what appeared to be the proof of her own eyes, convinced her that this had indeed been the case, and she had to satisfy herself with terrorizing the child.

"What did you mean by bringing that infernal creature into my shop?" she roared.

"I'm very sorry, madam," said Eddie with a hasty curtsy.

She attempted to dart from the room, but Zhenay caught her by the arm, and twisted it so painfully that the girl cried out.

"I've half a mind to keep you here forever," whispered the ogress, thrusting her face close to Eddie's, "and force you to be my slave! How would you like *that?*"

"No!" Eddie shouted, as loudly as she could. "Stop! Let me go!"

Arabella had been anxiously hovering at the bottom of the stairs ever since she had seen Madame leave the sales floor. But when Eddie screamed, her aunt swarmed up them at once and fairly flew into the room, wresting her niece from that merciless grip. Evidently, though, Arabella had only effected the rescue in order to castigate the child, herself.

"Edwardina! How could you?! When you promised me you would be good! I shall probably lose my place now, thanks to you, and we shall be thrown into the street when I cannot pay the rent!"

Eddie's lower lip trembled. "B   but Bella! I was only going after my turtle! I couldn't leave him to run loose in the house, could I? Imagine the fright he'd have given Madame, if she had stepped on him as she was getting out of bed!"

And with that, the child began to cry hysterically. Arabella was actually worried that the shock might induce a relapse.

"Wait! Who's minding the shop?!" bellowed Zhenay. And she tore downstairs, dragging Arabella and Eddie behind her. But all was well. For once there were no customers.

"Get her out of here, Bella!" cried the proprietor. "And come straight back! You'll work late tonight, to make up the time!"

"Yes, Madame! God bless you, Madame!"

And Arabella hustled Eddie out the door, surreptitiously removing the BACK IN TEN MINUTES' TIME sign that she had placed in the window.

Chapter 9

"There *is* a strongbox," said Eddie breathlessly, after Arabella whisked her round the corner. "A big locked one, next to the desk. The key is probably hanging from that ring she wears on her belt."

"Oh, sweetheart! You are invaluable!" cried Arabella, hugging her.

"Well, I could not have done it without Stupid-Looking," said Eddie modestly. She took the turtle from her pocket, brushed off the under-bed dust, and placed her lips upon his snout.

"Kissing turtles is a most unsanitary practice," said Arabella reprovingly. "I cannot think it advisable in your current compromised state of health, Edwardina."

"But he has served such a noble purpose," Eddie protested. "Don't you think he deserves to be rewarded?"

"Perhaps. But I doubt whether he is sensible of the honor you've bestowed upon him. It is typically frogs which reap the benefits of being kissed." Arabella brushed the worst of the dust from Eddie's pinafore and helped her into the carriage. "Although now I come to think of it," she added, "I am not at all certain that a prince *is* better than a frog. I, for one, should much prefer an unassuming little amphibian to Britain's own great walrus!"

"It hardly matters which is better, though, does it?" asked the practical Eddie, as her aunt was herself handed inside by the driver. "Stupid-Looking is only a turtle. And no one ever heard of a turtle prince."

"You're quite right, my dear; let us take this little hero back to the garden and set him free again. I have an idea that he would much prefer his liberty to a throne, or even to a kiss from a future famous courtesan."

Eddie smiled. "How will you get the key, though?"

"Never you mind," said Arabella. "I have a plan of my own for that!"

And after restoring her niece to bed and the reptile to its burrow, "Bella Daltry" returned to La Palais de Beautay, where she worked so hard and behaved so submissively, shooting occasional cow-eyed glances at her employer, that Madame Zhenay was sufficiently mollified to invite the minx to join her in a glass of claret after they'd locked up for the evening.

"There's a place I know of, not far from here," said Madame. "It's very discreet, and known only to women like ourselves."

But Arabella did not want to risk seeing someone whom she knew, who might unwittingly expose her for the fraud that she was.

"Couldn't we stay here, Madame? This is so much cozier, and I am not really interested in talking to anyone but you."

"Perfect," said her employer. "We'll go up to my bed-room."

Afterward, Madame Zhenay, who had told Arabella to call her "Cream Pot," fell asleep. And when a series of loud, wet snores indicated that she was well and truly under, Arabella, clad only in her shift, crept out of bed and tiptoed across the room. The great key ring lay upon the desk in plain sight.

But if you think that it is easy to locate a particular key on a large iron ring loaded with the blasted things, in semi-darkness, whilst simultaneously preventing them from clinking together, then the author respectfully recommends that you try it sometime. Arabella sorted carefully through the collection, searching for a tiny key that might fit the strongbox lock. Her task was ultimately complicated by the fact that there were three that might have done, and they weren't positioned together, but suspended at random between an assortment of larger keys. She was obliged to try each of the small ones in turn, and keeping the rest of them from jangling while she did this was no walk in the park. But finally, the last of the small keys turned in the keyhole with a satisfying click.

Arabella lifted the strongbox's hinged top to reveal an organizational arrangement of impressive efficiency. The interior was full of files, each tabbed with a last name and first initial. Some of these held routine business papers, but many contained sealed envelopes addressed to the designated persons or agencies where, presumably, they might do the most damage.

By the light from the moonlit window, Arabella read through the names with wonder: She either knew or had heard of most of these people, many of whom were socially prominent. Of course, they weren't all blackmail victims—the collection also included Zhenay's regular customer files. But there was no time to waste; "Cream Pot" might wake at any moment to apprehend her, and Arabella did not like to think what would happen if she did: Something in her employer's menacing mien suggested that murder would not be out of the question, and this was just the sort of situation that was apt to bring out the beast in her.

Costanze's letters were filed under *W*, toward the rear, where, in a folder of its own, Arabella also discovered a ledger wedged between the *Z*s and the back of the strongbox. She remembered the conversation she'd had with Eddie about the difficulties of proving blackmail without exposing Costanze's secret. "I expect I shall find proof of all sorts of dark doings," she had said lightly. This must be the index to the files, the "proof of dark doings." So she took that, also. And as she stuffed her contraband into one of Fielding's large unattached pockets, the lovely thief gave thanks to the benevolent universe: an ordinary reticule could never have contained so much.

She was about to close the lid again, when an impulse seized her that she could never afterward explain, and Arabella grabbed Lady Ribbonhat's customer file, closed the lid, and shoved the file into the other pocket.

"Just what do you think you are doing?"

A dark shape, swathed in blankets, rose up from the bed. It seemed impossibly huge in the half-light, like a threatening breaker that appears out of nowhere on a windless day. But Arabella had spent many childhood summers at the seaside, and knew from long experience that when one is confronted with a wave of this magnitude, the only practical thing to do is to dive straight into it.

"I must get back, Cream Pot," she said, hoping her voice sounded relaxed. "I was trying not to wake you, but I cannot find all the pieces of my clothing."

For a certainty she could not. Except for the pockets, which she still held in her hand, Arabella had intentionally scattered her clothes about the room as much as possible when taking them off. Zhenay was reaching for her spectacles, and in that split second, Arabella tossed the bulging pouches onto the vanity bench.

"Ah!" she cried. "There are my pockets, anyhow," and she moved toward them.

"Stay where you are," said Madame.

Arabella froze. There is a certain type of voice that compels obedience, and Madame Zhenay had one.

"I can't let you leave now; it's"—she brought the spectacles to her eyes and picked up a clock from the bedside table—"three o'clock in the morning! You'll never get a cab at this hour! Besides, I don't want to be told that your beautiful body has been found nude and lifeless in some alley. Bring it back to bed, love," she said, holding open the bedclothes, "and this time I'll light the lamp, so you can see what I'm doing!"

The younger woman was glad enough to comply—her feet were getting cold. Later, when the two of them were lying back against the pillows and blissfully smoking cigars, Arabella studied the numerous cracks in the water-stained ceiling, and the hideous, mold-colored wallpaper that was peeling and curling throughout the room.

"How much longer do you intend to live here, Cream Pot?" she asked. "A successful business woman like you should have a house of her own!"

"Why?"

Arabella was nonplussed. "Well, because . . . a woman is not complete without a house that reflects her tastes and passions. After all, what else is a home, but the mind made manifest?"

Madame grunted. "That may hold true for titled women and the like, but I'm working class, and proud of it! We live over our shops so that we may access them at any hour of the day or night. Because our work is who we are. To live otherwise would be unnatural . . . like a body without a heart."

"That's a moving sentiment, in its way," said Arabella, "but you're wealthy enough to move up in the world now! You should—"

"Don't tell me what I should do," said Zhenay flatly. "And don't worry your pretty head about it," she added in fawning tones. "I don't plan on living here forever, but the time is not yet ripe to make a move. My people come from Alsatia," she added, apparently changing the subject. "Do you even know where that is, Bella?"

Arabella shook her head. She *did* know, in fact, for her library contained a copy of *The Squire of Alsatia,* but she quickly decided that the gently raised Bella Daltry would not have heard of such a place.

"It's the district that lies between the Thames, the Temple, and Fleet Street," Zhenay explained, "the vilest slums in London. But that's where I grew up, you see. It's an official criminal sanctuary—no one can be arrested there—so you may imagine the sorts of things that go on."

"Remarkable!" said Arabella. "And you're to be congratulated on having escaped! But how did you come to open a cosmeticks shop?"

"Oh," said Zhenay, rolling over and flipping her cigar stub into her half-empty wineglass. (Or perhaps it was half full.) "That is a long story."

"The night is also long," said Arabella. "What more perfect place and time to tell it, than here and now?" She turned on her side, cradling her head upon her arm, adopting the manner of a person who is prepared to listen—forever, if need be—to the tales of her companion. Because people are usually quite keen on relating their life histories, and the rule holds true for villains and heroes alike.

If the Almighty were to grant mankind a gift, just one, something that would have to please the greatest number of people all over the world, it would have to be the gift of an appreciative audience.

"Years ago, when I was much younger," said Madame Zhenay, "I ended up in Paris on the eve of the revolution. The English were not popular in France at the time. Heads were being chopped off for no reason at all. And there I was, without a sou in my pocket."

"Dear God!" Arabella exclaimed. "What did you do?"

"I went to Alsace—the very place for which my old London neighborhood was named—where things were safer. Eventually, I found work as a laundress.

"My best clients were the members of a family that made skin emollients in their cellar. They were forever wiping cold creams from clients' faces and mopping up spills with their shirtsleeves, so I went there often, both to deliver loads of clean laundry and to collect piles of soiled.

"Once I'd become familiar with the premises, I found it easy to filch small items that no one would miss for a while, like teaspoons and candle snuffers. One time I even got a brooch, which the mistress of the house had foolishly left on a side table. I sold these things to the dolly shops, and didn't do too badly, but one day I realized I would rather be making the sort of money the family earned. From that time on, I began to focus my attention on the business itself. I asked lots of questions, which turned into suggestions, and the head of the family eventually took me on as his assistant."

"You must speak very good French, then," said Arabella, who was now even more at a loss to explain the stupid name of Madame Zhenay's establishment.

"Not a word, I'm afraid. My employer tried to teach it to me, but eventually he gave it up and spoke to me in English." She pushed herself upright and selected another cigar from the humidor next to her bed.

"After the troubles ended, I moved to Paris, opened my own shop, and made money hand over fist. The only drawback was that I had to rely on my blasted bilingual shop assistants, who robbed me blind. Finally, one of them denounced me to the authorities as an alien without papers, and I was deported back to England, penniless, once again. Years later, I learnt that the woman who denounced me had stolen my business."

"Well, how were you able to start La Palais de Beautay?

Which is not proper French, by the way. It should be 'Le Palais de Beauté.' "

"I know," said Madame, exhaling smoke through her nose, "but it's better for business this way."

Arabella blinked. "Why would mangled French be good for business?"

"Two reasons. One: The love of the English for exotic goods is ever at odds with their distrust of foreign ways. They would rather deal with English persons *pretending* to be foreigners than with *actual* foreigners. Two: Mistakes linger in the memory. French speakers, recalling the grammatical error, will remember the name of my shop, whilst non-French speakers will cling to the recognizable, almost-English words."

"But can that really be true?" asked Arabella.

"It *is* true," said Zhenay. "They want foreign things, you see; not foreign people. But the foreign things must seem to be sold by foreigners in order to appear genuine. The name of my shop takes full advantage of this prejudice."

"How cynically clever of you!"

"Yes. But it took time to get started again after my return to this country, skinned as I was, and with no family to speak of. I nearly starved that first year; couldn't even get work as a whore—the pimps all said I frightened the customers!"

Here she threw back her head and laughed a wild, murderous laugh that raised gooseflesh on Arabella's arms.

"I began by selling pots of lip rouge door to door. Then I got a booth, and hawked my wares at fairs and festivals. With very hard work, business gradually improved, until finally I was able to open La Palais.

"I am driven ever onward, Bella, by one very striking maxim. Perhaps you have heard of it: Behind every great man there is a great woman. And there is no overestimating her power: Just get the woman in your grip, my girl, and you will have the man!"

"I see," said Arabella. "So your cosmeticks business is really . . ."

". . . the means to an end. All wealthy women are obsessed with beauty. Either they lack it, and wish it above everything, or they have it, and wish to retain it for as long as possible. I promise them that eternal beauty *can* be theirs, for a price, and they flock to me like the geese they are, putting themselves in my power so readily that it is almost too easy!"

"I fail to take your meaning."

Zhenay squinted at her for a moment.

"I think I may rely on your discretion," she said, at last. "You don't yet know the world, Bella, but you're clever and a quick learner. You have already guessed what I am about to some extent, have you not? It must be apparent to you that I am doing more than merely selling beauty aids."

Arabella was silent.

"I sell face creams and hair dye," Madame continued. "That is all my customers know of me. Yet you would think I was a faithful old family retainer, the way I am trusted! Stupid cows! Confiding their deepest secrets, entrusting me with correspondence that could ruin their marriages, willingly doffing their clothes in unsecured bathrooms, and meeting their lovers in storage closets here on my premises. . . . How can I possibly *not* take advantage, when they are practically begging me to?"

Zhenay seemed on the brink of confessing to criminal activities, and there was no telling what she might say if she were given her head. But as abruptly as she had begun to speak, the older woman now fell silent, ruminating over God only knew what nefarious exploits. Arabella lay next to her in the big bed, half-mad with suspense, but smoking quietly and waiting for whatever should come next.

"Gentlemen use my products, too, you know," said Madame at last.

"Do they? But I have never seen any men in the shop."

Zhenay laughed that laugh again. "Of course not! Their housekeepers and whatnot make the purchases for them. They're ashamed to come to a ladies' beauty shop themselves. That's why I have decided to open an establishment just for gentlemen. I am going to call it Jackson's."

"Jackson's?" asked Arabella. "Why that? Who is he?"

"No one. But I mean it to put people in mind of John Jackson, the pugilist. The premises will have the masculine tone of a fine tailor's, with a male manager and shop assistants. It must be the sort of place that inspires manly confidence, yet I intend to sell them exactly the same products that I market to the ladies. Only the labels, and the shapes of some of the bottles, will be different.

"If women trust me with amorous matters," she added, "who knows? Perhaps men will trust me with state secrets!"

Her eyes seemed to glow as she spoke, and Arabella recalled an illustration she'd once seen of a gwyllion, the Welsh mountain demon that delights in leading solitary travelers astray.

"Soon I shall be able to retire from business for good," said Madame, with a grin, "for I am about to obtain what I most desire!"

Once again, she howled with glee, and her listener was reminded that one could always tell a gwyllion by its hideous laughter.

"Are you, really?" asked Arabella. "How exciting!" She had the feeling that whatever it was Madame wanted, it could not be a good thing. "I am happy for you, Cream Pot, even without knowing what it is! . . . What is it?"

Zhenay sucked the cigar, her gaze fixed on some unseen grail. "Revenge," she whispered, exhaling smoke like the dragon she was.

"Oh," said Arabella faintly. "Revenge against whom?"

"All of them. Everyone who has ever crossed me! I'll make

them all suffer; one person in particular! Yes," said Zhenay, nodding to herself, for she seemed to have forgotten Arabella's existence, "I'll have my revenge, all right. And when I have become the richest, most powerful woman in England, they shall all bow *to me*."

By the time Arabella finally got out the door, the sun was high in the sky and the city was bustling about its usual business. So! I've slept with a murderess! she thought. Zhenay had made no actual confession, but hints she had dropped concerning a "deal" she'd done left Arabella in no doubt that Zhenay had ordered the murder of Greely. She had probably had lots of people killed.

Arabella's wrist was jangling with Zhenay's gift to her: a new-pink-and-blue-enamel-flowers-and-birds-and-crystals-charm-bracelet-on-a-gilt-chain-with-silver-coin-pendant-clasp.

"Single bracelets are all the rage just now," Zhenay had said, fastening it about her shopgirl's slender wrist. And the shopgirl had thanked her, warmly. Now that she found herself alone in the hired cab and heading for home, Arabella stared at the bauble and thought about how it looked on her. It was ugly, and Costanze had one just like it. But then she thought back on the previous night, and about the confidences that she'd been told that morning, of which this bracelet was the sole souvenir. Arabella considered starting a museum, filled with mementos from her harrowing exploits: From the first one, there could be that portrait of Oliver Wedge that so offended Bunny, also the trunk and one tusk of a ruby glass elephant, which were all that was left of one of her favorite trinkets. From the second, she could display the saucy Roman tintinnabulum she'd plucked from the regent's collection, which currently hung from the doorway of her boudoir. From the current escapade, she would donate her awful bracelet.

It was a warm day. The sun seemed to promise brilliant futures for everyone and everything it touched, and this troublesome blackmailing incident was about to come to a successful conclusion. Arabella smiled to herself as she snuggled deeper into the upholstery. The sunshine *did* feel nice. It seemed set on exploring every inch of her torso, too, and Fielding's somewhat threadbare frock offered scant protection from the heated rays, especially where Madame Zhenay had rent those giant holes whilst tearing it off her the night before.

As the carriage rounded a turn in the road, Arabella sat up again and flung the bracelet out of the window.

Chapter 10

"Look, Frank! This is blackmail, pure and simple!"

Arabella had fanned out Costanze's amorous letters across her library desk, having previously read every one of them. (Despite the overall gravity of the situation, they had made her laugh heartily, and she had quoted some of the funniest lines in a recent letter to Belinda.)

Fortunately, Madame Zhenay was a thorough record keeper, and the Worthington file also contained copies of her own blackmail threats to Constance, including the first one, whose original was still in Arabella's possession.

"It's a clear case, all right, Miss Beaumont," said Constable Dysart, rubbing his chin and picking up two of the letters. The former Constable Dysart, we should have said. For he had lately been promoted to sergeant. "I'll take a man and go round to arrest her at once, just as soon as I've seen my little popkin here safely home."

Eddie's hair had been dressed by the incomparable Doyle, and she looked older than her eleven years as she posed in her new traveling frock (a gift from her aunt) in the light of the window, taking gracious leave of the servants. The staff were not nearly as composed as Eddie was, and Arabella was reminded of a tableau of grief she'd seen once in a Pompeian cemetery, as she watched them sniffling and applying their apron hems to their eye corners.

"This visit has done Edwardina a world of good," said Frank approvingly. "I have never seen her so happy or so healthy. Of course, her medicine must take the bulk of the credit, but I believe that your tender attentions had a hand in it, too."

"Do you, really?" asked Arabella, smiling up at him.

"Oh, yes! You know," said Frank, lowering his voice, "the doctor was amazed when I told him she'd made a full recovery; said he'd expected her to . . . to expire, after I told him I'd moved Eddie to your house."

"Dear me!" said Arabella, clicking her tongue. "And who was this paragon? Dr. Duckworth, perchance?"

"Why, bless my soul!" Frank exclaimed. "That's the very man! You have heard of him, have you? I am not surprised, for he is one of the greatest physicians in London!"

"Yes," said Arabella. "Wherever there is death and suffering, Dr. Duckworth is surely connected with it. Frank, would you be good enough to do me a favor?"

"Anything in my power! You have only to ask and, so long as it's legal, it shall be done."

"In future, if you or Edwardina should fall ill, tell me first. You would vastly oblige me by coming to Lustings to convalesce. My own physician is quite good, too, you know."

"Right you are."

"And if Sarah Jane should ever return to this country, she is free to consult Dr. Duckworth as much as she likes!"

Frank reached into his pocket. "I can never hope to repay you for what you've done, Miss Beaumont," he said, removing a tiny box. "But I thought, perhaps, you might appreciate having a souvenir from our adventure."

Inside was an earring, with a single pink tourmaline.

"Oh, Frank! It's the perfect memento! But, when did you . . . I mean, how . . . ?"

"Well," he said, "if I hadn't taken it, the grave digger would have. Besides, I don't imagine it's worth much. Do you really like it?"

"I cannot think of a better present," said Arabella. "And speaking of our adventure, I must tell you that Eddie has been a great help. You would not now have those letters in your hand but for her able assistance!" Seeing Frank's perplexed expression, she hastily added, "And how she was able to be so useful without once leaving her bed is another mystery, all to itself!"

Frank smiled, and regarded the envelopes in his hand.

"Yes," he said. "She's a clever sprat; there's no denying it! Now, as to these, I shall need to take them with me down to the station. Evidence, you know."

"Oh! But the scandal must not come out!" cried Arabella, in sudden alarm. "If Mr. Pollard gets wind of this, he'll drop Costanze, and I shall go to debtor's prison!"

Eddie crossed the room to take her stepfather's free hand in her own. "We shan't actually need Miss Worthington's letters, Frank," she said quietly. "Once you impound the strongbox, there will be dozens of her victims to choose from. If we make discreet inquiries, someone is bound to come forward in exchange for anonymity up to a point, to ensure Madame Zhenay's incarceration."

"Why, you clever little minx! That's very true!" said Frank. And he handed the letters back to Arabella, who regarded her niece with a thoughtful expression. The wild, impulsive little girl had gone quite away, leaving this calm, self-assured young lady in her place.

"Good-bye, Aunt Bell," said Eddie. "And thank you for letting me help."

"No; thank *you*, Edwardina, and good luck," replied her aunt. "You have the makings of an exceptional sleuth!"

"Oh, do you really think so?" asked the young lady eagerly, letting the child show through for a moment. "I am glad to be going home with dear Frank again, but I am sorry to leave you! How I wish the three of us could all live together!"

"I hardly think your mother would care for that arrangement!" said Arabella, stepping forward to shake the blushing Frank by the hand.

"I don't know what we'd have done without your help," he said. "Thanks to you, little Ed has got her health back, I've got my promotion, and we still have our life together."

"That is what family is for, Frank."

Arabella continued to stand in the drive, waving her handkerchief until the carriage was quite lost to view: She had received eight thousand pounds from Miss Worthington that afternoon, and could now afford to be sentimental.

"Only a drop in the bucket of what Costanze owes me," she observed to Doyle, who was helping her disrobe. "But a nice, comfortable sum, nonetheless. In any event, I shall be able to replace the frock I borrowed from Fielding—it's quite beyond repair, is it?"

"Quite, miss," Doyle assured her. "Mrs. Janks said it looked like it'd been trampled by wild boars and rent by helephants. She said 'twas a wonder you'd survived a'tall!"

And Arabella, recalling that terrible moment when Zhenay had suddenly risen up in bed like a volcano, wondered, too.

"Anyway, miss; who d'you think 'twas Mrs. Janks found standin' there, bold as ye please, when she opened the back door to throw that frock in the dust bin?"

"I cannot imagine."

"Wasn't it auld Lady Ribbonhat herself, with a bag o' table scraps?"

"What! Has the dowager duchess taken to foraging through people's compost piles?"

"Oh, no! They were nivver *our* scraps, ma'm. They were

hers. And nasty, as well, wi' flies an' auld moldy bones an' that!"

Doyle paused to pin up Arabella's hair, for her mistress was about to have a bath, and the chambermaid was placing the pins between her lips for convenience.

"Well? Go on, Doyle!" cried Arabella. "Don't keep me in suspense this way! What was Glen*deen*'s mother doing at my back door with a bag of kitchen scraps?"

"She was bringin' them to *us*, ma'm," said Doyle, speaking round the hairpins. "Said we might be glad of a bit more food, seein' as how ye give us so little."

"*What?!* Aren't you getting enough to eat, Doyle? Why ever hasn't anyone said anything?"

The chambermaid laughed, and nearly swallowed the pins, which she hastily removed from her mouth.

"Mother of God!" she cried. "And aren't ye the kindest, most generous mistress as ever was? No, we're not starvin' a'tall! If we were, we'd ask Mrs. Janks for somethin' t' tide us over till the reg'lar meal. No, y'see; there's a story behind Lady Ribbonhat's visit. Apparently, somethin' you said to her a while back made her worry she mightn't be allowed to enter heaven once her mortal span is over and done, and now she's tryin' like anythin' to make it right with the Creator."

"By giving rotten garbage to my servants?"

"Sure now, and isn't that Lady Ribbonhat all over?"

Arabella had to agree with her there.

"What did Mrs. Janks say?"

"Oh, that's the best part o' the story, miss! Mrs. Janks curtsied, nice as you please, and blessed her ladyship for being so thoughtful. Then she handed her yer ruined frock— Fielding's, that was—to make her a kind return! Well, Lady Ribbonhat tried to refuse it, but Mrs. Janks said if she wouldn't take it, then we wouldn't take her table leavin's, so she hadn't any choice. And in the end, Oy think the dowager was happy to have the frock, most like. Because then, you see, she could give it away t' someone else and so increase her standin' wi' the Almighty."

Much as Arabella had enjoyed this story, it was too nice a day to spoil with thoughts of Lady Ribbonhat. The drapes were open in her bedroom, and the glorious sunshine was peeping through the lace-edged under-curtains, which "let in the light but not the sight."

"You know, Doyle, persons of fashion are adding rooms to their homes, simply to house their bathtubs! I think I prefer bathing in the bedroom, though."

Doyle dragged the heavy copper tub up to the window, and straightened, stretching her spine.

"Well, Oy'd give it serious consideration, if Oy were you, miss," she said. "It'd mean a lot less wear and tear on the carpets." (She did not mention her back.)

"No. I enjoy bathing in the bedroom," said Arabella decisively. "And as I only have one all-over bath a week, it hardly seems worth the outlay required to add on another room. Beau Brummell bathes every day! I wonder if I should like that?"

Doyle groaned, but Arabella didn't mind. She liked to allow her servants perfect freedom of expression, as it made them feel better, and did not in the least affect her own decisions.

After the chambermaid had left the room, the mistress of Lustings set down her glass of cordial, shed her shift, and straddled the tub, as naked as the day she was born. Hers was not a graceful entry, since Arabella disliked getting her feet wet first. But just as she was lowering herself into the water, an errant draft suddenly caught the lawn curtain in front of her, tossing it straight up in the air and completely exposing her to the delighted gaze of a stranger!

This fortunate young man had been walking along the lane that skirted Arabella's garden wall when he happened to spy a peach on one of her fruit trees—the selfsame fruit that Eddie had once observed from the depths of her boredom. The early ripener was now a fully grown specimen of juicy perfection, and the lusty young fellow was only human. He scaled the wall, and was stretching his hand out for the golden orb, when Arabella's bedroom curtain suddenly afforded him the prospect of another pair of peaches, crowding each other behind a split fig!

Seasoned though she was, Arabella blushed from the unexpectedness of the encounter, and the errant curtain, as though shocked at itself, immediately fell back into place, shielding her from view a little after the fact.

Something about the fellow's expression reminded her of John Kendrick.

Who had left her a parcel.

Which she had allowed to languish at the rectory.

Arabella had said nothing to anyone about it, but Mr. Kendrick had been on her mind rather a lot, lately. She thought about him whilst stocking the shelves at La Palais de Beautay, and he was quite frequently the subject of her ruminations before falling asleep. In fact, she had applied to the Bishop of Bramblehurst for his address. After she got it, Arabella had stalled for a time, but in the end she had swallowed her pride and written to the absent rector, apologizing for her bad behavior, and imploring him to come back at once:

When one is admired by a person to whom one is neither promised nor tethered, one is tempted to presume that the admirer may be put aside, in a dish with a saucer over the top, to enjoy at leisure. This notion is much mistaken.

He had not answered her. But letters probably took a long time to travel between London and Puka-Puka.

Arabella left the tub and dried her limbs with a silky towel. Now that she could relax a little without fearing for her life or fretting over money problems, she found herself urgently desiring that parcel at the rectory. After all, her case was solved, and she had no other pressing engagements. Why shouldn't she see what John Kendrick had left for her? Quickly donning her clothes without calling Doyle, Arabella went downstairs and ordered the carriage.

"To Effing, Trotter," she told her coachman. And all the way out there, she puzzled over what the parcel might contain. Love letters? That he had written to her, secretly, and never had the courage to send? Arabella hoped it was that. She should cry when she read them, with longing and remorse and infinite sadness. But it would feel good to cry. And when she was through, perhaps she would know what to do next.

Mrs. Hasquith, the taciturn housekeeper, met her at the rectory door. This was the selfsame taciturn housekeeper who had watched over John Kendrick—fed him his meals, washed and pressed his clothing, looked after him when he was sick—and Arabella felt a sudden, unreasoning stab of jealousy. But Mrs. Hasquith was now employed by the Right Reverend William Clydesdale, and to *her* mind, it scarcely mattered whom she served; masters was all alike, more 'r less.

The visitor was shewn into the little reception parlor. Arabella had scarcely ever marked this room before, but how she noted it now! Noted it, and mentally berated herself for being unable to tell the Kendrick relics from the Clydesdale additions.

"Miss Beaumont."

The coldness of the voice put her off before she had properly seen the new rector, for he stood against the light, and Arabella had to rise from her seat in order to perceive the features: an impossibly large face, with enormous ears, and scant, pale hair, carefully combed across a broad forehead.

"To what do I owe the . . . honor of your visit?" he asked, by his manner implying that he was discharging a distasteful social duty. And so he was. The Right Reverend Clydesdale was not pleased to find a woman of easy virtue fouling his sacrosanct rectory air with her presence.

She curtsied, meeting his coldness with a coolness of her own. "How do you do? I believe your predecessor has left a parcel for me here."

Arabella had become very aware of teeth, since her first case had so hinged upon them, and she noticed that Clydesdale's were separated, each from the other, by a little space, like the tumuli at Avebury. He peered unpleasantly at her through his tiny, pale eyes, and at once advised her to come to the Lord and be cleansed of her sins.

"I'm afraid I have not got time for that today," she said, "but you would greatly oblige me by fetching my parcel, so that I may attend to the rest of my errands."

The rector was not accustomed to being dispatched like a common servant. Not, at any rate, by fallen women. He stood and glared at Arabella for the space of four heartbeats, at the end of which time Mrs. Hasquith rather unexpectedly saved the situation. For, having divined the visitor's purpose, the housekeeper now entered the parlor of her own volition, and handed over the parcel without comment.

"Thank you," said Arabella. And turning on her heel, she made a swift and stately exit, meaning to escape from the place at once. But outside the rectory door, the Effing Sunday School children had gathered in a body to embrace her. Reverend Kendrick had on several occasions taken them to Lustings to study the pond and bird life there, and Arabella had always treated the group to a wonderful cream tea afterward. She was not overly fond of children as a rule, but she liked the nice ones well enough, provided they did not share proximity with her for too long. Besides, *these* children had once been closely associated with her dear Mr. Kendrick, and she was therefore delighted to stoop down and receive their affectionate caresses.

But Reverend Clydesdale, following close on her heels, was aghast. He waded straight into the thick of the group and physically separated the innocent lambs from their false idol.

"Certain women are to be shunned, if you would grow up in the sight of God," he said sternly.

The children obediently fell away. Arabella didn't mind. She knew she should never again return to this place, now that she held the thing she had come for in her own two hands. She leapt into her carriage, slamming the door behind her.

Now that she had leisure to inspect her parcel, Arabella was both pained and pleased to observe that the package was the exact size and shape of a bundle of letters; pages full of longing, expressive of a deep and lasting love, and carefully smoothed out with a sensitive yet masculine hand before being bound together in a neat stack and wrapped in brown paper.

Are they love letters? she wondered. Penned to me during quiet nights and lonely dawns in the sanctity of his bedroom? Arabella resisted the urge to tear off the wrapping and plunge into the contents immediately—she would wait till she might be alone in her boudoir, because it wouldn't do for Trotter to hear her blubbering. The carriage had scarcely cleared the rectory drive, however, before she was attacking the string with the penknife she had brought with her for this purpose!

Inside, all she found were the notes and letters she had written to Mr. Kendrick. There were not many, considering the length of time she had known him. Here was a handkerchief of hers, too. And a glove and a hairpin. There was nothing of him. It was all her own.

Arabella was shocked by the insensitivity of the gesture. For a few moments she sat and stared blindly before her, but at last she gave herself over to tears. Not those hot, voluptuous floods of self-indulgent remorse that are so purging for the soul; these were the cold, peevish tears of disappointment, which must be squeezed out from under the eyelids in order to fall at all, expressive of nothing but hopelessness and abandonment. Grief of this type is good for neither the soul nor the mind, and all too frequently results, for the young, in a heart turned to ice that can never be thawed again.

Though the tears of desertion work differently upon different characters, the results are never good. In Arabella's case, the shock and emptiness she felt turned first to vexation, thence to fury. What a coldhearted thing to do! How could he profess to love her, and yet treat her thus? But by the time her carriage pulled into the drive, she was sitting up straight, perfectly composed and dry-eyed. There was only a dull, aching throb at the back of her head, which could not be detected by others. In fact, anyone observing Arabella walk into the house would have been arrested by her perfect poise and the self-controlled elegance of her demeanor.

It is a skill of a higher order, this trick of concealing one's emotions, and other people were not as adept as Arabella was. After his visitor had gone, Reverend Clydesdale found himself unable to rid his mind of her. He was not able to eat his dinner, and lay long awake that night, imagining he could hear her voice in his head. Gradually, the things she had actually said to him—"I'm afraid I have not got time for that today." "You would greatly oblige me by fetching my parcel." "Allow me to attend to my errands."—became things she *hadn't* said: "I have got time to oblige you." "Allow me to attend to you." "I am afraid of your parcel!" And eventually, he floated off into the sort of dreams that men of his profession are never supposed to have.

But that was nothing to the emotional display taking place on the other side of town, where a gaoler, in the company of a solicitor, was unlocking one of the prison cells.

"Where have *you* been?!" shouted the prisoner.

"I came as soon as I could. The regent is currently conscripting every able-bodied Tory lawyer to work on his divorce. I only finished up half an hour ago, and then I came straight over. I've had nothing to eat since breakfast."

Madame Zhenay made no reply, glaring balefully into the darkness ahead as she stalked down the prison passageway toward freedom. But what the solicitor fancied was the sound of an ancient bolt being dragged across the door of a distant cell was actually his client grinding her teeth.

Chapter 11

Lady Ribbonhat had tried to distance herself from her footman (the selfsame footman who had started all the trouble with Costanze in the first place) as he rapped the rhino knocker smartly against Arabella's front door. But there wasn't much room on the doorstep, and her ladyship's enormous crinoline limited the available space even more. When ladies went calling, it was usual for them to remain in the carriage whilst their footmen plied the knockers, but Lady Ribbonhat knew that her servant's livery had only to be recognized, and Lustings's door would be slammed in his face. So she was taking the precaution of standing near the entrance, in order to be able to push herself forward (a thing at which she excelled) before this should occur. Her gown, though, was overly commodious to quite an outrageous degree. So much so, that when Fielding opened the door, the footman lost his balance and was unable to avoid collapsing into the foyer on top of her.

"Get up from there, Harry!" exhorted his mistress. "This house may be run like a brothel, but that does not entitle you to take advantage of the fact, nor does it excuse you from your duty to me!"

Harry picked himself up, and helped the hapless Fielding

to her feet. When he attempted to brush off her skirt for her, though, he only received a sharp kick in the shin for his pains, after which Fielding pushed him back out onto the doorstep.

"Good day to you," said Lady Ribbonhat imperiously.

Fielding responded with a stony stare. Like Lady Ribbonhat's pugs, she knew her mistress's enemy by sight, and though she refrained from snarling and snapping, she was nevertheless disinclined to shew the dowager any respect.

"Whatsoever it is you come for, th' answer is no."

"I have brought you and your fellow servants a gift of uplifting tracts," replied the duchess, attempting to hand the maid a basket full of nasty, dog-eared leaflets, "which contain any number of moral and improving sermons. Perhaps you would like to read them on your off day. Or, if you happen to be illiterate, you might ask one of the more educated servants, should your mistress employ any, to read them to you."

"What are they about?" asked Fielding suspiciously, placing her hands behind her by way of rejecting the basket.

"All sorts of wonderful things!" Lady Ribbonhat replied, and she picked carefully through the soiled pamphlets so as not to stain her gloves. "*The Right Way to Remove Mucus from the Nasal Passages*; *Living Off the Land: How to Make Soup from Dirt*; and *Looking Within for Reasons to be Thankful You Are Poor*. That will give you the general idea. I believe there is also a leaflet with instructions on how to curtsy when a duchess calls, and not keep her waiting on the doorstep."

Fielding snorted. "Sounds like utter rubbish! An' if you think they're so wonderful, why are they all stained and crusted-looking?"

"One or two of them might have seen duty at the bottom of the canary cage, but that in no way reflects upon their fine, moral tone. Anyway, I should like to leave these with you," insisted Lady R., thrusting the basket rather more firmly at

Fielding's stomach, "and I wish to have a talk with your mistress. Is she at home?"

"'Course she is! Where else would she be at *this* hour?" asked Fielding rudely. "The question's not whether the mistress be at 'ome, but whether she be at 'ome *to you*. I'll go see what she says, but you'll 'ave to wait outside. 'Ere, gimme them pamphlets; she'll be more apt to see you if she's 'ad a good laugh."

After Fielding had grabbed the basket and slammed the door, Lady Ribbonhat turned toward her footman, nearly knocking him off the porch. "Wait at the carriage," she said, "but be ready to assist me if I am attacked."

It was very early in the morning, and ordinarily, Arabella would still have been deep in the arms of Morpheus (or Henry, or Thomas, or somebody). But today she was up and about, for there were Things to Be Done at her club, and she was having a light breakfast before leaving the house.

"Lady Ribbon'at's at the door, miss," said Fielding.

"What on Earth has she to do here?"

"Dunno, miss. She says she wants to talk to you, and she give us *this*." Fielding held out the basket of tracts for inspection, but her mistress recoiled from them.

"Faugh! Keep those things away from the butter, if you please! You didn't let her in, I hope!"

"Naw. She's outside, on the step."

"Good work, Fielding. I shall see her directly. I've finished my 'toast and post,' but you needn't tell *her* that. In fact, you needn't tell her anything. Just remove that foul receptacle from the dining room, if you would."

"Yes, miss. Would you like us to read through the pamphlets, and tell you about the funniest bits?"

"Yes, why not? Thank you, Fielding," said Arabella distractedly, for she had just noticed a missive from Frank on the letter tray.

Dear Miss Beaumont,

I am sorry to tell you that Madame Zhenay has been released from prison and has found out it was you turned her in. We could not hold her for she has friends or at least supporters in high places and someone here must have shown her the report which names you as the principal informant. I thought you should know because you will need to go careful now. I don't have to tell you that the woman is dangerous. Please let me know at once if she tries to get back at you.

Yours respectfully,
Frank Dysart

Her blood seemed to stop its course through her veins: To be on that woman's bad side was not a pleasant prospect. "Well," muttered Arabella under her breath, "and isn't that *just* what I needed!"

All this while, Lady Ribbonhat had been waiting outside. Ordinarily, a self-respecting dowager duchess would have quitted any place where she was so emphatically unwelcome. But Lady Ribbonhat had fully expected this type of reception, for she knew herself to be in enemy territory. So she stood there alone with her hands folded across her stomach and humming a hymn through her nose, prepared to wait till doomsday, if need be.

"It is early for social calls, Lady Ribbonhat," Arabella remarked, standing in the open doorway and pointedly not inviting her adversary to enter.

Lady R. ignored the reproof. "I have brought a gift for your staff."

"So I understand. Generally, we take deliveries through

the rear door, but deliveries of garbage do not, as a rule, come into the house at all."

"Since last we met," said the dowager duchess, ignoring this remark, "I have been considering what you told me, and have decided that there may be merit in your counsel. Accordingly, I am here on a mission of goodwill. Ask me in, if you please, for I bring urgent news which may be of use to you."

Arabella was so surprised by the courteous form of this address that she actually did let her adversary in, and led the way to the drawing room.

"Will you take tea?"

"I think not. This is a pilgrimage of contrition; not a social call."

"Suit yourself," said Arabella, picking up the silver teapot with the curlicue handle. "I am going to have some. What was it you wished to say?"

"First of all, my son, Henry, your generous protector, will wed Madame Zhenay as soon as his ship returns. So, were I you, I should make other financial plans for the future."

Arabella arched an eyebrow as she poured the fragrant stream into a pink and gray teacup as fragile as a fingernail. "Is he, indeed? Henry never mentioned it to me, and I have just had a letter from him. One would think he'd have included an item of such great personal import."

"He does not know of it, as yet—Madame Zhenay and I have arranged it between ourselves in his absence."

"That is the single most incredible thing I have heard this week," said Arabella, stirring her tea. "I am afraid I don't believe a word of it."

"It is quite true, nevertheless. But that is not what I came to tell you. Madame Zhenay knows that you turned her over to the police, and now she is sworn to have her revenge. Your life is in danger."

Arabella smiled and sipped. The fact that she had already

had a warning from Frank enabled her to mask her concern with perfect equanimity.

"I am not afraid of Madame Zhenay. I run faster than she does."

"Don't be a fool!" cried the dowager with sudden vehemence. "Zhenay's not coming after you *herself!* She'll be sending hired thugs to do the dirty work."

"Then what would you suggest I do, Lady Ribbonhat? Take up the javelin? Wear chain mail under my gowns? Learn to operate a trebuchet?"

Arabella's visitor rose from the chair and gathered her things. Lady Ribbonhat badly wanted a cup of tea, but it would not be seemly to ask for one now.

"Well," she said, glancing at the ceiling as though to invoke God's attention and approval. "I have tried my best to help her, but it is clear that there is nothing more to be done here."

Arabella walked her nemesis to the door, to make sure she didn't steal anything. The dowager duchess had once owned Lustings, and before her son had given it to Arabella, she had planned on spending her retiring years in this place. She still looked upon the house and its contents as rightfully hers, and for this reason could not be trusted in the vicinity of any of Arabella's portable objets d'art.

When they reached the door, the courtesan held it open as wide as she could, both to accommodate her visitor's voluminous skirts, and to be able to slam it after her as loudly as possible.

"I should like you to return the basket when your servants have finished reading those tracts," said Lady Ribbonhat, her foot upon the threshold. "And remember: Whatever happens to you via Madame Zhenay, you shall not be able to fault me for it."

"Not for that, perhaps," replied Arabella, leaving her listener to imply the rest. "Good morning."

The prospect of Madame Zhenay stalking her through the streets was not a pleasant one, but Arabella could not afford to waste time worrying about it now, with the Bird's opening night just round the corner. After quickly finishing her tea and donning her hat and gloves, she struck out for town, inhaling deep lungsful of spring air as she walked. It was clean today, for a wonder, and smelt faintly of the countryside.

As she stept off the kerb, Arabella noticed the driver of a brewery wagon across the road, who slapped the reins across the broad rumps of his draft horses at precisely the same instant. The next thing she knew, the wagon was heading dead at her! Arabella held her ground, assuming that the driver had not seen her yet. For to run away now, either to the right or left, would have been equally dangerous, should the wagon veer in either of those directions. It is also thus with life in general: the middle of the road is usually safest.

But the rumble and clank of the wagon grew ever louder, seeming almost to explode in her head like the last sound she was ever to hear in this life. And then, for the briefest instant, Arabella's eyes met those of the driver, and she saw that he fully intended to run her over. She whirled about upon the instant, making the kerb only just in time. And as she stood there, shaking like a gooseberry jelly, she saw the man pull up his team and grab a cudgel from the floor of the wagon. Then he jumped down, and in very much less time than it has taken to describe all this, was running at Arabella, with his club held high and ready to strike.

London is widely reputed to be one of the most crowded places on Earth, and in the main, I expect it is. But one of the most peculiar things about this most peculiar city is that it only becomes crowded at a certain time of the day—after ten in the morning, to be exact, and it was just gone 8:30 when our heroine was nearly run over. So there was no one at hand to step in and accost her attacker, as there would have been a mere two hours later.

Fortunately, Arabella had, from her grandmother, inherited the gift of automatic reflex. And before she quite understood what the fellow was even doing, she had turned and fled from him down St. James's Street. This was lucky for her, because St. James's Street, as we have seen, is home to London's most exclusive gentlemen's clubs. Many a gallant member, who lived elsewhere but was staying temporarily in town, or who had sat up gambling on the previous night until it was too late to return home, was already stationed at some bow window or other. Because of the early hour, some were clad in dressing gowns and slippers; others still had their curl papers in, but virtually all of them were drinking coffee and waiting to observe life with wry amusement and caustic remarks, as soon as life should wake up and display itself before them in all its amusing variety. They were not amused by the sight of a fine lady chased down by a ruffian, however, and immediately began to pour forth from their various front doors to come to her assistance.

But the brute had a head start on them, and he was evidently accustomed to running, whereas Arabella was not. Although she had nearly reached the Cyprian Society, she doubted whether she should be able to make it up the steps, for her assailant, who was closing on her quickly, seemed to have energy to spare, whereas Arabella was practically out of breath. But just when she thought she could go no further, the Cyprian Society's burly doorman, Rivers, came down the steps and seized her by the arm.

"Quickly, Miss Beaumont! Up with you, now! Mr. Tilbury!" he shouted over his shoulder to the porter. "Help, Mr. Tilbury!"

And before she knew what was happening, Arabella found herself handed inside to the porter and rushed through to the cloakroom.

"This way, miss," said the porter. "Hurry, if you please!"

Someone else took her from his capable hands, and then another servant opened the secret panel.

"In here, miss," he said, and he shut it behind her.

All this may seem rather melodramatic. Because once inside her club, with Rivers and half the bucks of London confronting her assailant outside, Arabella was more than safe. She probably would have been much more comfortable on the panel's other side, too, where there were servants and fellow Cyprians to soothe and care for her. But all the phases of her rescue had been quite properly observed in accordance with Arabella's newly instigated emergency drill. There would not always be time to assess the level of threat from without, nor the threat's potential for coming inside: London was a dangerous place. On the other hand, it was not inconceivable that a CS member in jeopardy might be wanted by the police or by bailiffs, who would of course be capable of following her right into the precincts of the club itself. Hence, the drill. And this first run had been entirely successful.

There was no knob on Arabella's side of the panel, for the architect had explained that criminal gangs were known to inhabit these ancient subterranean passageways, and the club precincts must be made fast against them. But at the bottom of a short stone stairway there was a lantern, with a flint and steel provided for the candle inside it. A faint light came through the small window above the door panel, sufficient to see to strike them by, and Arabella had also ordained a decanter of brandy and a comfortable chair, for she had envisioned this place as a haven for the persecuted. Naturally, she never dreamed that she herself would be first to make use of it. As she sank onto the seat cushion and poured herself a generous tot with trembling fingers, the president of the CS scarcely knew whether to laugh or to sob with relief. Only one thing seemed certain at the moment: She was safe!

It was a pity she had to be safe in here, though: Arabella

was missing the drama out on the street, where her assailant was being beaten within an inch of his life. Rivers was a former middleweight champion, which was one of the reasons she had hired him, and the clubmen who had chased down the cudgel-wielding ruffian now stood about in a tight circle, preventing the criminal's escape. No doubt the brute was wondering whether the fee he had received from his client was worth the violence now being visited upon his person, but it is equally probable that his mind was otherwise occupied, and I'm afraid we shall never know.

As for our heroine, once her nerves had settled, she picked up the lamp and began to make her way forward. The tunnels had not yet been mapped, though, and before long, she was completely and utterly lost.

Chapter 12

But if there was one thing with which Arabella was thoroughly familiar, it was her own city, and she knew that, wherever she might emerge from this labyrinth, she was almost certain of finding her way home again. So being lost beneath the streets was not a frightening prospect for her. What *was* frightening was the possibility of stumbling onto a nest of thieves or worse.

She noticed as she walked that the acoustics were strange down here. Take that drip from the ceiling, for example; Arabella could see by the light of her lantern that it was splashing into a pool, and that both were located on the other side of a vast open space. Yet it sounded as though it were mere inches away, and on her right, rather than her left. Then there was that low, uneven murmur, doubtless a subterranean stream, that sounded uncannily like distant voices. Where was that coming from? No stream was visible anywhere, but the farther she went, the more human it sounded. And then suddenly she caught the words: "See whether you can find any . . ."

Arabella blew out her candle and stood perfectly still. She was hoping to escape detection in the dark, and also trying to establish the location of the voices without the added distraction of her eyesight. In the darkness, though, her mind was only too ready to paint pictures for her: Now she was being flayed alive . . . now turned on a spit, like a capon . . . now cut up into pieces, roasted on sticks and eaten with pickled onions, as a kind of ploughman's lunch. Rape scenarios never even entered her head, for Arabella was thoroughly frightened by this time, and beyond the reach of more diverting possibilities.

The voices seemed to issue from somewhere to her right. So she would turn down this tunnel here, on the left, and distance herself from them as swiftly as she—

With a smack and a grunt, Arabella ran straight into a man holding a dark lantern, nearly knocking it from his hand. And just before she fainted dead away, she had a single, instantaneous impression of half a dozen desperadoes, crouched in a circle round the lantern holder, all staring at her in astonishment. Then followed a pleasant period of unconsciousness, devoid of all fear and discomfort. But it didn't last.

"Arabella! Miss Beaumont! Can you hear me?"

She came woozily to her senses to find herself stretched at full length upon the ground, lying on a man's coat. The next instant she was sitting up, half-embraced by Someone's strong, supporting arm.

"Here," said Someone, pressing a cup to her lips. "Drink this. You'll feel better shortly." The voice was familiar.

"What's happening?" she asked, drinking the brandy.

"You fainted. From fear, I shouldn't wonder. What on Earth are you doing down here?"

Arabella craned her neck round to look at her nurse.

"Elliot!" she cried, with mingled joy and relief. It was the friend she had met aboard the *Perseverance* the previous year, one of the people who had been so helpful in procuring her Pan statue. She didn't know these other fellows, who were grouped around them, looking concerned, but she concluded that they were not dangerous. This conviction was based in part upon their gentlemanlike appearance and demeanor, but chiefly upon their weapons, for rather than pistols, knives, and cudgels, they brandished compasses, engineering transits, measuring tapes, and collecting sacks.

When Arabella had recovered, Mr. Elliot assisted her to her feet.

"I am delighted to see you again," he said, "but I regret that I am unable to converse just now, as my work here is of the utmost urgency. However, if you should be free tomorrow night, perhaps we might meet for supper. And then we can tell each other what we were doing in this place."

"I shall very much look forward to it, Elliot. Will eight o'clock suit you?"

"The question is, will it suit *you*," he replied. "Evidently it does. Excellent! I'll call for you at eight. I only regret that our present encounter must be so brief."

"Where, exactly, am I?" she asked.

"Directly beneath Green Park. Permit me to escort you to the nearest exit."

Cecil Elliot had the most exquisite manners. It was what Arabella liked best about him. Or at least, it was one of the things. When he had shewn her the way out, he said, very quietly, "May I see you tonight? It may not be possible for me to get away, but if it is, I could be there round midnight. Would that be convenient?"

"Of course, Elliot," she murmured. "I shall be quite alone."

Well born ladies of the era generally spent their days paying social calls, or being called upon in their turn by other well-born ladies. It was a tedious business in Arabella's opinion, and sometimes she wondered in her idle moments whether the system hadn't been thought up by men, in order to keep women from making important scientific discoveries or developing new mathematical theories or contributing in a general but substantial manner to the betterment of man- (and woman-) kind.

In her *idle* moments, reader. But Arabella had not got many of those. For whereas less fortunate ladies were compelled to call on one another to no purpose, *she* had been barred from this pointless activity by virtue of her lack of same. It therefore behooved her to demonstrate her gratitude by putting her free time to good use. Just now, for instance, she was writing a novel.

It was a scurrilous piece of work, full of villains and stabbings and cloaked figures stealing down crooked stairways at the bottom of streets, and Arabella wrote furiously for a couple of hours. But in the end, her fingers cramped up, and she slumped back in her chair, turban askew, surrounded by the scattered pages of her first draft, and wishing for an uncritical audience to hear her fresh pages. Bunny had heard her the last time, when Palomina Breasted, Arabella's heroine, had found herself cornered in the deserted caravanserai:

> The wicked Prefecture of Police was about to seize her, when, to his utter surprise and extreme vexation, Palomina withdrew a pistol from her muff and pointed it at him.
>
> "You must be mad!" he cried.
>
> "Perhaps! But you are obviously a dullard, sir. Because it is sheer stupidity to antagonize the person who is holding you at gunpoint. Allow me to demonstrate!"
>
> She fired straight at his heart.
>
> "You see?" she said, addressing only herself now, as there was no longer anyone else present to hear her. "Given a choice, I should take insanity over idiocy every time!"
>
> And she stepped lightly over the body, dropping the firearm onto a conveniently situated refuse pile.

Bunny had said she liked it, but added that it was not likely to go over well.

"Why not?" Arabella had asked.

"Because it's not what people are used to, and that is what they like. Now, if you were to change 'Palomina' to 'Paolo,' say . . ."

"Never! Most of my best lines are gender-based!"

"You're a good writer, Bell. Why not write about real situations?"

"Such as . . . ?"

"Such as your detecting adventures."

"Don't be silly, Bunny! Nobody wants to read detective stories! Your judgment has undoubtedly been compromised by this," she said, picking up the book Belinda had just been reading. "*Pride and Prejudice!*"

"There is no detection in that. Anyway, I got it from the lending library, and it is very good! Have you read it?"

"Yes," said Arabella, curtly. "And I suppose you prefer her work to mine."

Belinda said nothing.

"This author," said Arabella, "who signs herself 'A Lady,' is too timid to use her own name. And her novels, whilst the writing is tolerably good, deal with well-behaved little ladies who stay at home and wait for men to come by and discover them. Wouldn't you prefer an independent heroine like Palomina, who doesn't need to form an attachment to a man? A woman who is not afraid of anything? Who travels to exotic lands and knows how to handle firearms?"

Belinda persisted in maintaining her silence.

"Well, *I* do!" huffed Arabella. "Evidently, I am ahead of my time!"

She smiled now, to recall the scene. Oh, how she missed Belinda! Thankfully, Cecil Elliot would soon arrive to help divert her sad thoughts from the people she missed. After all, Cecil would actually be present, unlike Bunny and Mr. Kendrick, and a popular maxim holds that a bird . . . or some other thing . . . in the hand is worth two in the bush. Still, Arabella thought, a certain *type* of barnyard bird, in a certain *type* of bush, was better than any number of other possibilities. She was by now convinced that she should never see Mr. Kendrick more, and concluded on that account that the healthiest thing she could do was to forget him completely the moment Mr. Elliot arrived with his bird.

She would receive Cecil in her boudoir, which was properly neutral. That is, it contained neither bed nor bathtub, yet still hinted at intimacy via its close quarters and sumptuous appointments. By half-past eleven, the pink porcelain stove was glowing like a satisfied lover, and the plump cushions on the boudoir divan were most friendly and suggestive. Arabella looked tempting, yet sophisticated, in a semi-transparent peignoir that seemed fabricated from early morning mist. She pulled the neckline a little lower, and was fluffing the ruffles clinging thereto, when Doyle appeared in the doorway.

"Someone to see you, miss," said the chambermaid, "but don't be gettin' yer hopes up, now, for 'tis not the party you're thinkin' it is."

"Dear God!" cried her mistress. "I thought Glen*deen* was still at sea!"

Arabella and the duke had a tacit understanding about entertaining other friends while separated, but in sudden and unforeseen circumstances, reactions were apt to be unpredictable.

Doyle hastened to reassure her. "No fear; 'tis only Miss Worthington. But she won't be put off, and insists on seein' ye, right away!"

"Constance?"

"No, miss, if you please. She says we must call her 'Costanze' now."

"What on Earth does she want at this hour?"

"Is it me yer askin'? Oy've nivver known why that eejit does half the t'ings she does, and I doubt whether she could tell ye, either!"

Mistress and maid repaired to the dressing room, to search for a suitable dressing gown. "Very well, Doyle," said Arabella, after covering up in a robe of heavy, salmon-colored satin. "Ask her up to the boudoir."

A moment later, Costanze burst through the door like a cannonball in purple feathers. Having begun her soliloquy on the staircase, she merely kept going, never minding that her audience had missed out on the beginning.

". . . fate you know so it wasn't *my* fault but whatever am I to do now?"

"Costanze, stop. I have not the faintest notion of what you are talking about."

The-woman-who-now-called-herself-Costanze ceased talking and goggled at Arabella, as though her eyes would burst from her head.

"Breathe, Costanze," said Arabella.

The visitor gulped in a double lungful of air and continued to goggle.

"Again, Costanze. Don't stop. Keep breathing again and again and again. Never stop, in fact."

The visitor obeyed. Then she began to hiccup, and Arabella poured her out a tumbler of water.

"Here," she said. "Now, I want you to relax, yes! And think back to the beginning of your problem. You do have a problem, do you not? Isn't that why you have come here at this inconvenient hour?"

Costanze nodded, and because she was trying to drink from the tumbler at the same time, spilled a quantity of it onto her feathered cloak, and swore a blue streak, as they say.

"Oh, for heaven's sake!" cried Arabella, quite at the end of her patience. "*Will* you get on with it?"

"It is Lady Ribbonhat!" gasped the other, at last. "She is going all over town performing good deeds so that she'll get into heaven despite the fact that she's been utterly horrid for so long and she decided to give some of her old hats to me but they were all smudged and greasy and most all the plumes were broken and I didn't want them so I really don't see how she expects to get into paradise on the strength of that do you?"

"Is that what you've come to tell me?"

"No that is only the pry-and-bull honestly Bell sometimes you can be so obtuse anyway she sent the hats over with her footman you see."

"Not with Harry?"

"Yes with Harry so there he was on my doorstep again and Pigeon was away dining with Lord Melbourne I think it was in Cheapside or no that was that other time so I suppose he must have been dining with his grandmama if it was a Thursday, because Pigeon always dines with family on Thursdays but now I think of it I could have sworn the Lord Melbourne dinner was on a Thursday—do you suppose they are related?"

"No. And either it wasn't Lord Melbourne or it wasn't Cheapside, because you would never find the one in the other. It's too preposterous."

"Well anyway Pigeon was away somewhere and one thing led to another and it was just like the last time except for the hats I mean and so we started up again and I'm being black-mailed again only this time I know who it is—it is Madame Zhenay because she said I was to tell you that you'll never see a penny of the money I owe you."

"Wait," said Arabella. "This is not making sense. How does she propose to blackmail you? The woman has no proof."

"Yes she does—she has my letters to Harry."

"No she doesn't, Costanze. *I* have those letters, remember?"

"You have the old ones but she has the new ones!"

"What! Are you telling me that you have written to him, *again?!*"

"Yes Bell I just said that!"

"*Why* does Madame Zhenay have your new letters?"

"Because I gave them to her to give to Harry."

"Costanze," said Arabella slowly. "If you had been born a rabbit, or a pig, or any type of animal other than a human being, your mother would have eaten you at birth."

"That is not a nice thing to say!"

"You are not a nice thing to *be*. You are quite simply too stupid to live."

"So what? I can be stupid if I like. That's my right."

"Not when it impacts me, it isn't! Now listen carefully, Costanze. Because I am going to kill you if you fail to do exactly as I say."

"*Tsk!* Oh, very well then."

"You are going to make Pigeon take you to the seashore. You will leave London tomorrow morning for Brighton, and you will stay there until I write and tell you that it is safe to come back."

"I can't. I'm in a play, remember? *The Bird?* Opening night?"

"They'll have to get along without you."

"But it's my debut! Besides, Pigeon is coming and he will be frantic if he doesn't see me in the cream puff chorus!"

"Pigeon is going *with* you, Costanze. I want you to stay in Brighton, where you'll be out of harm's way."

"Oh, all right, Bell, seeing as how you're going to kill me if I don't. But why will I be out of harm's way in Brighton?"

"Because Harry won't be there."

"Oh. Does that mean I cannot invite him to visit me?"

"Yes. That is what it means."

Chapter 13

Cecil Elliot had not been able to keep his midnight assignation, after all. But the following night, he arrived at Lustings at half seven on the dot. And when Arabella made her entrance at Grillon's upon his arm, she was gratified by the awed hush—to which she had long been accustomed and yet had never taken for granted—that fell over the restaurant. She was looking her best, in a rich gown of cobalt velvet with flame-colored gloves, and a rather famous sapphire necklace. The first time Belinda had seen her in this ensemble, she had remarked on Arabella's resemblance to a sea slug, but she had meant it kindly. The Beaumont sisters were well-versed in matters of natural history, and knew nudibranchs to be among the most beautiful, colorfully diverse creatures in all creation.

Arabella seldom wore bright colors. That she had elected to do so tonight was a gesture of defiance, for she had not been out since the attempted assault two days ago, and that, coupled with the warnings she'd received from Frank and Lady Ribbonhat, had prompted her to make a public showing of herself. *Here I am,* she seemed to be saying. *Come get me, if you dare!*

"You are without doubt the loveliest creature ever to grace this establishment," said Elliot, holding her chair for her. "And I hope that you can find it in your heart to forgive me for engaging this private dining chamber."

"But why should you apologize?"

"Because, in that gown you should expect to be widely admired all evening, and here there is no one but myself to pay you homage."

"No woman could wish for a better audience," said Arabella graciously. "Besides, I presume you have a good reason for bringing me here."

He smiled. "I have, as a matter of fact. What I am going to say must not leave this room. I know I may trust you, my dear, as your tact and discretion are legendary."

She bowed her head in acknowledgment of his approbation. "But if it's so secret, why tell me at all?" she asked. "You don't have to, you know."

"Yes, I do. For I would seek your permission for something, and I doubt you would grant it without an explanation."

"I am all agog."

Elliot lifted the lid of the soup tureen and inhaled the aroma wafting up therefrom. "I have heard," said he, ladling the contents into their bowls, "that you have been conducting an investigation of one Madame Zhenay."

"I was, yes. And the woman was duly arrested. But now she has been released from prison, and is apparently trying to have me killed."

If Arabella expected Elliot to be outraged by this—and she probably did—she was sorely disappointed, for he casually spooned up his broth as though he were more interested in whether it contained sufficient saffron than in her safety.

"Hmm," he said at last. "I presume you are taking prudent precautions."

"Well, there is really not much I *can* do, you know," she replied, "other than maintain vigilance at all times."

"Quite right. I certainly hope that your adversary fails in her purpose." He smiled, and moved his foot to touch her own beneath the table, but Arabella did not care for his attitude and moved hers away.

"She nearly succeeded! When I encountered you beneath the street, I had just escaped her hired ruffian, who chased me down the road, with a club!"

"How terrible for you. Speaking of clubs, I shall be requiring access to the tunnels directly beneath yours. Have I your permission to search the area?"

Arabella was really annoyed now. Elliot seemed indifferent to her assault, and oblivious of the dangers that lay before her. This was not like him; he was extremely attentive, as a rule.

"You don't need my permission," she snapped. "Surely the streets and whatever lies beneath them are city property."

"One might think so. But a peculiar charter, drawn up in 1324, grants the rights to that particular stretch of tunnel to the owner of the property above it. One of my investigators informed me of this yesterday, shortly before you appeared out of nowhere and fainted in my arms. Was not that an extraordinary coincidence?"

Then he caught sight of her expression and chuckled, tenderly taking her hand.

"Now, now, Miss Beaumont," said he. "I detect that you are hurt over my apparent indifference to your plight. But let me assure you that nothing could be further from the truth."

"Couldn't it?"

"No. And I hope you will forgive me for not devoting more conversational time to your personal safety, but you see, I prefer action to words."

"I don't follow you, Elliot."

"I intend to see to it that you are protected whenever you go out."

"You do?"

"Indeed. Nevertheless, I should advise you to be especially careful at your theater opening. The henchman has failed in his purpose, and your Madame Zhenay strikes me as the sort of woman who is accustomed to doing things herself, in order to be certain that they are done properly."

"Do you really think she would risk coming out into the open?"

"There *is* no risk, so far as Zhenay is concerned. That woman has the city of London by the short hairs. The law cannot reach her."

"You seem to know an awful lot about Madame Zhenay," said Arabella. And after a pause, she added, "I still don't know what it is that you do, exactly."

"That is as it should be," he replied gently. "I am not at liberty to discuss my occupation, but I *will* tell you that I, too, am conducting an investigation, just now."

"Beneath my club?"

"In part, although the scope of our search is much wider. Are you aware that the prime minister was assassinated last year?"

Arabella raised an eyebrow. "Do you take me for a simpleton?"

"Hardly. But I know how you loathe politics, and that you go to great lengths to avoid the subject."

"Well, I could hardly have missed hearing of *that*."

"True. At present I am . . . looking into the matter."

"Then you're a little late, I fear. The assassin has already been apprehended and executed."

"Ah! How readily you take my point, dear lady!" (Arabella, ever attentive to double meanings, actually blushed.) "You are quite right. And this selfsame John Bellingham was hiding out in the tunnels for some days prior to committing the crime. My team has discovered certain ambiguous articles at a couple of his camps, which may indicate the involvement of Irish radicals. Their main bivouac appears to have been located directly beneath your club, so we simply must search that area. Will you grant us permission to do so?"

"Of course," said Arabella. "And who are 'we'?"

"Why, thou and I, Miss Beaumont!" he said, kissing her hand, and ringing for the waiter. "Do you still have those enchanting blue bed curtains with the golden pineapples?"

"Pray, do not insult my intelligence, Mr. Elliot. If you cannot name the agency for which you work, just tell me so."

"Very well, then. I cannot name it."

"Then can you tell me what it is that you are seeking in my tunnel?"

Here he gave her a look so salacious, so unmistakably ribald, that she actually blushed again!

"No," she faltered, in pretty confusion. "I meant the one beneath the CS." A waiter appeared, and was dispatched for a quill, a bottle of ink, and a rolling blotter. But the instant he left, Elliot seized Arabella's hand again, and began planting kisses along her arm as he spoke.

"We are trying to ascertain the identities of these other parties," he murmured. "Bellingham burned some papers in the tunnel, but left certain others behind. The bits we have managed to piece together so far form a tantalizing puzzle. And while my team searches for the co-conspirators, I shall endeavor to discover who paid Bellingham and the others to commit the assassination—the mastermind behind the grand plan."

Writing implements were produced at this juncture, and Elliot paused in his amorous activities whilst Arabella read and signed the writ.

"Now," he said when she had finished. "I am free to devote the rest of this evening exclusively to your pleasure."

And Arabella was happy at last.

"Listen, my dove," said Elliot, "would you mind terribly much if we didn't attend the opera tonight? I have a sudden desire to see your bed curtains again."

"Why, no; I should not mind in the least," said Arabella, smiling. "After all, it is only Gluck. And I have seen it before."

Chapter 14

"You have *not* seen it before," Mrs. Anybody admonished her grumbling husband, as their carriage pulled up to the theater. "Nobody has! It is Sheridan's newest play, which was only finished early this morning!"

"Well, then, I daresay I've seen somethin' just like it! Plays are all the same: just a bunch of silly, conceited actors struttin' about the stage sayin' God knows what to each other, and ladies flutterin' their fans. That's all it is, just a lot of struttin' and flutterin,' with an occasional bellow whenever somebody tries to sing!"

The Bird o' Paradise's opening night was a brilliant event, in every sense of the term, but not all the attendees were sensible of its allures.

"Oh, for heaven's sake, Mr. Anybody!" said his wife, as he helped her out. "Why, the costumes alone are worth double the admission price! All those feathers and furs and what-nots!"

"By Jove!" cried he. "If it's feathers and furs you wanted, an' flutterin' and bellowin', I should have taken you to the zoological gardens! Though I don't imagine it will be open at this hour. Sorry, my love, but I simply didn't realize where it was you wanted to go. There's nothing to be done now. I suppose we shall have to go home again."

His spouse regarded him with icy hauteur. "As you are not to be reasoned with in this mood, Mr. Anybody, I shall not deign to answer you," said she, taking his arm.

"No, of course not," he grumbled. "And quite right, too. After all, there is nothing you *can* say, as I have seen it all before."

His mate was on the brink of responding, despite her resolution not to, when she passed through the doors of the Bird o' Paradise, and her tongue quite froze in astonishment. She was right, though, and her husband was wrong, for he had *not* seen anything like this before.

The Morning Post would later describe the scene as:

> . . . a sensual feast, from the lobby's thick carpets to the international scent of the spectacular floral arrangements: Dutch tulips, English roses, French lavender, Chinese chrysanthemums. Here and there, one might also have caught the elusive scent of cigar smoke, which is rather exciting at a distance. The chandeliers sparkled with golden light, reflected in the giltframed pier glasses, and a kind of informal musical arrangement was effected from the combination of cultivated voices in the lobby, snapping fans keeping time to the nodding of ostrich plumes, the sneezing of snuff takers and fluting of champagne glasses. Here and there, one encountered people horning in on conversations, fiddling with their opera glasses,

drumming up support for the Cyprian Society, harping on the lack of police protection within city limits and chiming in with opinions upon the economic prospects of Puffing Billy, the new steam locomotive. Laughter was widespread, though subdued, and some of it was probably genuine.

The heavy window curtains had been pulled back to display the opulence within to the common without. Not that they weren't welcome, too: The theater was open to all humanity, from the grand persons who would shortly be holding court in the private boxes, to the cheerful rowdies who would pack the pit. In the theater proper, the seats were cushioned and comfortable. New gas lighting had been installed for the wall sconces, and the ceiling was painted with classical scenes. (Isn't it odd how readily the art patron accepts nudity, provided it is confined to ancient Greece? If, instead of olive groves and classical temples, the same naked nymphs and youths had been depicted chasing each other in and out of parliament or the Bank of England, there would have been a general outcry.) As it was, the patrons were charmed to a man, and Arabella was satisfied that all had been done in the best of taste.

Everyone had come, from aristocrats, war heroes, and foreign dignitaries, right down to the painters, playwrights, poets, and politicians. More significantly, at least as far as Arabella was concerned, they had brought their wives. She had expected this, of course, for a theater was one of the few places where courtesans and society's leading ladies might freely mingle without fear of damaging one another, but it still gave her a thrill to find them here, at *her* place.

In the back of her mind, though, she remembered Cecil Elliot's warning, and her eyes searched the crowd for Madame

Zhenay. But there was no sign of her so far, and Arabella felt a little rush as her confidence returned.

I should think so, too! She was truly resplendent this evening, in an off-the-shoulder gown of white silk, with a froth of satin roses clustered at the top and spilling down one side to the hip. An ombre effect (the color technique, not the card game) had been achieved here—the roses passing from purest white down to palest green. To complete her ensemble, Arabella had chosen pale green satin slippers, a shawl of white silk velvet trimmed in pale green braid, a silver fan, and a reticule of emerald-green velvet. Her throat, bosom, arms, and slender fingers were all bare of decoration. Whilst the other ladies blazed with jewels, their hostess preferred to let her silk roses do for the main adornment—there was, besides, a set of silver combs, set with moonstones, in her rich auburn hair—and the effect was exactly what she wished it to be: In all that flashing, shining, diamond-studded crowd, Arabella stood out as the elegant focal point.

Now the outer doors were closed, the bell was rung, and the audience surged up the staircase in a body, like the restless tide of civilization assaulting the hillsides of a new continent. Seats were procured, the company settled itself, and then . . . out of the wings walked the legendary Sarah Siddons herself; retired, now, but briefly back onstage for this one special occasion.

She did not say much, nor remain upon the stage for very long, but the audience, in its enthusiasm, stood and clapped and clapped its elegant gloves, and some of the ha'penny stalls cheered out loud, for she had been a very great actress.

Arabella was extremely gratified by the general enthusiasm. Observing the scene from her box, she reflected on her supreme satisfaction with the evening thus far. As usual, after having made her entrance, London's premier courtesan had been mobbed by elegant gentlemen who knew her well, knew her slightly, or wished, ardently, *to* know her, and they had swum after her up the grand staircase (for those who credit Leeuwenhoek's astounding hypothesis) like so many spermatozoa after an egg cell. Her box could only accommodate six persons at a time, however, so each group was allowed just ten minutes in which to see their idol and attempt to fix assignations for later dates, before being obliged to make room for the next lot. The initial five aspirants had enjoyed a slightly longer audience, since no interruptions were allowed during Mrs. Siddons's dedication. But now that it was finished, gentlemen were once again thronging the passage outside Arabella's box, and striving for admittance to the inner sanctum.

Pierce Eagan, the celebrated sportswriter, was passed by the ushers.

"I have a young American friend outside," said Pierce, after kissing Arabella's hand, "actually, he's my second cousin, though I have only just met him—who urgently wishes to make your acquaintance."

"Americans tend to be badly brought up. Has he nice manners, Eagan?"

"Exceedin' nice."

"Is he good-looking?"

"I should say he was your ideal type."

"Oh, very well. Please inform him that my price for an introduction is one hundred pounds."

"One hundred pounds? Wasn't it fifty, only last Tuesday?"

"It has gone up. If your kinsman wishes to be presented now, he may jump the queue and come in at once. Otherwise, there is a host of others waiting their chance for admission."

"Oh, he'll want to come in, of course! Meeting you will be the pinnacle of achievement in his life so far!"

"You exaggerate, sir! After all, the Yankee will no doubt have fought wild Indians, and skinned grizzly bears with his teeth."

Arabella shooed her visitors out of the box as a baker

shoos flies from a confectionery window. All obeyed her, albeit with greater or lesser shows of reluctance, until she was alone at last. And into this sudden void stepped the man who had ogled her through her window as she was preparing to bathe! He was even younger and more handsome up close, but how changed! (Evening clothes do, indeed, make the man, but they *also* make the woman.) Arabella could never resist a male in formal attire, and her heart seemed to flutter in her throat.

"Miss Beaumont," he murmured, with an elegant bow. "Or, as I should say, 'Miss Beau-*mound!*'"

It was very much the wrong remark to make, and Arabella took exception to his insolence. Such vulgar familiarity presumed on so short an acquaintance was not to be borne, even if they *were* alone. And then he said, with a sheepish grin, "I'm afraid I can't afford your price, ma'm. Y' see, I only just got to England, and all I had in the world was my letter of introduction to Eagan."

"Then what are you doing in my box?" she demanded. "Mr. Jones, please show this 'gentleman' out immediately!"

The usher entered and took hold of the American's arm.

"Wait . . . I can explain . . ."

But Arabella had turned again to face the stage, covering her ear with her folded fan.

"I will *not* listen!" she replied. "Go!"

The fellow shook off the usher, straightened his waistcoat with both hands, bowed, and withdrew. Under the circumstances, he could scarcely have done otherwise, and yet, Arabella owned that the manner in which he took his leave was not without dash.

The reader may wonder at all this drama occurring off the stage and yet during the performance, but the fact is, other than the audience in the pit, and possibly one or two patrons in the stalls, few people attended the theater in order to actually see plays. Those up in the boxes could not hear the actors, in any case. But they liked it that way; audible dialogue would have interrupted their conversations. And this play was fairly stupid, anyhow—it seemed to consist of a lot of pies standing about, taking it in turns to disparage a theater critic who had panned Sheridan's last production. However, the fact that the *actual* critic was in attendance lent a certain frisson to the evening, and the audience hoped to see a dust-up between critic and playwright during the coming interval. Someone had already shouted to Sheridan, offering to hold his coat for him.

"Hmm," said Lord Foley, who had entered Arabella's box and was settling himself with a printed program. "*Pride and Pastry: A Short History of Eggles the Baker.* What is it about?"

"For heaven's sake, Foley," said Arabella. "If your intention in coming here was to watch the *play*, you should've stayed in the pit!"

Foley apologized, and said that he was only asking in a nominal sort of way.

"Well," said Arabella, relenting, "as I make it out, that man there, Mr. Puff-Pastry, is a playwright who is having a dream about a bake shop. Only, because it is a dream, you see, the pastries stand up and walk about, expressing indignation over the hero's ill-treatment at the hands of that man in the second row. Can you see him? In the bottle-green jacket? That's Mr. Mock. Sheridan has portrayed him as a butcher. He'll make his entrance in a minute—the butcher, I mean—and when he does, I would have you note the blood upon his apron."

"Why?"

"Because it is actual blood—human, not bovine. Sheridan had it sent over from a hospital this afternoon. It is meant to be symbolic, in a realistic sort of way."

"Sounds perfectly awful," said Richard Sharp, who was seated behind Foley. "Not to mention, derivative. Hasn't Sheridan any *new* ideas?"

"As the play's importance *as* a play is *not* important," said Arabella, "I don't care whether he has or not. Mrs. Siddons was here, the cream of society is in attendance, and the venue itself is a wonder to behold. Never you fear; the Bird o' Paradise has been well and truly fledged!"

"But what of the playwright?"

"Foley," said Poodle Byng. "You're snuffing the mood, old man."

"Snuff, did someone say? What a cracking wheeze!"

Then there was nothing for it but the snuff boxes all had to come out, and Poodle, who had purposely engineered the conversation to flow in this direction, was able to shew off his new carnelian-and-onyx-snuffbox-featuring-miniature-portraits-of-his-unmarried-sisters-framed-in-gold-beading-with-names-engraved-upon-inlaid-ivory-cartouches-and-having-open-spaces-adorned-in-brightly-enameled-flowers. His presentation was greeted by a chorus of appreciative sneezing, even though everyone knew it was only a ploy to try to get his sisters married off.

"Still," Lord Foley persisted, "I cannot help feeling sorry for Sheridan. He was 'all the go' only last year!"

"Sheridan is having the satisfaction of expressing his displeasure to an influential audience," said Sharp.

"Yes, but after tonight, everyone is going to be on the side of the critic, and I doubt that was his intention. Poor chap! I warned him about his excessive drinking, but I fear that the fellow has quite drowned his talent."

"Perhaps," said Arabella. "And I am afraid that your time is up, Foley. Make way for the next man, if you please."

"Beg pardon, Miss Beaumont," said one of the Wellesley brothers, leaning across from the neighboring box. "But did Foley just ask you what the play was *about?*"

"Indeed he did, sir."

"Good God! Now I've heard everything!"

Wellesley turned and repeated the story to Colonel Hangar,

who guffawed in surprise. "D'you mean to say the fellow dressed in his evening clothes and rousted out his coachman to bring him here . . . actually paid for tickets even, just to watch the play?"

"Remarkable," Wellesley agreed. "Although, mind you, there are any number of legitimate reasons to attend the theater. I, for one, put in an appearance in order to attend upon Miss Beaumont—I say, may I come over there, Miss Beaumont?—but I'm also deuced fond of the intervals."

The others heartily concurred, and Arabella indicated that she was willing that Mr. Wellesley should visit her box.

"Speaking of intervals," said Poodle Byng. "Is it nearly time for the first one?"

"No," said Arabella, observing the stage through her opera glass. "But I believe we are about to have an unscheduled break."

Apparently, the play was so bad that the cheap seats were staging a riot. With cries of "Boh!" "We want action!" and "I'll slice *your* pie, you cream puff!" persons in the pit and front rows were climbing onto the stage and chasing the poor little dinner rolls into the wings.

As Arabella had predicted, the interval was called early, in order to clear the theater and pitch out the troublemakers. But that was just fine with the audience. The wave of outraged, upper-crust humanity washed back down the staircase again, to revel in champagne and oysters. Arabella had no sooner descended the last step, when a man rushed up to her. He was a short, rather stout fellow, with a florid face and a flat head top, and she instinctively recoiled, recalling Elliot's warning and her unpleasant street encounter with the wagon driver.

"Miss Beaumont, I must speak with you!" he said. Then he bowed, with exaggerated deference. "My name's Cackletub. My professional name, that is. Clifford Cackletub, but do call me 'Cliff.' I had to find you and congratulate you

upon the magnificence of this theater. It would be *parfait*—
just right, you know—for staging the play I wish to produce,
and I should like to talk to you about engaging your premises
for that purpose."

"Then you should speak with the business manager."

"Oh, of course! But first I wanted to tell *you* about it! *You*
are the genius behind everything! One word from you and
the business manager will have no choice but to accept my
proposal."

Arabella was fond of hearing herself referred to as a genius.

"What play do you propose?" she asked. Not that it mattered. But she had privately decided to have no more bake
shop productions. Happy audiences tended to be better behaved, and consequently less destructive than angry ones.

"*The Quadrupeds, a Tragedy for Warm Weather.*"

He was trying to deceive her by referring to the play's second and third titles only, but Arabella was not fooled. It was
The Tailors, that infamous production that eight years previously had so insulted London's hard-working tailors that
they had arrived in a body to prevent the performance,
nearly destroying the Haymarket in their fury. In the end, it
had been necessary to call in the Life Guards.

"No," said Arabella, turning away. "I won't have that."

"Oh, but I am changing the incendiary elements!" cried
Cackletub, running after her. "It's not even *about* tailors anymore!"

"Why on Earth," said Arabella, rounding on him, "would
you want to revive anything Samuel Foote produced?"

"Because I love to make people laugh!"

"People do not generally laugh whilst they are rioting,"
said Arabella, "and I do not share Mr. Foote's brand of humor.
In a word, Mr. Cackletub, it is lowbrow."

"Exactly, miss. That's the sort that sells tickets!"

Arabella paused, and looked at him. Sometimes commercial considerations must supersede aesthetic standards, and this might be one of those times.

"Very well," she said. "How do you propose to change this terrible piece so that people will queue up to see it?"

"Spectacle, miss! Live horses! The four quadrupeds of the Apocalypse, swung out over the audience on chains!"

"That might create a *slight* problem, you know. The audience will be *underneath* the horses, after all, and the poor beasts are apt to be frightened out of their wits."

"Yes!" cried Cackletub, barely able to contain his mirth. "But that's the cheap seats, do you see? Most entertaining for the people in the boxes!"

Arabella sighed. "I am afraid that is a bit *too* lowbrow for me, Mr. Cackletub. Oh, Richard!" she called, waving her program at the playwright/director of her current disaster. "I must speak with you!"

Cackletub still refused to give up. "We could always clear the first five rows!"

But Arabella was walking away from him, again. "In that case," she said, "we shouldn't be able to sell as many tickets, should we?"

"*Dead* horses!" he cried, galloping after her. "We could get them from the knackers!"

"I would never be able to justify backing such a bad play to my investors," she said, over her shoulder. "Has no one ever discussed with you the futility of flogging lifeless equines?"

"Oh, that's all right, miss!" he called out. "I got the backing, all right! Madame Zhenay owes me a favor!"

At the sound of the name, Arabella stumbled on a ruche in the carpet. Someone grabbed her arm, and she felt a sudden, sharp pressure on the left side of her rib cage. A man with a knife—where had he come from?—lifting his arm to stab her again. Then she was knocked to the floor by sheer force. People were screaming and exclaiming, running toward her, or running away. From her strange viewpoint—face-up, ankle-level—Arabella saw two men apprehend her assailant, force the knife from his grip, and secure his hands behind him with a pair of manacles. The third man, the one who had shielded her from further assault and who was now lying on top of her, raised up on his arms and smiled into her face.

"Are you hurt?" asked the American, apparently knowing she wasn't, and using a tone of voice normally reserved for bedrooms. He rose when she shook her head, and helped her to her feet.

"I do not think so," she said. "It was my . . . the roses on my gown. Do you see? They are so thick, just here, that they prevented the knife from penetrating my . . ." She touched herself beneath the breast, and her protector's gaze eagerly followed the movement of her hand.

"What a dress!" he said approvingly. "A brilliant design! Practical, too."

By this time, a crowd of concerned onlookers had gathered round them.

"Excuse me a moment," said Arabella, and she turned to thank the two rather elegant fellows who had caught her would-be murderer. "How came you to have manacles with you this evening?"

"Mr. Elliot sent us, Miss Beaumont. We have been looking after you all night, though we very nearly bungled it. You see, *we* were watching the other fellow, the one who kept talking about dead horses and following you about. This villain had us completely fooled. He's dressed all wrong, you see. One doesn't expect murderers to wear evening clothes. Well, as they say, one shouldn't judge a sausage by its skin!"

"Nor constables."

"Beg pardon?"

"Haven't you come from the police station?"

The two smiled slightly, in the manner of nobility who've been mistaken for delivery boys.

"Not exactly, madam. But we *are* headed there now, in

order to see that our distinguished companion here is suitably accommodated, according to his merits."

Arabella knew better than to pursue her saviors' identities, for they were, after all, connected with Cecil Elliot.

"Well, thank you again, gentlemen," she said. "I am *very* much obliged to you. And please thank Mr. Elliot for me. Now I should like to have a word with this fellow, before you take him away."

They waited, whilst Arabella inspected her assailant's countenance. "You're the same man who chased me down the street, aren't you? The man with the cudgel. Who sent you after me?"

She knew the answer, of course, which was just as well, as the man declined to provide one. He refused to speak at all, and persisted in staring stonily at a spot on the ceiling, above Arabella's head.

"That's all right, miss," said one of his captors. "I expect we'll be able to get the truth out of him without too much trouble!"

And so, nearly everyone left the theater happy that night: Elliot's men had caught the attacker, the audience had been treated to smoked oysters and a really terrible play, a few lucky persons had nearly got to see a murder, Arabella had the satisfaction of a brilliant grand opening, and when the American left the theater, her hand was safely tucked within the crook of his arm. Only the playwright and the hired killer were completely unhappy. Also, our heroine's triumph was just a *little* marred, for her beautiful gown had been ruined beyond all hope of repair.

The trouble with summer in the south of England, thought Constable Norton, as he made his way along the marine parade under threatening skies, was its blasted unreliability. Yesterday had been fair; today it looked like rain. You never knew where you stood with the weather down here. It was like a woman. Like a capricious blonde woman, utterly spoilt and vicious when crossed. Like Maddy, he thought, with sudden rancor, who'd refused him and run off with an aerialist. The part of his mind that had been wont to think of her tried to fill the void by searching the crowds for faces like hers. Mrs. Walter Fairbottom's, for instance. She was a newlywed, and the spit and image of Maddy, who may well have been a newlywed herself by this time.

Constable Norton had researched the Fairbottoms. He had found out their names, where they were staying, and what their routine was. Thus armed, he made a point of swinging past their accustomed promenade when he knew they were likely to be there, and entertained himself by inventing little tragedies in which, after Mr. Fairbottom was swept out to sea, the good constable stepped in to comfort the grieving widow.

Blast and damnation! It was starting to rain! The Fairbottoms would not be taking their accustomed walk today. When it rained, they stayed inside and behaved like newlyweds. Well, there was no point in staying out here to get soaked. He would repair to a coffee stall and flirt with the waitress until the sun decided to show itself.

But he had no sooner turned around, when what should appear but a vision! Mrs. Fairbottom, the lovely Mrs. Walter, running toward him, obviously in acute distress, without her husband, her hair all wet, her gown soaked right through and clinging to her body most suggestively! And screaming against the rising wind, those magical words: "Constable! Come quickly, for God's sake! There's been an accident!"

Arabella kept the American with her until late the next day. Her brush with death had produced a peculiar effect upon her emotions, and when she learned that his middle name was "Kendrick," she wanted him by her side for as long as possible.

Garth Provenson claimed to be nineteen (she had thought he was older) and said he had come over with his mother in the hopes of making his fortune.

"Most people go *to* America *from* here to do that," said Arabella. They were lolling about in her big, soft bed, drinking madeira and nibbling cheese before breakfast.

"Well, it's kind of a problem when you start out over there," Garth replied. "You see, Momma and I thought we were rich, but when Poppa passed over, it all popped like a soap bubble. The creditors moved in right after the funeral, and left us barely enough to pay our passage to England."

"But why come here?" she persisted. And that's when she learned, to her consternation, that Garth was godson to Madame Zhenay.

He's not going to kill me, she thought. If he had wanted to, he had the perfect opportunity when we were alone in my box. He shielded me at the theater. He wouldn't have done that, unless . . . unless Zhenay instructed him to win my confidence first. But why do that?

"Are you . . . fond of your godmother?" asked Arabella.

"Heck, no! I never even knew she existed till Momma told me about her a few weeks ago. I guess I must've met her at my christening, but I don't remember much about that. My parents took me to America when I was just a tad."

"Pardon?"

"A tadpole. You know; a baby. I'm not even sure how Momma knows Zhenay. They don't seem very chummy. But I have to act nice to her, on account of . . . well, you know."

"The money," said Arabella. "Of course."

"Well, yeah. All the way over, Momma kept saying how we were going to be all right—better than all right, because my relations on both sides were really, really rich. She had her facts wrong," he said, "as usual. I'm related to the Eagans on my father's side."

"*They're* not wealthy," said Arabella.

"No, I know. Still, Pierce is a great sportswriter. I'm prouder of that than if he was the richest man in the world! On Momma's side, there is your neighbor, Judge Harbuckle. That's who I was going to see the day I first saw you in . . . the window."

"Harbuckle?" cried Arabella. "He's the meanest man alive!"

"Yeah. So I learned. My visit was a short one, though he *was* kind enough to tell me the name of the beautiful woman who lived at this house."

Arabella was pleased. "Really? You asked Justice Harbuckle about me?"

Garth nodded. "I didn't know anything about you, except where you lived, and I *had* to meet the owner of the most bewitching little—"

"So it was lust, then, that drove you on?" she asked.

"What do you think?"

Once again, Arabella found herself pinned under that wonderful physique, and she abandoned herself to the moment. But before they got totally carried away, she sensibly suggested that they dress and go down to breakfast.

"I am certain that things will turn round for you, Garth," she said. "In the meantime, at least you can still afford to dress well."

They both looked over at his evening clothes, which lay where he had shed them, in a heap near the fireplace.

"Eagan lent me those."

"Oh. Well, that was nice of him. Come, my love; let us dress and go down, for we have expended ourselves overmuch, I believe, and require more sustenance than mere cheese and wine may bestow."

"I love the way Englishwomen talk!" said Garth. "It's so refined and old-fashioned!"

"I was doing that on purpose," said Arabella. "How would an American woman have put it?"

Garth picked up one of his stockings and, using it like a puppet, said, in a falsetto voice: " 'I'm just about *starved*, dammit! If you think you can fuck me all night without feedin' me up good next day, then you got another think comin'!' "

"How delightfully crass!" cried Arabella, laughing. "It must be wonderfully freeing to speak without thinking!"

"Well," Garth admitted, as he buttoned her up the back. "They don't *all* talk like that. Just most of them."

"*Most* of them? Most of the women in *America?* Goodness! You have rather extensive experience for a nineteen-year-old!"

"Yep."

The Lustings breakfast room had been renovated by John Soane himself, and boasted his signature handkerchief ceiling, but with a convex mirror instead of a skylight. Arabella was pleased to see that the reflection of Garth and herself was so striking: She did not suffer at all in comparison with a youth of nineteen.

They continued their conversation at the table, over apple pie and sausages.

"I presume that at some point you called on Madame Zhenay," said Arabella.

"Momma did. She hadn't heard from Zhenay in years, and was always kind of scared of her, but she was our only hope. And as things turned out, it was lucky we found her: I'm her heir."

"Really! Well, congratulations, Garth! The Palais de Beautay fortune is reportedly worth millions. So, why are you borrowing Eagan's evening clothes? Surely Zhenay can manage an advance on your inheritance?"

Garth shook his head. "She won't give me anything now. But she wants me to manage this gentlemen's shop she's opening in the fall. Zhenay doesn't trust anyone, but she says

I'm the best bet, since, if I steal from her, I'll be stealing from myself. Can you imagine what it's like, Miss Beaumont? To have financial expectations and then suddenly discover . . ."

". . . That it's all turned to fairy gold? Yes, indeed," said Arabella grimly.

"Well, it's happened to me a few times, now, and I have to say, this last arrangement seems kind of underhanded. Where I come from, a healthy, sober white man has to really work at it if he wants to be poor. There's opportunity everywhere, and practically no limit to how far a fellow can go, unless he's Irish. But it takes time to get established, and I got my Momma to think of. She's been in low spirits since Poppa died, and she's unwell, to boot. So when she wanted to come to England I figured it might be dangerous to refuse her."

"I'm sorry to hear that your mother is unwell," said Arabella, pouring him another cup of coffee.

"Zhenay's probably going to outlive her. But as long as Momma has that fantasy inheritance to cling to, she is a little more cheerful, at least."

"Have you spoken to Zhenay recently?"

"Sort of; I saw her just before she left."

"Oh. I had not heard she was going away. When was this?"

"Yesterday. Said she was meeting some friends at a place called . . . what is it? . . . Peach Head or something. You folks have the funniest names for things! Anyway, I was surprised that she had any friends."

"Do you mean 'Beachy Head'?"

"That's the one! You know it?"

"Mmm-hmm. I've heard of it, anyway." (This was good news. With her enemy out of town, perhaps Arabella could relax her vigilance.) "How did Zhenay seem when you saw her?"

"Furious." Garth chuckled to himself. "I never saw a body in such a state! Pacing up and down, swearing revenge on some woman who'd put her behind bars—to tell the truth, I wouldn't be surprised if the old witch winds up back in prison pretty soon, for murder!"

Arabella cut herself another slice of pie. "Did she say who this person was?"

He shrugged. "Someone who used to work for her under a false name."

Garth regarded her for a moment and grinned.

"Actually," he said, "it was you, wasn't it?"

Arabella stood by the open door, marking her visitor's progress as he swung off toward town. He had a marvelous walk, marvelous legs; and that rear portion of his anatomy, to which the legs were attached, was marvelous, also.

He's an altogether marvelous man, she thought dreamily, and then realized, with a start, that when she had said good-bye, she had called him "Kendrick."

"Garth? Is that you?"

"Yeah," Garth replied, hanging his hat on the vestibule hook.

"Where on Earth have you been?"

"Staying with a friend, Momma," he replied, entering the sitting room of their rented lodgings. "I went to the theater, and it got so late I decided to sleep over."

Though the day outside was riotous with sunshine, in here the heavy drapes created a twilit netherworld of quiet shadows, which might have been pleasant, but wasn't: the mingled smells of vomit and alcohol rendered it nauseating. Mrs. Provenson, a pale, frail woman in a soft cap and ribbons, reclined upon an Empire sopha with a fur rug over her legs. She was drinking tea . . . and something more.

"Well, thank heaven you're back, anyhow. I was worried sick. I don't know what I'd have done if—"

"Nothing's going to happen to me," said Garth. "I just

didn't want to come in at all hours, disturbing you and the rest of the household."

"You just missed Zhenay," said Mrs. Provenson, sipping her tea. "She was hoping to see you before she left."

"I thought she left yesterday."

"Her trip was postponed. She wanted to talk about the will before she went off to Eastbourne, but you're too late to catch her now."

"I thought she was going to Peachface."

"Beachy Head is *in* Eastbourne. Or near it, or something."

"Ha!" he exclaimed, pouring himself a glass of hock. "Wanted to discuss the will, did she? Excellent!" He drank down the contents in a single swig and glared at the empty glass. "German wine! And last night I was drinking prissy little cordials! What I wouldn't give for a good bottle of whisky! I thought they had that here."

"Oh, they do. Or at least, they did. Zhenay says most of it came from Scotland, until the English taxed it or shut it down or something. So now it's illegal, and hard to find."

"Don't they make it in Ireland, too?"

"Probably. Zhenay will find us some when she gets back."

"Hmm," said Garth. "How far away is this place she's gone to? Maybe I should follow her."

"There's no need, son," said his mother. "She wasn't bringing very good news. Garth, she's going to be married."

"Married?! That battle ax?! Who in his right mind would marry her?"

"Englishmen have queer tastes, dear. Anyway, she still plans to settle some small amount on you, and you'll have your job at her shop, of course, but Zhenay says she is changing her will in favor of her husband-to-be."

"*What?!*" Garth slammed his glass down on the table so hard that it broke. "*Again?!* Goddammit, Momma! We're right back where we started!"

"Well—at least you'll have a job, now."

"A job!" He stared at her. "I don't want a *job!* Money's what I want! Enough of it so I'll never have to work *again!*"

"But you seemed so pleased about the manager's position!"

"Don't you understand? That was all dumb show, for the sake of your ugly friend! It was *supposed* to lead to something better! Now it's all there is! I wasn't born to work," he muttered, "and by God, I'm not going to!"

"I'm so, so sorry, darling!" said his mother. "You know I don't like your drinking, but this has been a terrible shock. There's a bottle of malt whisky in the cupboard. Let's both have a glass."

"You've been holding out on me!" he cried, opening the cupboard and seizing the bottle. "Why, this thing's three-quarters empty! How could you be so selfish?"

"If I'd told you about it, we wouldn't have any now, when we need it."

He savagely pulled out the cork with his teeth, and swallowed straight from the bottle—once, twice, three times, four . . .

"Hey!" cried his mother. "What about me?"

"You've already had yours," he said, throwing the empty bottle into a trash receptacle, and wiping his mouth with the back of his hand. "Well, at least I won't have to pretend anymore. I'm so goddamned sick of pretending all the time!"

The letter from Belinda had inexplicably gone astray at Hamsterhead, and consequently was delayed for some days:

Dear Bell,
 My heartiest congratulations on Madame Zhenay's incarceration! Now we can all breathe easier, knowing you won't be plagued by creditors anymore!

Arabella cast a rueful glance at the post tray, where the latest pile of vendor demands lay awaiting her attention. It had been a full week since the Bird's opening night, but there had been no new developments in the case. Obviously, Belinda had written this before receiving the explanation that the chase was not only resumed but reversed, with Arabella as the quarry this time.

> *Of all the rooms in the Redwelts model, I am proudest of the grand saloon, which has been the most exacting. The draperies, alone . . .*

Arabella skipped the descriptions, knowing full well that Belinda would tell them to her all over again when she returned.

> *The quarantine is lifted at last, and I am starting for home on Tuesday!*
> *I cannot wait to get back to you, and out of this place, lovely though it is. Sir Birdwood-Fizzer is the most considerate of hosts, but I cannot say as much for his friends, who fair give me the chills. They look at me, and then at each other, sidelong; not in an open, admiring manner, but furtively, with evil grins, the way I imagine wolves must smile at one another when they exit from a forest to discover a lone, unguarded sheep. There are horrid books in the library, and the torture devices in the dungeon show signs of recent use. Last night, when one of the guests got up from table, there was blood on his chair. I know that*

you'll say I am being silly. In fact, I can hear
your voice now: "They are only men, Bunny, how-
ever they might remind you of beasts." And really,
I am not worried, for I am understood to be under
Birdwood-Fizzer's protection. But I should hate
to think what might happen, if I were not.

"Express post, miss," said Mrs. Janks, entering the library and handing Arabella an additional letter. "This just arrived. I think you'd better open it at once."

"Oh, all right," grumbled Arabella, holding out her hand for it. "It's probably just another tradesman's bill."

It was postmarked Brighton, though. Arabella laid Bunny's letter aside, in favor of this new one, and read the brief contents with mingled horror and disbelief.

"Oh, dear God!" she exclaimed, half rising from her chair.

"What is it, miss? What's wrong?" cried the housekeeper.

"Constance is in prison for the murder of Madame Zhenay!"

Chapter 15

"The situation looks bad for your friend, I'm afraid," said Sergeant Dysart, returning to his desk with a sheaf of documents. "It says here, 'Deceased discovered under pier with crushed skull. Accused apprehended next to body, with large stone.' "

"Who wrote that?" cried Arabella indignantly. "You must sack him at once! The fool has left out all the articles, as well as the past tense singular form of the verb 'to be'!"

"It's a faster way of writing, miss," Frank explained. "A formal version is written up later, but this abbreviated style saves time in the field."

"I thought you said the body was discovered at the seashore."

"Yes, miss. Saves time there, too."

The Bow Street office was littered with loose piles of papers obscuring a motley multitude of desks and tables. Unsightly wooden floors that cried for carpets revealed every scuff, stain, and splinter in the relentless light from naked windows that could only be *shuttered*—plunging the room into total darkness, or *un*—with no way of filtering the sun on rare days like today, when there was too much of it. A few hard benches, placed at random for the public's inconvenience, stood against the dirty walls, where a ponderous clock ticked away the doleful minutes, heedless of the busy men who worked against it.

Arabella's sense of order was offended by the place. Her fingers fairly itched to hang up curtains and set it to rights.

"Costanze could not have murdered Madame Zhenay," she said with conviction, striving to maintain both her balance and her dignity upon a wobbly chair in front of Frank's desk. "She hasn't the sense to plan a course of action."

"Well, perhaps she didn't plan it. Perhaps it was a spur of the moment occurrence."

Frank lifted off the first page of the preliminary report and read from the second: "Suspect apprehended with stone unable to account for self."

"I've never met a stone that *could* account for itself," sniffed Arabella, though she had to admit that Costanze never could, either. "What is that document, again?"

"The field notes section of the police record."

"And what is that?"

"A report, written by the first officer to arrive at the scene of a crime. It's a new idea, but a sound one, and destined to become standard practice."

"Very sensible. What else does it say?"

" 'Deceased found floating in large puddle seawater. Depth: six inches.' "

"The tide was out, then?"

"I presume so. The report doesn't indicate one way or another."

"Don't you find it odd that a member of the local constabulary should be taking a stroll on the beach while on duty? And that he just happened to find himself under the pier in time to apprehend Costanze, moments after she supposedly murdered Zhenay?"

"Oh, it wasn't a constable found the body; it was a couple.

A Mr. and Mrs. Fairbottom. Newlyweds, spending their honeymoon at Brighton. The husband held fast to Miss Worthington, whilst his wife went to inform the authorities."

"I see. And I presume that the stone was admitted as evidence?"

"The which?"

"The alleged murder weapon. I should like to examine it."

"I don't believe anyone thought to bring it in. I don't see it listed on the evidence report."

Arabella flung up her hands.

"What have they got working down in Brighton, chimpanzees?"

"We're doing our best, miss," said Sergeant Dysart. "But it's deuced difficult sometimes. Detection is still a very young science."

"It's more art than science, at this point," replied Arabella, making an effort to control her impatience, "and bad art, at that. I am sorry, Frank; I did not mean to insult your profession. It is just that, if Costanze had really used this stone on Madame Zhenay, it would have been covered in blood, hair . . . bits of brain, perhaps. And if, as I suspect, it bore no traces of any such things, she should have been cleared of the murder charge by now. What else can you tell me?"

Frank consulted the report again, this time reading from the formal write-up: " 'The victim was last seen alive making her way to Eastbourne, where her companion was expecting her.' "

"Her companion?"

"Lady Ribbonhat," Frank explained. " 'The two were planning to stay at an hotel there, where—' "

Arabella interrupted him. "But Eastbourne is more than twenty miles from Brighton!"

"Twenty-four, miss . . . 'where, according to the witness . . .' "

"What witness?"

"That would be Lady Ribbonhat, again. We have been instructed to use official jargon as much as possible when writing up cases. You see? We *are* attempting to establish standards. Soon this kind of lingo will seem completely natural, though it's bound to be a bit confusing to a lay person like yourself."

" 'Lay person,' " said Arabella thoughtfully. "I like that expression."

Frank suddenly became so engrossed in the report that his ears burned bright red from concentration. "Anyway," he continued, " 'the victim and the witness were planning to meet, by mutual arrangement, at Eastbourne . . .' "

"Why is Lady Ribbonhat a witness? She didn't actually see anything, did she?"

"We questioned her, miss. So we have to call her *something.*"

"Then why not call her 'Lady Ribbonhat'?"

Frank read on: " 'In order to meet the witness's son, Vice Admiral Seaholme, the Duke of Glen*deen,* who was going to be married to the victim. According to the witness—' "

"Frank," said Arabella firmly. "Would you mind referring to the parties by name, rather than designation, in view of the fact that it is only I whom you are addressing, and not a fellow professional? I am only a 'lay person,' you know."

The scarlet hue of concentration was spreading to Frank's cheeks. "Very good, miss," he said. "I'll carry on reading from the final report. That's got all the grammatical bits put back in.

> *"According to Lady Ribbonhat, she retired early, as the vic—sorry, Madame Zhenay—was not expected to arrive until very late that night.*
>
> *Around noon the next day, the body was found floating in a large sea puddle beneath the Brighton pier. The limbs were scratched and bruised, and the back of the head was crushed. The suspect—I mean, Miss Worthington—was*

apprehended at the scene, with a large stone in
her hands and unable to satisfactorily account
for herself."

He looked up and added, "A little digging on the part of
the Brighton Police turned up Madame Zhenay's blackmail
attempt against Miss Worthington."

"Frank! You *told* them about that?"

"I didn't have to. A Brighton constable came in requesting
to see any records we had pertaining to the accused. When
you informed on Madame Zhenay, I had to make out a report, miss. That's standard procedure."

Arabella groaned. "So they've established a motive! How
do you think the prosecution will present the case?"

"They'll probably say that Miss Worthington lured Madame Zhenay to Brighton with regards to the blackmailing
matter, promising to make her a payment of some kind. Naturally, Zhenay wouldn't want her prospective mother-in-law
to know she was a blackmailer, so she changed coaches at
Eastbourne and proceeded to Brighton, planning to meet
with the duke and Lady Ribbonhat later the following day.
Then, at Brighton, she was done to death by the suspect
under the pier."

"How do you account for the scratches and bruises?"

"There was a struggle."

"But Frank, this theory cannot possibly hold water, if
you'll forgive the expression. Why should Madame Zhenay
have started out for Eastbourne, and then changed for
Brighton in the *middle* of her journey? She couldn't have received word from Costanze whilst traveling by coach, and if
she had planned to see her before leaving London, she would
have gone to Brighton direct."

"Well, perhaps she did, miss."

"Have you found the coachman who supposedly took her
there?"

"Not yet; no."

"Well, I do not think you will ever find him. Because I do not believe he exists. Zhenay went to Eastbourne."

"We have not found anyone who claims to have taken her there, either."

"How strange! Well, moving on: According to the Brighton field notes, the newlyweds apprehended Costanze moments after she killed Zhenay. The body must have been fresh, then? Still almost warm, was it?"

"I don't know any more than you do, miss. If it's not in the field notes, we can only guess at what might have happened."

"Is there a doctor's report? Surely they called in a doctor to establish the time and cause of death?"

"No. It doesn't appear that they did. It's Brighton, miss. The police don't see as many murders down there, so they don't always know what to do when they get one. And between ourselves, the investigating officer, this Constable Norton, does not strike me as being particularly quick off the mark."

"Well," said Arabella, "if Costanze and Zhenay had struggled, Costanze, too, would be covered in scratches . . . and probably bite marks," she added, recalling the ones bestowed upon her own flesh by Madame during the course of their erotic encounter. "I have my own reasons for suspecting that the victim would not hesitate to use her teeth in a physical altercation. Ask the gaoler at Brighton, if you would, whether Constance shows evidence of similar abuse on her own person. Zhenay was taller, heavier, stronger, and a good deal cleverer than Costanze. If those two had ever come to blows, I am quite certain that Miss Worthington would have been the one to end up in the puddle."

"What's your theory, then, miss?"

"I do not presently possess one, but neither can I accept

your approximation of the prosecution's probable version of events."

"What do you think Miss Worthington was doing under the pier with that stone?"

"God knows. Does the report reflect any of her actual remarks?"

"No. It only states that she was incoherent."

"Yes. Costanze is always incoherent. But she has not murdered Madame Zhenay; of that I am certain."

Certainty and proof are two different animals, however. Arabella knew that if she were going to recover her money, she would first have to establish Miss Worthington's innocence beyond a reasonable doubt. And she had a feeling that that word, "reasonable," which was always difficult to prove in any matter involving Costanze, would be something close to impossible, in this case.

There had been no time to apprise Bunny of this, for she had already left Redwelts, and could not be reached—was due to arrive in St. Albans the next day, in fact, where accordingly, Arabella drove out in the brougham to meet and to dine with her at the Cocks.

"How is dear old Birdwood-Fizzer?" asked Arabella, after the two had exchanged kisses, hugs, and typical reunion sentiments.

"Just the same," Belinda replied, removing her gloves "All mouth and no trousers."

The waiter entered the private dining room that Arabella had engaged, with two pints of ale for the weary travelers.

"Bunny," said Arabella, after he'd gone to get their dinner, "something rather awkward has come up since you left Scotland." She outlined the situation as briefly as possible.

"Well, well!" chortled Belinda. "This is splendid! With Madame Zhenay dead, Costanze needn't worry about being blackmailed anymore, and you're out of bodily danger, at last!"

"Costanze needn't worry anymore? Whatever *can* you mean? She is in gaol for murder, Bunny, and if she swings for this, I shall never see another farthing of the amount she owes me!"

"Oh. That is true, I suppose. But what a strange way you have of putting it. I almost have the impression that you are more concerned over your money than you are over the fate of poor Costanze."

"Well, I am."

"Bell!"

"Stop pretending she's a dear friend. We both loathe her. Do you remember that book of gallows etiquette she insisted on reading to me when I was accused of Euphemia's murder? If I thought her capable of comprehending the irony, what joy I should take in reading it to her now!"

Belinda was going to protest, probably, but the waiter returned at that moment with a tureen of oxtail soup, and the weary traveler, suddenly finding that she was ravenous, fell to.

"Personal feelings toward Costanze aside," said Arabella, who was less hungry than Belinda, and therefore able to speak at greater length, "I shall have to go to Brighton and see what can be done for her."

Belinda nodded whilst chewing on a slice of bread and reaching for her glass.

"And, as there is a good chance that the Brighton Police are even more inept than our London ones, I am afraid there is no time to be lost."

Her sister drained her glass and said, "Well, I shall be very sorry to miss you again, after we have only just been reunited, but I *do* understand."

"I knew you would, dear," said Arabella. "So finish up your soup, and we'll be off directly. I have packed the brougham with everything required for our immediate needs, and the servants have been sent on ahead to make everything ready for us."

"*Us?*"

"Why, yes! I shall require my little sister's wise counsel and unflagging support if I am to get through this."

"Oh, but, Bell!" cried Belinda. "I have only just returned! I am exhausted! All I want to do is go home and keep to my bed for a few days!" The young woman could not help whimpering a little, as she added, "I really do not think I am fit for more traveling right now!"

Arabella was unmoved. "I am afraid that you cannot go home, dearest, as there will be no one to look after you there. You can sleep on the way. I shall read a book, or something."

"But where shall we lodge? Brighton will be full up, surely!"

"Uncle Selwyn has kindly sent me the keys to his town house. You'll like it there, Bunny! Fresh ocean breezes and sea views from all the front windows! We shall go riding on the marine parade in all our gay apparel!"

"What apparel?" wailed Belinda. "Everything I own is packed up in the hired coach I took from Scotland!"

"Which I have engaged to follow us down to Brighton. So you shall have your summer clothes *and* your Scottish clothes, for starters. We can purchase additional sea togs when we get to town, if we like."

Belinda was so dispirited at the thought of another day's travel that even the prospect of shopping failed to revive her. And she further suspected that she should *not* be allowed to sleep in the coach, for she knew Arabella. Sure enough, despite the elder sister's promise to read a book, once they were somewhat uncomfortably ensconced, Arabella was unable to resist the opportunity of unburdening herself concerning her newly discovered feelings for Mr. Kendrick.

"Oh, Bunny!" she cried, after a lengthy discourse on her

sufferings. "I cannot bear it! He is gone, because of me, and I have not realized until now how much I esteem him!"

"Esteem him?"

"Admire and appreciate him!"

"Admire and appreciate?"

"Love . . . him. Belinda! I love John Kendrick! I see that now! And it is too late!" So saying, she threw herself into her sister's arms, there to indulge her feelings with a really good cry. Belinda patted her wearily upon the back.

"Well," she said. "It is *not* too late; Mr. Kendrick will have to return to England sometime. And then you can see him and tell him how you feel."

"No," Arabella sniffled, plucking the tucker from her sister's gown and blowing her own nose upon it. "If he ever comes back at all, he will come back married, like they all do!"

"Who 'all' do you mean?"

"Jilted lovers in novels. They always go abroad, even if it's only to Croyden, and then they come back with a bride."

"You cannot judge real life by novels, Bell."

"But you *can!* Mr. Kendrick is an avid reader of novels! That is why he is doing this; he would never have had the idea to go away on his own . . . a mission!" she said, scornfully. "When he scarcely even believes in God! No, it's too ridiculous. But he has done it anyway, and he will marry. And his bride will have facial tattoos, or plates in her lips, and her teeth filed to points, like a shark's!"

"Now, now," said Belinda soothingly. "You know perfectly well that Mr. Kendrick dotes upon you. He has never so much as glanced at another woman in your presence. Or out of it, either, probably. And this separation will help him to sort out *his* feelings, too. He will probably come home in a year or so, and when he does, he will come to Lustings direct and take you in his arms, and you will live happily ever after."

"He will be married, I tell you!"

And she went on at some length, in a similar vein to that given above, but Belinda only snorted. Or so Arabella thought at first. On closer inspection, however, her sister appeared to be asleep. It is remarkable, is it not, the way in which that non-articulate noise, which in itself is so expressive of scorn and derision, resembles the unconscious sound of a person completely dead to the world of opinions?

Their uncle's town house was elegant, and the Lustings servants had rendered the rooms most comfortable. After a good night's sleep, both sisters awoke feeling generally refreshed and better about the world. Brighton was almost exactly the way Arabella remembered it from her childhood: raucous, vulgar, crowded, and loud, and she shied away from reflecting that, but for Costanze, she would not have to be here at all. Because she mustn't resent the accused. Not while there was work to do, at any rate. Poor Costanze! How terrible all this must be for *her!* Charged with murder; locked up in gaol . . . even so, our heroine did not sufficiently trust her temper to actually go down and see the wretch just yet; Belinda could do that, whilst Arabella examined the area under the pier.

"But why?" Belinda asked. "The arrest was made over a week ago! What are you searching *for?*"

"For something I hope I do not find. Now, go to Costanze, and see whether you can discover just what it was she was doing under there with that rock."

Chapter 16

"Building a staircase," said Costanze.

Belinda had discovered the prisoner to be living in circumstances much more comfortable than she had imagined, for the ever-attentive Mr. Pollard, who was currently seated in a chair outside the cell, had been providing the accused a steady supply of blankets, books, pillows, and foodstuffs with which to keep up her spirits. Today he had brought her the best gift of all—a feather bed.

"Building a staircase?" Belinda repeated, bewilderment showing in her countenance. "That is what you were doing with the rock? A staircase to where?"

"Up one of the posts."

"One of the posts that hold up the pier, d'you mean?"

"*I* don't know what they're for, Belinda! They're just *posts* with . . . branch things at the top. And they're down under the pier you know but they're quite a lot taller than I am so I had to build a staircase in order to get up there."

"And why did you want to do that?"

"Well because there was a gull's nest at the top with a gull sitting on it."

"Oh," said Belinda, in some relief. "And you wanted the eggs, I suppose?"

This was not so stupid, after all—lots of people ate gulls' eggs.

"No—I wanted the gull to teach me her language so that Pigeon wouldn't be the only one of us who could talk to birds. After all a seagull might teach me the secret of flying as well as a pigeon even better if you like because gulls can soar and kind of hover can't they whilst pigeons only flap."

This comment rang a vague bell in Belinda's memory, which Costanze kindly amplified for her.

"Pigeon speaks to pigeons," she said, with a fond glance at Mr. Pollard, "but Bell won't allow me to ask him to ask them how they fly so when I saw the gull up there I decided to see whether I could speak Gullah and ask her myself."

Belinda was suddenly glad that Arabella was not present. "You decided to *see* whether you could speak *Gullah?*"

This was so mixing that she felt herself beginning to go light in the head.

"Yes I have never tried to speak it before you know so I don't know whether I can or not."

"In the first place," said Belinda, "Gullah is not the language of seagulls . . ."

"You have asked me what I was doing under the pier and I am trying to tell you but you keep interrupting to lecture me! Do you want to know what happened or do you just want to show off your knowledge?"

Belinda opened and shut her mouth. "I am sorry," she said at last. "Pray, continue."

But Costanze had not finished following up her newest thought. "Now I *know* that *you* cannot speak Gullah Bunny you do not speak anything but English. And isn't it wonderful," she added, "that out of all the countries in the world you were born in the only one which speaks your language?"

"This *isn't* the only one, Shortcake," said Pigeon kindly, as though, but for this slight factual error, the rest of her statement were perfectly sensible. "There's America and Australia and New Zealand, too. And Canada."

"Yes but Canada does not count for they speak French there as well."

Belinda's head was fairly buzzing by this time.

"Well there's not much more to say really," said Costanze, returning abruptly to her original tack. "I was building stairs so that I could climb up the pole and ask the seagull how she flew and then this couple came strolling along and the woman screamed which startled me so that I dropped the rock and the next thing I knew the man was holding me by the arm and shouting to the woman to fetch a constable."

Pigeon was stroking Costanze's arm through the cell bars. The sight made Belinda queasy, for some reason.

"Then what happened?" she asked.

"Well after a bit the woman came back with a constable and I was brought to this place and Pigeon came to see me. He's been ever so kind to his widdle birdie-brain sweetheart hasn't you moochie-woochie? . . ."

Whereupon, Pigeon and his widdle birdie-brain sweetheart began to bill and coo at one another through the iron bars.

"We shall never be able to explain such a ridiculous story to the jury," fumed Arabella, when Belinda had given her a full account of the morning's proceedings. "And you may be certain that the prosecution will attempt to cross-examine her on exactly that point."

"Which may be all to the good," said Belinda. "If Costanze can be certified as a lunatic, they will not hang her. I am glad she has Mr. Pollard's devotion. It is very touching, though observing them together makes me seasick. He calls her 'Shortcake.' "

"Does he? I should have thought 'Fruitcake' more apt, especially if the court has her certified. I have also heard him call her 'Pet,' you know; probably because she reminds him of his first horse."

"But," said Belinda doubtfully, "I remember you said, if Costanze is officially declared insane, she will go to the madhouse, and you will never see your money."

After a moment's thoughtful silence, Arabella cleared her throat and shifted uncomfortably in her chair. She and Belinda were sitting on the narrow balcony, facing the sea.

"Oh," she said, "that's true. I seem to be unable to collect my thoughts here—the wind confuses me and scatters them everywhere. But you and I needn't worry about it, in any case. I have engaged Sir Clifton Corydon-Figge, a barrister of more than ordinary assiduity and perspicacity. He will surely know best what's to be done. I shall interview the newlyweds, and lay all my findings at his learned feet."

"Good," said Belinda. "How went the pier inspection? Did you find your bloody rock?"

"Not a bit of it, thank God!"

"Hmm. And did you by any chance find a heap of stones next to a piling?"

"Yes," said Arabella. "As a matter of fact, I did."

"So Costanze's story is true, it seems."

"Don't be silly; of course it is! Costanze is constitutionally incapable of conceiving a lie. Lies require cunning, and the ability to plan. Speaking of plans, have you made any for this afternoon? I thought perhaps you would care to accompany me to interview the newlyweds."

"I am sorry to disappoint you," said Belinda, "but Lord Tittington has invited me to the matinee. *The Three Chumps* is on offer there. So many of our friends are in town, Bell! Why not postpone the newlyweds and join us, instead?"

"I thank you, but French farce is not to my taste. It always features people injuring one another, and the audience is expected to laugh."

"They *do* laugh!"

"In France, perhaps. But remember, that is the nation where, not so lately, they made life-sized puppets from the headless corpses of guillotine victims. The French laughed at that. I feel certain that British people would not have."

"I never figured you for a Francophobe!" said Belinda.

"Nor am I!" Arabella asserted. "If you will recall, I have paid France the compliment of wanting to live here, as though it were there. Paris is wonderful beyond words, I believe. I love champagne, and French food, and French furnishings. And I remain an ardent admirer of Voltaire's—though even he resorted to torture and disembowelings to get a laugh. Consider: Who or what is the most famous French comedian of all time? Punch, a puppet, whose very name denotes a violent act!"

"Punch is Italian, actually."

"It's the same thing! People being injured is not in the least funny. I wonder that *you* can like it, Bunny!"

"Come now," said Belinda. "You have laughed at Punch and Judy shows."

"When I was a child! And in any case, I was not laughing at the *violence*, but at the absurdity. Punch was pretending to be a cripple, and claiming he couldn't walk because of a bone in his leg."

"I do not recall specifically what it was you were laughing at," Belinda admitted, "but violence can be funny, sometimes. It all depends on who is being attacked, you see; authority figures and whatnot."

"I disagree."

"Really? Picture this: Lady Ribbonhat is lecturing the poor, deriding them for their lax morals and slovenly ways. Suddenly, a very short person, a dwarf, in fact, goes right up to her and punches her in the stomach. Just one punch. And he doesn't say anything."

For a few moments, Arabella stared straight ahead, her

face expressionless. Then her mouth started to wobble, and shortly thereafter she was shrieking in a fit of uncontrollable laughter.

"How," she gasped, "did you ever manage to think of that example?"

"It's from a play that I am writing in the small hours, when I cannot sleep. Do you really like it?"

"I love it! What is it called?"

"*Lady Ribbonhat Gets Punched in the Stomach by a Dwarf.*"

"What! Do you mean that's the title?"

"Why not? What would you suggest I call it?"

"I don't know. I have not read your play, although I hope you will let me read it when it is finished. But don't you think the title will spoil your best scene?"

"Not at all!" said Belinda. "The audience will be expecting it, you see. The anticipation builds and builds, until finally . . . it happens!"

"Hmmm. It will have to be a very small dwarf, because the dowager is nearly a dwarf herself. If it ever gets produced, I think you must expect to hear from Lady Ribbonhat's solicitors."

"I know. I shall give them free tickets."

"But what else happens?"

"What do you mean?"

"Well, something else has to happen, besides that!"

"Why?"

"Because the audience will want to know what comes next, or what came before. I mean, that isn't a story by itself."

"Isn't it?"

"No! This scene needs to come at the end or the beginning or in the middle of a story. We need to know how Lady Ribbonhat *reacts* to being punched in the stomach."

"Oh!" said Belinda. "I forgot to tell you that part! She falls down."

"No, I mean . . . look, Bunny; don't you think that's awfully short for a play?"

"Well, of course! It's a one-act!"

The Fairbottoms—greedy, surly, superior—were prime examples of that hard new breed that proliferates in towns with lots of offices where the men can make money, and lots of smart establishments where the women can spend it. Our couple was sharp and ambitious; they were nobody's fools, who, despite their youth, thought they knew more about the world than all the great thinkers who have ever lived in it, and consequently believed themselves entitled to anything they wanted.

For the Fairbottoms saw themselves as the human embodiment of the tree of all knowledge: Art, science, philosophy, and the great inventions of civilization were mere baubles dangling from the ends of the stately Fairbottom boughs. When they spoke of the illustrious achievements of other individuals, they used the term "we," as in: "We discovered America," or "We invented movable type," readily claiming their share in the glory, even if the person whose discovery or invention or idea it actually was merely hailed from the same nation or continent as themselves, or belonged to the same race.

Mr. and Mrs. were spending their "tinsel weeks" in a honeymoon cottage with a Dutch door, and Mr. Fairbottom spoke to Arabella from over the top of the bottom half, without inviting her in.

"The police have already questioned us," he said, with all the arrogance and suspicion of a man who is determined that no one shall put anything over on *him*. "Why should I tell it all over again . . . to *you?*"

"Because I am a friend of the accused, and I know that she could not have done such a thing," Arabella replied.

"That," said Mr. Fairbottom loftily, "has been said of

every murderer since Cain. The truth is, anybody might commit a murder, given the right circumstances."

"Oh, not *anybody*, Walter," simpered his wife, who was standing behind him in order to hear everything without directly involving herself. "*You* could never murder anyone!"

"I'm afraid we have nothing more to add," said Mr. Fairbottom firmly, preparing to close the top half of the door. "Good day to you."

"One moment, if you please." Arabella's tone conveyed such unassailable authority that even the great Walter Fairbottom stayed his hand.

"I should have introduced myself to you earlier: I am Arabella Beaumont."

Mrs. Fairbottom gasped. Arabella was counting on this couple to be just snobbish enough, and common enough, to want to enhance their own prestige in the eyes of their acquaintances by being able to say, "We met Arabella Beaumont on our honeymoon!" The bride could add, "It was quite all right—Walter never left my side the entire time she was in the room!" And the groom, in an aside to his cronies, might embroider the truth a bit, by hinting that she had given him some wonderful advice for the bedroom when his wife was out of earshot.

In any event, the realization that they had come face-to-face with a living, breathing celebrity had the desired effect. Mr. Fairbottom not only refrained from closing the top portion of their door; he opened the bottom half, too, and so Arabella was at last admitted to the inner sanctum.

When Belinda returned from the matinee, replete and rosy from the ardent attentions of her escort, as well as from the effects of an afternoon of laughter and a paper cone full of toffees, Arabella felt an unaccustomed stab of envy. She herself had spent a miserable afternoon with the newlyweds, who had had nothing to tell her, yet would not let her leave.

"Lord preserve me from middle-class mooncalves!" she replied, when Belinda asked how the interview had gone.

"Were they no help at all, then?"

"Well, the wife mentioned that the corpse was barefoot, but that hardly signifies, I think. And the husband *would* not stop talking! I had to hear all about the linen drapers', where he is almost certain to be tapped for a management position before Christmas; the highlights of his honeymoon thus far and his erudition in surmising that something rum was afoot when he spied the shoes."

"The shoes?" Belinda asked. "I haven't heard those mentioned before."

"No, well, neither had I, until my enchanting encounter with the Fairbottoms. He said the shoe ribbons were tied together in a knot, and then wound round the corpse's arm."

"*Hmph,*" said Belinda. "That can hardly have anything to do with the murder, I think. Still, it *is* rather singular."

"Oh," said Arabella dismissively, "I suspect Zhenay went wading in the sea, and tied her shoes together to keep them from going astray. I also had to listen to Mr. Fairbottom's account of his brilliant deduction, on finding Constance and the body in close proximity to one another. Then he began dropping the names of various illustrious persons I have never heard of, with whom he has a nodding acquaintance in London. All the while, his wife kept up a little accompaniment of her own, saying things like, 'Ooh, yes, that's right! You certainly know your way around the block, my love!' and 'Such a heavenly holiday, and we've only just come here, you know!' But as she could not get a word in, they spoke at the same time. You can imagine the cacophony! It sounded as though she were interpreting for him. And all of it was the stupidest rubbish! I swear, if I *had* found that rock of Constance's, I'd have brained them both with it!"

"You poor dear!" said Belinda. "It sounds as if your entire day were a complete waste of time."

"Not quite. Because I called upon the local magistrate after getting clear of the bores' nest, and with the aid of a letter from Sergeant Dysart—which I was clever enough to obtain before coming away to Brighton—I have managed to arrange for Costanze's transfer up to London."

"Oh!" cried Belinda. "But I am certain she will have better treatment in the little Brighton lockup than she can hope for at Newgate or someplace!"

"It isn't a question of Costanze's comfort," said Arabella severely. "At the moment, I am more concerned about the inconvenience to my attorney, who cannot be forever coming down here to question her and so forth, and the additional strain upon my already straitened finances."

"You sound as though poor Costanze deserves to be in gaol!" cried Belinda.

"So she does! Not for Zhenay's murder, but for the willful idiocy which got her into this scrape in the first place . . . no, in the *second* place! When I saved her from blackmail the first time, Madame Zhenay was still alive, and everything was hunky dory—that's American slang for 'splendid.' An expression I learnt from Garth Kendrick Provenson. But was Costanze satisfied? Was she grateful? No! The first chance she got, she went and joined her giblets with that Harry footman's again!"

"Well, perhaps, as you say, she *wasn't* satisfied."

"Don't you be an ass, too, Bunny! I've had my fill of morons for one day!"

"I'm sorry. But Costanze really cannot help being dim witted, you know."

"Dim-witted? Not a bit of it! I have lately come to realize that the woman is horribly cunning. She manipulates people by refusing to use her brain, and as others are always willing to make excuses for her, she is free to do as she pleases. It fair makes me sick!"

"I think you are wrong, Bell."

"Well, naturally! You *would!*" Arabella retorted. "Because she has manipulated you, too!"

Chapter 17

Dim-witted or not, the next morning found "poor" Miss Worthington gorging on strawberries in her prison cell, courtesy of Pigeon Pollard. In his haste to see her, Costanze's benefactor had stridden down the passage ahead of Arabella and the gaoler, and by the time they caught him up, he seemed to be attempting to squeeze his big pudding face between the bars of his lady love's cage.

"Good morning, my dove!" he warbled. "I have the most wonderful news! Miss Beaumont has obtained a writ for your release! Now we can go home!"

"I am afraid it's not as simple as that, Mr. Pollard," said Arabella. "I have merely obtained permission to have Costanze transferred to a London lockup. She is still suspected of murder, you know. Get your things together, Costanze, and make haste; your police escort is arriving momentarily."

"It is 'Constance' again," said the prisoner, dribbling cream from the side of her mouth as she spoke. "I can never remember how to spell 'Costanze' because I always want to put an *n* between the *o* and the *s* and if I do that then it sounds as though I am trying to spell 'Constantinople' not that I would ever *want* to because the Turks are so fierce and

I pray I never meet one that's a sweet gown Bell but I do not wish to go to London yet. I am on holiday."

"Constance," said Arabella, "you are in gaol."

"Yes, but I am in gaol in Brighton."

"What difference can that make?"

"I know you for a beef wit Arabella but *do* make an effort *please!* People come to Brighton on holiday they don't stay in London if they want to get away because Brighton is everything nice: the sea, the sun . . ."

"But your cell has no window! You cannot see the sun!"

"Yes. 'The sea, the sun . . .' That is what I just *said.*" Constance looked sideways at Pigeon, as though to say, "There! Do you see what I mean? The woman is thick as custard!" "Really Bell," she continued, "if you cannot do anything but stand there stupidly repeating everything I say you may as well leave for you are of no use at all and I find your presence irritating!"

Arabella considered: There was really no need to bring Constance back to London. The Brighton lockup was undoubtedly cozier than its London counterpart would prove, and sensible persons did not, as a rule, endeavor to bring Miss Worthington closer to themselves. Distance was the thing, and the more of it there was, the happier the circumstances for all parties concerned. In arranging the transfer, Arabella had been thinking chiefly of the convenience to counsel, and of her own pocketbook. But mightn't it be better if the barrister couldn't speak to Constance? Especially since Arabella now knew for certain that Miss Worthington's testimony would be of no use, except, perhaps, as proof of insanity?

So, leaving the lovebirds to nuzzle through the bars, Arabella re-traced her steps to the entrance. But Pigeon followed her up.

"Miss Beaumont? Do you really think this case will go to trial?"

"I am almost certain that it will, Mr. Pollard."

"And you have retained counsel, have you not?"

"I have put Sir Corydon-Figge on retainer, yes."

"Excellent! I shall write to him, too." He dipped into his pocket and removed a very large packet of crisp, new hundred-pound notes, neatly bound with a circlet of white paper. "I know that you have been put to some expense, and no little inconvenience on my little Shortcake's behalf," said he. "This should cover it, but pray let me know if you should require more."

So saying, Pigeon handed her the packet, took his leave, and returned to Constance.

Arabella was still staring at the bills in her hand when she was hailed by a troop of courtesans, coming toward her down the passage. She returned their salutations with a grateful heart: The Cyprians had come to Brighton to offer her their support! Now Arabella should have all the assistance she required in the way of money *and* company! They could be her advisors, and she might dispatch them on little errands she would rather leave to others. This was exactly the sort of thing she'd had in mind when she started the CS—a tightly knit group of female allies, aiding one another through life's difficulties.

"To what," asked Arabella, modestly, "do I owe the pleasure of this delightful encounter?"

"We have come to see Costanze," May explained. "The poor dear must be simply wretched in this awful place!"

And Arabella now saw that they were carrying food hampers and packages of books. "On the contrary," she replied sourly. "I think you will find Miss Worthington in wonderful spirits."

Outside the lockup, Marine Parade was chockablock with holiday makers. Hordes of them were strolling along the street, shouting, eating, riding the ponies, pushing each other and laughing, shoving each other and cursing, punching each other and having to be separated, purchasing spun sugar wands and painted bladder balloons and having their fortunes told, or their silhouettes made. Many of them, of course, were engaged in watching the various performances: fire eaters, conjurers, jugglers, a trained monkey. One of the largest groups was massing round a makeshift puppet theater, where the antics of Punch and Judy were eliciting loud, communal guffaws.

Arabella recalled her recent conversation with Belinda, and wondered whether she should still find Punch funny after so many years. The moment she stepped off the pavement, our heroine found herself caught up in the eddying swirl of color and noise all about her. She believed herself far above this society of simple gawkers, and yet she was part of it, too; part of the very center of it, in fact, with bits of dancing bear, and winkles, and toy tin trumpets poking out round the edges.

Has the reader had occasion to observe the way in which mature minds revert to childhood pleasures when they want to relax? Take this puppet theater crowd, for example. Arabella noticed that there were easily more adults than youngsters, including that child-sized adult who was pushing her way through the children in order to obtain a front-row view of the . . . goodness! It was Lady Ribbonhat! What was she doing in Brighton, the Happy Kingdom, when her best friend had just died? But then Arabella remembered that Henry's ship was due to come in. It already had, probably, and perhaps Puddles had wished to loiter in town for a bit. Only, he was nowhere to be seen. Lady Ribbonhat was attending the performance alone, without so much as a footman to clear the way for her.

Up on the stage, a pirate was attempting to make Punch walk the plank, forcing him out at sword point, and laughing into his black beard. But each time, the wily Punch saved himself by clutching the plank with his little legs as he fell, and then climbing back onto its upper surface, his arms still tied behind him.

Arabella took a closer look at the dowager. She certainly didn't appear to be grief-stricken. In fact, she seemed to be thoroughly enjoying the show, if "enjoyed" was the proper term for what she was doing. Well, no; perhaps it wasn't.

Lady Ribbonhat stood very close to the stage, watching the action with the concentration of a cat waiting for the cuckoo to emerge from a clock. Her eyes were wide open and glazed, like one of Dr. Mesmer's patients. Her lips were moving, too, and Arabella edged in closer, to try to hear what she was saying.

"Get him!" muttered the dowager, who seemed be siding with the pirate.

Punch had re-boarded the ship, and was being forced to re-walk the plank. The crowd shouted with approval when his self-preservation maneuver was repeated.

"Kill him!" cried Lady Ribbonhat, her voice rising about the tumult.

When the puppet was planked for the third time, he remained suspended beneath the board and upside down, in order to lure the pirate out onto the beam to dislodge him. Anticipating some clever trick on the part of their hero, the audience began shouting suggestions. And Lady Ribbonhat's voice rose above the rest in a horrible shriek:

"Tie his feet together next time!"

Arabella reflected that her old adversary was growing progressively more eccentric with the passing years. Shouting at a puppet was, well, it was childish. Perhaps Lady Ribbonhat was become senile at last, and it was time for Puddles to have her shut up at home.

I shall miss her, thought Arabella. For such interesting nemeses were not easily come by. And without enemies, as we know, there can be no victory.

Watching Lady Ribbonhat today has made me wonder: Could pirates have kidnapped Madame Zhenay in Eastbourne, taken her aboard a boat and then sailed to Brighton? Not pirates, exactly, but somebody like pirates? Take that troll I met at the pub, for instance, Gun Jensen, what was it he said?

She flipped back through her notes to locate the earlier entry:

"We aim to find the bastard who ordered [Greely's murder]. We won't stop looking till he's found." Or words to that effect.

Could Mrs. Greely have sent a retributive army after Madame Zhenay? No doubt there were scores of people who wanted her dead, but Gun Jensen's oath struck me as both determined and sincere.

Zhenay would have been too powerful to be taken by a single assailant. One person might hit her over the head, and then tie her up whilst she was unconscious, but he would never be able to remove her to a boat unaided.

So let us say there are three murderers. They bundle her onto a boat, sail to Brighton, and then what? Tie her shoes together and push her overboard? That makes no sense. If Zhenay knew how to swim, she could easily have kicked off her shoes and make for shore. And if she didn't know how, why tie the shoes together?

Murderers who drown their victims at sea usually tie their arms, not their shoes, like the pirate puppet did with Punch. No. I am quite certain that Madame Zhenay took off her shoes and tied them herself, so as to keep the pair together.

By the end of their second day in Brighton, the Beaumont sisters had effectively changed position with respect to their opinions of the town. Belinda had just wanted to go home, but now she was finding it ever so gay, and Arabella, who had originally viewed their journey thither as an immediate necessity, was nearly beside herself in her longing to leave.

"There is no privacy," she complained. "I don't know what Uncle Selwyn was thinking when he bought this house . . . it is on the street! People passing by can look straight into the lower windows!"

"I think he must have *wanted* to feel a part of the summer festivities," said Belinda, "and I quite agree with him! Everyone needs to join in the fun and forget who they are from time to time."

"I've no choice, have I?" cried Arabella. "Everyone *else* has evidently forgotten who I am! Unless I meet with one of our friends, I am not recognized when I go out—not a single stranger has doffed his hat to me and reverentially murmured my name!"

"Oh, Bell! The post is crammed with invitations every day, and the salver is brimming with visiting cards! Everyone wants to see you!"

"I cannot accept invitations right now," said Arabella perversely. "I am working, as you know. But since Constance has made up her mind to stay on, there is no longer any reason for my presence here. We shall return home as soon as may be. I cannot wait to leave this horrible place!"

"I am sorry to hear it," said Belinda. "I think Brighton is a nice town!"

Arabella sniffed. "It may be for you; I have no great liking for the hurly-burly of the hoi polloi!"

"Oh, but even you must admit that the sea is beautiful, Bell! Look there—today it has the color of emeralds. Yesterday it was gentian blue."

And greatly to her sister's surprise, Arabella burst into tears.

"I cannot *bear* to look at the ocean!" she wept. "Every

time I do, I think of John Kendrick, living on the other side of it! We should not have come to this house, with its sea views from all the front windows, but I did not know it would affect me in this manner!"

Belinda patted her and made sympathetic noises, and she genuinely *was* sorry for her sister's pain, despite the fact that Arabella had brought it on herself. But Bunny, who was straightforward when it came to expressing her own passions, could not understand why it had taken Arabella so long to acknowledge her love for John Kendrick. How could anyone be confused by such a simple emotion?

Fortunately, Arabella had got started on one of her nostalgic tangents again, and did not, for the moment, require understanding. All she wanted was her sister's undivided attention.

"When he looked at me in his rajah disguise," she said, through her tears, "all his submissive slavishness was gone. It's true, he *was* bringing me a cup of punch, but that was out of sheer politeness. I think by that time he had already made up his mind to leave, which freed him of his obsession for me. For the first time I saw the actual *man* who'd been hiding behind all that tedious adoration. It fair took my breath away."

"Hmmm," said Belinda shrewdly. "Are you saying, then, that the key to your heart is indifference toward yourself?"

"I don't . . . no!"

"You don't know?"

"Yes."

"Well, if you are unhappy here, we had better leave at once."

"We can't."

"Why not?"

"Because," said Arabella, "I have had a letter from Uncle Selwyn today. He is coming to town tomorrow, and wants to spend time with us."

"Oh, that is splendid!" Bunny replied. "It is ages since we have seen him! You must vacate the master bedroom, Bell."

"He means to stay at his club," said Arabella. "The dear soul says he is loath to incommode us."

Two years earlier, Lord Selwyn had returned from the Indian colonial service in poor health, and no one, seeing his frail physiognomy, expected him to live very long. His wife had died abroad, so that he was alone in the world, and it was doubtful whether he would survive to see another Christmas. Then, greatly to his nieces' satisfaction, he had married an old flame, a woman for whom he had long carried a torch. (Was she the flame *in* his torch, Arabella had wondered, or had he been wanting to carry his torch *to* her flame, in order to light it?) At any rate, as the woman had herself been recently widowed, and was also in delicate health, the pair had hoped to be a comfort to one another in their waning days.

But to everyone's surprise, instead of fading away, both had flourished under an agreeable matrimonial regime, and had promptly purchased a number of houses, envisioning their remaining years (not weeks or months) as a pleasurable round of short trips and extended visits to those parts of the country which they liked best.

Brighton was one of those parts, and thanks to what their elder niece deemed the Selwyns' "poor taste and lack of propriety" (for it will be remembered that Arabella thought Brighton vulgar), she and Belinda had managed to find comfortable lodgings in a fashionable resort, at the height of the season, and absolutely free.

Lord Selwyn having said in his letter that he was longing for a picnic on the beach, his nieces gave orders accordingly, and the next day sunshades, rugs, and a luncheon hamper were set up at the water's edge. Mrs. Selwyn arrived unexpectedly (she'd been visiting a brother in Saltdean) to lend her delightful presence to the party and render her husband's happiness complete. Thus, the family whiled away a pleasant afternoon, idly chatting and watching the rollers wash in, whilst swatting at the sand flies and picking grit out of their sandwiches. Belinda was worried about the depressive effect of the sea upon Arabella's spirits, but there was nothing for it, since their host had his heart set on spending a day in the sand.

"I hear you're working on a murder case, my dear," he said, passing the olives. "It's been mentioned in nearly all the papers, and when Mrs. Selwyn (Mrs. Ironmonger-that-was, you know) first read me the account, I was practically bowled over!" He smiled at his wife, fondly patting her little hand.

"Bowled over? But why, Uncle?" asked Arabella. "You know I have a tendency to mix myself up in situations of this kind."

"Of course, yes; it was the *connexion* which came as a surprise, you see. Because I was personally acquainted with the victim."

"You knew Madame Zhenay?"

"Well, not actually *knew* her. I met the woman once, many years ago, when she nearly snagged your protector."

"What?"

"Of course, she wasn't calling herself Madame Zhenay in those days; went by the name of Jeanette or something. In fact, I would never have made the connection from seeing her name in the paper, only I happened to have bumped into her for the second time only a few months ago."

"I beg your pardon, Uncle?"

Despite the fact that she was seated upon a rug at the shore, Arabella was beginning to feel herself very much at sea.

"You see, Mrs. Selwyn swears by Zhenay's products (don't you, my dear?), so I went to that Palais whatever-it-calls-itself on my way to a meeting once, when I was in London. Because Mrs. Selwyn asked me to look in. Normally, I should never dream of invading any place that was so obviously meant for . . . for ladies and their beauty secrets, but I went there, for *her*, you see; yes. For my *wife*. It was her idea, wasn't it, Miranda? Anyway, whilst I was there, buying Cleopatra's Moisturizing Immortality Lotion for Mrs. Selwyn, I saw this Zhenay behind the counter."

Arabella briefly wondered whether her uncle had gone there for the type of voyeuristic amusements enjoyed by Charles and his friends, or whether he was simply trying to hide the fact that he bought Cleopatra's Moisturizing Immortality Lotion for himself.

"It took me a moment to place her," he was saying, "because it's been more than twenty-five years, and time had not been terribly kind to the poor woman. But when I realized where I knew her from, and told her who I was, she acknowledged the connexion at once, and told me she was finally going to be married to her duke, after all, with his mother's blessing!"

"How had you met, originally?" asked Belinda.

"I was friends with Glen*deen*'s uncle. Good old Dagan Brody. A self-made man . . . but Irish, you know, and not shy about expressin' his views on Irish home rule and Catholic emancipation. The Tories did for him in the end; ruined his business and blackened his name, and he shot himself whilst I was in India."

Selwyn looked down at his naked toes and shook his head regretfully. "He was a good man, old Brody was. I still miss him, but I am glad he did not live to see his sons convicted, in the Luddite uprisings."

"Oh, no," Arabella groaned. Her uncle nodded.

"After their father was ruined, the boys had found honest work in the weaving trade, but the power loom came along a few years later, when they all had young families to support. They were put out of business and their families starved. You know the rest: When the angry weavers destroyed the new looms, the angry government executed the weavers."

"Well, we can't have that!" said Arabella bitterly. "Machinery is revered, but *new* machinery is sacred! What's a few starving families to the glories of progress?"

This was why she so hated politics. The stories were never happy, and the innocent never triumphed—they seldom even *survived*. Sometimes she fancied she could see the future writ large upon the walls of the banks and the big companies and the government buildings. And what she read there froze her to the marrow.

"In any event," said her uncle, "long before all that happened, I was dining with Brody at his house when Glendeen arrived, with Jeanette. They didn't stay long, and after they'd gone, Brody told me in strictest confidence that his nephew had made up his mind to marry the girl. Lady Ribbonhat wasn't to know about it, he said. So I kept mum, of course. But it must have been difficult for Brody to keep such an important secret from his sister. They were very close, you know."

"I cannot believe it!" cried Arabella.

Lord Selwyn nodded. "It did seem strange that the duke would want to marry a commoner, but you'll have to take my word for it; Madame Zhenay was quite striking when she was younger, and she had this . . . I don't know . . . this powerful presence. You could feel it, the moment you met her."

"No," said Arabella. "I mean I cannot believe that Lady Ribbonhat was ever close to anybody."

"Oh. Well, she quite doted on old Brody. But wasn't that remarkable of me? To recognize Madame Zhenay again, having met her only once, and after she had so much changed in appearance?" Selwyn tapped his forehead. "The old noggin may have gained some wrinkles and lost its hair on the outside, but the inside is still as sharp as ever!"

"What happened?" Belinda asked.

"I got older."

"No, I meant what happened between Madame Zhenay and the duke? Why didn't they marry?"

"Lady Ribbonhat found out. And had the girl deported as an undesirable."

"*What?*" cried Arabella.

"She was sent to France, poor thing, when they were chopping off the heads of foreigners left and right."

"Uncle Selwyn, didn't Glen*deen* ever try to bring her back?"

"He never knew where she was. His mother told him the girl had run off with a tradesman. But the duchess admitted to Brody what she had actually done. That's how I came to know of it."

"Interesting," said Arabella that evening as the sisters were preparing for bed. "One would hardly think Zhenay was the type to forgive and forget. Yet she was thick as thieves with Lady Ribbonhat right up to the time of her death."

"Perhaps Lady Ribbonhat apologized," said Belinda. "She has supposedly turned over a new leaf, remember, and I should think having somebody deported to a war zone would seriously hinder one's chances of getting into heaven."

"It's highly unlikely," said Arabella, "given Lady Ribbonhat's temperament, and yet it's possible, too, I suppose, given her new fear of God. "

"What other explanation can there be?"

"Well," said Arabella, brushing out her hair, "I am certain Zhenay remembered Lady R., but perhaps Lady R. failed to recognize Zhenay."

"Oh, but she must have done," said Belinda. "Otherwise, why ever should she associate with a commoner?"

"You heard Uncle say that Zhenay was much altered since her youth."

"No. Lady Ribbonhat's kindness to Zhenay was an act of penance," said Belinda firmly, smearing her face with Palais de Beautay's Soothing, Softening Syrup. "I am as certain of that as I am of never again finding a night serum that performs as this one does." She sighed and gazed into the depths of the jar. "This will only last me another week or two."

Arabella half turned. "Is that the jar I sent you during my apprenticeship?"

"The same. It is wonderful stuff. And there won't ever be any more of it."

"What would you say if I told you that you could have as many Palais de Beautay products as you liked for the rest of your life?"

"What's the use of your saying that?" asked Belinda crossly, "when you know perfectly well that La Palais de Beautay is no more?"

"The *shop* is no more, I'll grant you. But on the night I retrieved Constance's letters from Madame Zhenay, I also pocketed a ledger, which I took to be a file index, listing the victims. When I actually came to look at it, however, I found it contained the receipts for La Palais de Beautay's beauty formulas!"

"Huzzah!" shouted Belinda. "That's the best news I've had since . . . since I cannot remember when! To know we shall never run out of wonderful creams and lotions and serums and soaps!"

"Better than that," said her practical sister, "now, no matter what the future holds in store for us, and regardless of what happens to us financially, we may someday have to lower ourselves by working in trade, but we shall *never* starve!"

Three days later, the Beaumont sisters were back in London. And Lady Ribbonhat, who had preceded them by a day, found that, with the exception of Madame Zhenay's absence from her life, everything was much the same as before. Almost exactly the same, in fact: She encountered Mrs. Drain once again, on the same stretch of Piccadilly Street where they had met before, on the same day of the week. The missionary's wife was even wearing the same dress, and Lady

Ribbonhat had a sudden presentiment that she would be running into Arabella again, as well. So, rather than stand there talking of nothing and worrying about everything, she was obliged to invite her tiresome acquaintance to tea at Charburn House, in order to be able to make her excuses and hurry away.

But Mrs. Drain's visit, which took place later that afternoon, proved unexpectedly stimulating: The Drains were to go abroad again in the near future, and Mrs. Drain was not happy about it!

"My husband has been posted to Puka-Puka," she said, and the hostess was gratified to note the visible droop in her visitor's countenance.

"No!" exclaimed the duchess.

"Yes! He'll be relieving Reverend Kendrick, who has come into the title."

Lady Ribbonhat had not known of this, but nor had anyone. The fact had been communicated to Mr. Drain direct from the Bishop of Bramblehurst, in the very strictest of confidence. Drain had told his wife, though, and that good lady, with the generosity typical of her faith, had decided it was too good a piece of news to hoard all to herself. Hers was a sacrifice without purpose, however; Lady Ribbonhat had no interest in Mr. Kendrick's doings. Having ascertained that the rector would not be returning to Effing, where he might have been of some use to her, she lost all interest in him.

"It might interest you to know, Mrs. Drain," said the dowager, "that I have had a change of heart since our last meeting, and have undertaken a program of local good works."

"Yes," said Mrs. Drain dryly. "So I have heard." And something about the way that she peered into her teacup whilst stirring the contents told Lady Ribbonhat that her visitor was attempting to close the subject.

But this was not acceptable! In the first place, the duchess doubted that Mrs. Drain had heard about her acts of selfless-ness *in detail*. And in the second place, she wished to brag of her good deeds, and be complimented and admired for them.

"Yes," pursued the duchess. "I really think that the Lord Almighty is best pleased with me now, and is reserving my preferred place in paradise. I have distributed reproving tracts to the poor, and I have . . ."

But Mrs. Drain was not inclined to play this game. She se-cretly admired the opulence with which she was now sur-rounded, and her heart was reproaching her for the poor matrimonial bargain she had struck. Why, it demanded, had she doomed herself to a life of hardship posts, when with any luck she might have married a peer, like her hostess had?

"Do you suppose," snapped Mrs. Drain, "that taking bas-kets of refuse to random servants will gain you forgiveness? Can you actually anticipate admission to paradise on so slim a claim?" (Evidently, then, she really *had* heard of her host-ess's saintly exploits.) "He isn't fooled, you know! You haven't fooled anyone! If you've any real hopes of achieving heaven, you'll have to do much better than that!"

Mrs. Drain was in a position to know this, because she herself really *was* one of God's favorites, having earned that position through the suffering and privation commensurate with being the wife of *Mr.* Drain.

Lady Ribbonhat's brow puckered beneath its powder. "What would you suggest I do?"

"Regular church attendance and heartfelt prayers are what we typically recommend for newly converted heathen," said Mrs. Drain, "but I confess I haven't much experience with *English* prodigals. You really should ask your pastor. He is certain to know about the expectations for lifelong urban Christians."

"No!" cried Lady Ribbonhat. "Not that! I *hate* Reverend Clydesdale!"

Mrs. Drain pulled herself up straight. " 'Hate' is not in the

Christian lexicon," she said severely. "Especially directed against a rector! I am afraid, Lady Ribbonhat, that you may not be a good candidate for the Elysian Fields, after all—you still have so very far to go!"

"Oh, all right, then!" grumbled the dowager. "I'll go and talk to the old windbag, if I must! You're certain that it's the only way?"

"If there is another," said Mrs. Drain, "God has not seen fit to shew it to us!"

Chapter 18

Arabella, in her writing turban (which was striped like Madame de Stael's, but with narrower stripes) was once again seated at her desk, surrounded by the crumpled balls of her rejected drafts. She had not been working on her novel this time, but on a last, heartfelt attempt to induce Reverend Kendrick to return to England. It wouldn't come right, though. Probably because she wasn't clear about what it was she truly wanted to say.

> *You are the bravest and dearest man I have ever*
> *known, and I realize that I do not deserve you.*
> *But if you will only come back, I shall do every-*
> *thing in my power to endeavor to.*

No good! She'd ended with a preposition! Besides, just *how* was she going to endeavor to deserve him? Give up being a courtesan? No, no, no, no! And yet, she earnestly desired Kendrick's return: Arabella had never wanted anything so much in her life. Grown accustomed to the instantaneous gratification of her slightest whim, she was experiencing this challenge to her will as something new and irritating, like a rash.

Finally, she gave up on trying to write her letter, and turned instead to read one that had just come in. It was from Puddles:

> Dearest One,
>
> I am recently returned from Brighton, and hear that you are, too. How I wanted to see you whilst we both were there! But the PR asked me to call upon him at the palace, and once I was inside, he would not let me out again, knowing I should have come straight to you. And so I remained there, trapped in overheated apartments, dining on over-fussy food, obliged to inspect the latest architectural plans (he's going to re-do the palace as some kind of Taj Mahal-on-Sea) and admire his new Egyptian-red-gold-watch-with-inlaid-enamel-face-and-mother-of-pearl-hands-on-a-sterling-silver-chain-studded-with-diamonds-and-pearls-and-hung-with-ruby-and-sapphire-fobs-designed-to-look-like-giraffes-and-monkeys-with-hats-on, and forced to play at cards until past midnight each night. He wouldn't even let me write to you! I cannot imagine what my darling must have done to make him hate her so. But then, I do not think I <u>want</u> to know this. Please write and tell me when I may call upon you, for since my release, I have bought you many fine presents.
>
> Your very own
> Sea Tiger

"Mr. Provenson's here, miss," said Doyle, putting her head round the door. "And tea's been set up in the aviatory, as ye requested."

"Excellent," said Arabella. "Where's my sister?"

"She's in the aviatory, too, miss."

Arabella went downstairs to receive Mr. Provenson. "Hello, Kendrick," she said, extending both her hands to him. (Having once called him by his middle name in error, she had decided to do so henceforth, for she especially liked the name.) "I was sorry to hear about your godmother!"

"You were?"

"Yes. You see, a sort-of friend of mine has been accused of her murder, and if she is convicted, I shall be bankrupted."

"And that's the only reason you're sorry?" he asked, as they headed down the passage. "Isn't that a little cold-hearted?"

"Perhaps, a little," she conceded.

"Hmm. Well, if I am supposed to be a gentleman, I'll have to say something even colder, won't I? So as to cover up for you? All right, then: I was *not* sorry to hear about my god-mother, whose death was one of those occasions where the phrase, 'It's God's will' is on everyone's lips. By all accounts, she was a very unpleasant person. And now I am going to inherit her money, which makes me very happy."

"It's really too bad, though," said Arabella, handing him an umbrella. "She was on the point of marrying a duke, you know. You'd have been a good deal richer."

"Poorer, you mean," said Garth. "She was about to change her will, and make everything over to *him.*"

The droppings of exotic birds spattered their bumber-shoots as they made their way toward the little rotunda, snuggled like an egg in its nest of tropical foliage.

"She was?" asked Arabella. "And you knew about it?"

"I . . . well, you see . . . she'd told my mother . . ."

But by this time, they had arrived at the rotunda, where

Belinda awaited them at the little table, along with a perfectly splendid tea.

"Bunny, this is Garth Kendrick Provenson. My sister, Belinda."

He bowed over the dimpled hand, and Arabella at once perceived that her sister disliked him.

"Kendrick has just been telling me what a wealthy man he's become, now that his godmother is dead," said Arabella, picking up the heavy silver teapot. "Do you know, I don't believe he feels a bit sorry about it?"

"I really don't," he admitted, smiling. "I hear she was ruining the lives of a lot of people. It's better she's gone."

"And *you* call *me* coldhearted!" cried Arabella.

"I'm an American," said Garth. "We didn't win our independence from you through being impractically sentimental!"

"So," said Arabella, after he had gone. "What did you think of him?"

Belinda picked up a bright little pail of painted tin and began collecting kumquats with it. She could do this without leaving her chair, as the shrub grew hard by the rotunda, and had inexplicably begun producing fruits out of season.

"Do you want the truth?" she asked.

"I could tell you didn't like him. There is much about the boy that's objectionable, I suppose, but he's American, which is not his fault. He is also young, and that's not his fault, either. The nice thing about very young men is that they're such *ardent* lovers, a quality that makes up for a multitude of faults."

"Then I am happy for you," said Belinda.

"Well, I hope you can find a way to dislike him less, dear, because the connexion is likely to last a while. Particularly now that he is in a position to afford my company."

Plink. Plink. Plink.

"What I feel for your friend goes beyond dislike," said Belinda quietly. "I think he murdered Madame Zhenay."

"Oh, Bunny, how could he? Kendrick was with me when it happened!"

"I wish you would not keep calling him that. You sully the name of a good man every time you do. Anyway, he probably hired someone, the same way Madame Zhenay hired someone to kill *you*."

"He saved my life, you know."

Plink. Plink. Plink-Plink. Plink.

"The newspapers credited the roses on your gown."

"Well, yes; but Kendri— I mean, Garth, helped, too. Hmm . . ." she said. "He certainly had a plausible motive, though, didn't he?"

"For murdering his godmother? Yes. He did."

"But so did any number of other people; Zhenay was blackmailing half of London! Anyway, Ken—Garth was here with me when the corpse was recovered, and he says he didn't find out about the will till he got home."

"Perhaps he decided to have her killed before that," said Belinda, "so as to get his hands on the money without waiting for Zhenay to die of natural causes. The timing might have been a coincidence."

She chose a kumquat from the pail and began to chew it.

"Well . . . I don't think so. Anyway, there is no *need* for us to find the killer. All we have to do is establish Constance's innocence, and I don't suppose we really even have to do that."

"What do you mean? Of course you'll have to do that!"

"No, dear; in this country the accused are innocent until *proven* guilty. And the burden of proof rests with the prosecution."

"I think you're trying to avoid the issue," said Belinda, "because you want to go on sleeping with the Yank."

"That's not it at all! I simply disagree with you. You don't know Garth like I do; I don't believe him capable of such an act."

"It wouldn't be the first time," said Belinda.

"I have heard from Glen*deen* today," said Arabella, abruptly changing the subject. "He says he has presents."

"Presents?" The dark cloud was lifted from Belinda's mind, and the sun shone in, again. Actually, she was only too glad to have something else to talk about, because Arabella's apparent attraction to danger disturbed her, and she knew instinctively that no amount of discussion about it would make the slightest difference. The prospect of presents would provide a welcome distraction, even if the gifts were not intended for herself, personally. Besides, her sister was always generous about sharing the duke's largesse.

"I shall invite Glen*deen* to call on us when I return from my legal consultation," said Arabella. "So whilst I am gone, I would advise you to look through your jewels and shawls, and see what sorts of additions you might be requiring."

That was interesting, thought Arabella, as the carriage bore her townward: Bunny usually liked everybody, but she had not cared for Garth. Somehow Arabella felt that John Kendrick would not like him, either, and she felt a sudden stab of longing for her absent friend.

Longing is a tedious, painful emotion. It is quite common though, I believe. At least, "common" would certainly be one word for what Reverend Clydesdale was doing, in order to relieve his own longing for Arabella. Because he was seated in his library, with a large, open book upon his lap, and open trousers below that! The book, at least, was innocent enough— Reverend Kendrick's album, no less, and Mr. Clydesdale had turned to a study of Arabella's head, which Kendrick had once sketched from memory. But the rector was engrossed (and I think you'll agree that this, too, is the perfect expression) in privately expressing his admiration for this piece, when the housekeeper entered to announce Lady Ribbonhat.

Fortunately, the album was of sufficient size to conceal the activity taking place beneath it, and the reverend further reduced the chance of discovery by roaring at his servant.

"Don't ever *dare* intrude upon me again without knocking! Is that clear? The next time you disturb me in this fashion, you'll be sacked without a reference!"

Mrs. Hasquith never turned a hair. "Your visitor can 'ear you," she said. "What would you like me to do, send 'er packin', or open this door wider, so's she don't miss a thing?"

And with that, the servant quitted the room, leaving Reverend Clydesdale with his pants down, so to speak. He hastily buttoned them up again, though, slicked back his hair with one hand, and went forth to greet his bread and butter.

"You do me honor, Lady Ribbonhat!" simpered the rector, displaying all of his tombstone teeth. "To what am I indebted for this flattering visit?"

"I would have you know, sir," said the duchess grimly, "that I hold you in the lowest possible regard. You are everything I detest in a churchman: a pompous prattler, an arrogant fool, and probably a secret practitioner of vice and corruption. But for extreme necessity, I should not be here."

The reverend tilted his head deferentially to one side, and smiled as though she had paid him a compliment. Outright rudeness was the prerogative of the wealthy. After all, they could afford it.

"I have not led a blameless life," said the duchess, once she was comfortably situated with a cup of tea. "In fact, some of the things I have done might be construed in certain circles as selfish, or cruel . . ."

"One moment, Lady Ribbonhat. If you came here for the purpose of confessing your sins, I must caution you that I am not a Catholic priest, nor is this a Catholic confessional. You would know that, if you attended our church more often."

"Do you take me for a fool?" she cried. "This is exactly

the kind of thing I meant when I told Mrs. Drain why I didn't want to come here! I would never trust my secrets to you, under any circumstances!"

"Then why *have* you come?"

"Because I was led to believe that you could provide me with instructions on how to get into heaven. If I've been misinformed, I would be obliged to you for telling me so at once, rather than prolonging this tedious interview!"

A light went on behind the rector's eyes. "A *course of instruction,* did you say?"

"No, that is *not* what I said! Course of instruction, indeed! Do you think I'm going to drive out here every day? Just tell me what to do, and I'll do it."

Over the ensuing quarter of an hour, the duchess described her predicament without naming her sins directly, but including Mrs. Drain's observations concerning her conduct.

"So you see," she concluded uncomfortably, "I have . . . made some slight errors here and there, which, though not important in themselves, might add up to . . . well, Mrs. Drain is convinced that my prospects for heavenly admission are slight to nil."

The reverend smiled with those teeth again, rested his elbows on the arms of his chair, and placed the tips of his fingers together. "I shouldn't worry, Lady Ribbonhat," he said. "*All* the well-born get admitted to heaven, you know."

"No, they don't," she replied. "What about the rich? And the needle in the camel's eye? Besides," she added somewhat uneasily, "not all titled persons are born to their titles. Some obtain them through marriage."

"Insofar as the rich are concerned, the needle's eye applies only to those who fail to support their church. And as for titles, God sees marriage as the ultimate union, in which man and woman become one. Therefore, the personal attainments of the husband, whether by birth or merit, become the provenance of the wife, also."

"Truly?"

"Lady Ribbonhat . . . my *dear* Lady Ribbonhat—may I call you so?—I am a man of God, ordained by the church. I would not lie to you. Indeed, I *could* not, or I should be sent straight to . . . a place that is better not mentioned in polite company. Yes, I speak truly when I tell you that you are guaranteed a place in heaven, provided that you donate generously to your—and by 'your' I mean *this*—church."

Arabella had once consulted the great barrister Sir Clifton Corydon-Figge upon a legal point concerning her life expectancy, but she had never engaged him to argue a case for her. Therefore, she was uncertain as to whether he would be amenable to discussing strategies with a female client, or whether he would act pompous and patronizing, refusing to entertain her theories, since he, the legal expert, obviously knew better. The only way to find out was to try him.

"I'm anticipating a swift acquittal," she said. "After all, they have not got the murder weapon, there were no witnesses to the act, and there is no proven explanation as to how the victim even got to Brighton."

"You're forgetting the motive," said Corydon-Figge. "Miss Worthington had a very good *reason* for killing Madame Zhenay; the woman was blackmailing her."

Arabella was gratified to note the absence of condescension in his voice or manner. It would have been so tedious if she had had to battle her barrister as well as the prosecution.

"And there is another problem," said Corydon-Figge. He stood with his back to the large window of his sumptuous offices in the Inner Temple, and fixed Arabella with a bright, shrewd eye. "Your friend's protector insists that the case be heard in the House of Lords, before the greatest collection of unpredictable ninnies this world has ever known. As Miss Worthington is the late Earl of Nutchester's daughter, she does have that right, unfortunately."

"Oh, dear!" said Arabella. "I had quite forgotten that! What are our chances of prevailing?"

"Slim, I fear. Peers tend to be somewhat inconsistent in their views, but in this case I think they will probably all find her guilty if they can. Because by joining the demi-monde, Miss Worthington has let her side down. The prosecution will therefore have no difficulty in persuading a passel of privileged prats that a fallen woman from their own ranks has fallen still further. They are hypocrites to a man. Of course," he added generously, "the *women* of the peerage are an altogether different matter." (Arabella was the daughter of a baronet.)

"As are barristers," she added astutely. (Corydon-Figge had been knighted by the king, in gratitude for having successfully defended the reprehensible royal family against a multitude of lawsuits.)

"Of course," said Sir Clifton, "*you,* as the client, could always reject Mr. Pollard's request for the House of Lords hearing."

Arabella shook her head. "I have paid you with monies provided *by* Mr. Pollard," she replied, "and on that account, I am afraid we must honor his wishes. How do you propose to proceed?"

"Well," replied her counselor, "I very much fear that unless we can discover the actual murderer, Miss Worthington's prospects are bleak, indeed. It would help us greatly if we had her testimony. Does she still refuse to speak?"

"I am afraid it would do no good at all to put her on the stand."

The barrister sighed. "As you have engaged me, Miss Beaumont, I shall follow your instructions, but I really should be vouchsafed at least one interview with the accused, if only to determine that her testimony not come out in court."

"I cannot allow it, sir. If you heard Miss Worthington speak, if you *ever* heard her speak, it would prejudice you against her in such a way that you might be unable to go forth with your defense."

"Very well. And what, may I ask, is your own theory of the case?"

"Suicide," said Arabella, who had been thinking about this on the way over. "Madame Zhenay, fearing that she was about to be arrested again, for arranging the murder of one Tom Greely, decided to take her own life, and jumped off of Beachy Head. (Which is a favorite spot for suicides, if I may just point that out.) Her body either struck against the cliff on the way down, or was hurled against the rocks at the bottom, where it received the injuries sustained, including a smashed skull. The cadaver was then washed down the coast to Brighton, and lodged under the pier, where the accused was attempting to build herself a stairway up one of the posts to obtain the eggs from a gull's nest."

The barrister smiled. "Gulls' eggs? I *love* those!"

"So does Constance, Sir Clifton."

"I wish I could see it your way, madam, but I am afraid the prosecution has two very good arguments against suicide."

"And what are they?"

"That the victim was going to be married to a duke—"

"I thought of that," Arabella interrupted. "But, as the woman was also being investigated for murder, she knew she would have been hanged in any case. Perhaps she preferred a free fall on her own terms."

"And her shoes," said Corydon-Figge.

"Yes? What about them?"

"They were tied together by the ribbons that, when the shoes are worn, are normally wound round the . . . er, lower leg, as it were. The point being that the lady took care to tie her shoes together, presumably so that she could put them on again before leaving the beach, where I believe she was. Why should she remove her shoes before leaping to her death? And even if her fall were accidental, why take them off at all?

I don't believe she ever went up there, Miss Beaumont, and I'm afraid we'll have to rule out suicide, for the prosecution certainly has."

Arabella bit her thumbnail. "It might, as you say, have been an accidental fall. The body would still have been carried down the coast by the current, and might still have washed up beneath the Brighton pier."

"Yes, but the fact is, we have no proof that Madame Zhenay ever *went* to Eastbourne *or* Beachy Head. When Lady Ribbonhat woke up that morning, she says she found a note, purportedly from the deceased, indicating her arrival there during the night. But the note was subsequently destroyed, so we cannot verify that it was in the victim's handwriting. No one has been able to find the coachman who drove Zhenay from London to Eastbourne. Nor any driver who might have taken her from there to Brighton."

"No," agreed Sir Clifton. "Not as yet."

"Madame Zhenay had many enemies. Nearly everyone who knew the woman wanted her dead, and somebody finally found the opportunity, it seems. But if we agree with the prosecution that it was *definitely* murder, then everyone will be looking, consciously or not, for the murder*er,* and Constance is the most convenient suspect, since she is already in custody.

"We shall stand a much better chance for acquittal if we contend that the death was an accident. After all, if Zhenay were carrying her shoes, and someone clubbed her to death, she would have dropped the shoes, or they would have dropped from her when she lifted her arms to defend herself. But, if she waded into the surf, with her shoes around her arm, she might have been caught up by a wave and dashed against the rocks, which would not necessarily have unwound the shoe ribbons from her wrist."

"That *sounds* logical," said Corydon-Figge, "but it isn't, really."

"No. It isn't, really, but the only people you need to convince are those nincompoops in the House of Lords. And coming from you, with your unassailable oratorical style, the case for accidental death will sound perfectly rational. You can work out the details—say whatever you think best—but let us start from that premise, that there *was* no murder, only an accident. And that Miss Worthington just happened to be in the wrong place at the wrongest of times, innocently searching for gulls' eggs."

Sir Corydon-Figge regarded her for a moment with a penetrating stare. Then he began to smile. Arabella felt pleased. She detected, in the lifting of his mood, a ribbon of repressed ebullience, and another of cautious optimism. What could be more natural than to braid the two together, sling them at the facts, and launch the resultant theory into the chasm of the court?

Chapter 19

Madam:

I write to remind you that I am a man of the cloth, and though my church is Anglican, we, too, are familiar with the ways of the succubus! You come to me in dreams, and haunt my waking hours. Your voice echoes in my head whenever I am alone. I know you to be in league with the devil, but <u>you will not prevail!</u>

"Bla bla bla. Bla bla bla. Oh, blablablablablablabla!"

I shall offer you one chance, and one chance only, for if you are willing to repent, even now, I shall be only too happy as a Christian to offer you a course of instruction in <u>The Ways of Godliness</u>, and <u>True Salvation</u>. Please write to advise me of the dates and times you will be available. We shall need to meet thrice weekly for the remainder of this year. If you refuse this chance, I shall enjoin

> *my flock (which includes many of the tradesmen*
> *you are accustomed to patronize) to shun you ab-*
> *solutely, and refuse your custom in future.*

Arabella sighed. "And I had supposed that only papists believed in succubae," she murmured. "What do you think, Bunny? I have had a letter from Reverend Clydesdale. He is clearly obsessed with me, and yet I only met him once."

Belinda made a disgusted noise. "I have never met the man, and from what I have heard of him I hope I never shall."

"He is odious," Arabella agreed, "but sufficiently vocal to constitute a nuisance—he threatens to warn off all the proprietors in whose shops I currently enjoy credit, unless I subject myself to a course of 'religious instruction' at his hands. I am all too familiar with the type. Reverend Clydesdale's methods are bound to include humiliation, flogging, and nudity."

"The fiend!" cried Belinda. "What will you do?"

"Sleep with him, I suppose."

"Oh, no, Bell! You can't!"

"Yes, I can. It will dissipate the tension. And after he's explored his base lusts and scourged himself, or whatever it is that men of his kidney do after they have sinned, he'll reflect, and pray, and ultimately forswear me forever more."

"Well, perhaps. But I am sorry you have to sleep with him."

"So am I. However, I shall put him off, for the present, until I have dealt with the matter in hand."

"Yes, put him off, by all means! Perhaps he will be exposed and defrocked in the meantime, and you won't need to worry about him at all."

"Defrocked and exposed? He would probably like that! You see? He is amusing me already! I am fairly certain, Bunny, that when I do have time to 'rein in' this Clydesdale, the adventure will prove an inexhaustible source for humorous stories."

Arabella looked again at his letter, and read the closing aloud:

You shall not hide your wickedness from me, for I see it plain as day, beneath the smothering layers of your blarney . . .

"What?" cried Bunny. "Is the man insane?"

Her sister did not answer her at once, and Belinda, looking round, saw that she was sitting up straight, with her eyes opened very wide.

"What is it?" she asked.

"Sorry," said Arabella. "Will you excuse me for a moment?"

The desk in her boudoir contained a secret space at the back of the central drawer, and in this little chamber, our heroine was accustomed to storing small items that she was desirous of keeping to herself. From this private space, Arabella drew forth the letter, forgotten until now, which she had taken from Lady Ribbonhat's file in Madame Zhenay's strongbox. It was addressed to someone of whom she had never heard, in Blarney, Ireland, and Arabella recognized both the writing and the seal as Lady Ribbonhat's. She held the letter up to the light, turning it now this way, now that, in an attempt to read the contents through the envelope.

The following morning was hazy, and smelt of smoldering garbage, which, as a matter of fact, was why it was hazy. Everyone in Brompton Park seemed to have had the idea to burn trash at the same time, and there was no breeze today. Consequently, Arabella had ordered that the windows be shut. Then the curtains had to be drawn, to keep the temperature down.

"This is what people have to do in the tropics," she explained to Belinda. "Though I don't suppose they have to contend with poisonous air unless there's an active volcano in the vicinity."

Her sister, who was reading about Madame Zhenay's funeral in the paper, sat very still and tried not to breathe. Not because of the rank air, though: Puka-Puka was a tropical island, and if Arabella should make that connection, Bunny would have to listen to another litany about the man who got away.

But the association evidently failed to occur to her lovelorn sibling, who was busy constructing a riddle.

"Who do you think this is, Bunny? 'Relieved of a great weight, he becomes more himself.'"

"I don't know," said Belinda, who was trying to read the paper. "I can't think."

"Peniston! If one removes the 'ton,' one is left with 'penis'! Only . . . that doesn't really describe Mr. Pollard, does it? He's certainly very nice to Constance. In fact, if he weren't so much *like* Constance, I might actually have considered him a friend."

"That's odd," said Belinda.

"Why?"

"No, I mean the fact that Lady Ribbonhat's name does not appear on the list of attendees, nor did she send a floral tribute in Madame Zhenay's memory. I thought you said they were such great chums."

"Hmm!" said Arabella. "Like Klunk and Stupid-Looking."

"What?"

"Do you recall those turtles Neddy brought to the house two years ago?"

"What about them?"

"Eddie and I were talking about it recently. Listen, Bunny, I need to go out for a bit. Will you open the windows once the air clears outside?"

"Yes. Where are you going?"

"To Charburn House. I am going to have a chat with Lady Ribbonhat."

"What? Are you mad?"

"Very possibly. I don't know whether she actually murdered Madame Zhenay, and I don't see how she could have, but I suspect that the duchess knows more than she has told the authorities."

"She won't talk to you."

"I think she might," said Arabella, producing the letter. "Provided I offer sufficient inducement."

"What is that?"

"The letter by which Madame Zhenay was blackmailing her."

"Blackmail!" Belinda exclaimed, dropping the paper. "What's it say?"

"How would I know? It's sealed, as you see. Sir Clifton will most likely prevail in the House of Loonies, but we cannot leave it to fate, Bunny. We simply *must* make certain of Constance's acquittal."

Henry Honeywood Seaholme, Duke of Glen*deen* and disappointed bridegroom, had been restless ever since his return from Brighton. Actually, "disappointed" might be overstating it a bit, as Glen*deen* had not even known of his impending nuptials until after his bride-to-be had expired. Nor would he ever know who Madame Zhenay had really been. All he *did* know, in fact, was that he wished to escape the depressing influence of his mother and pay a call upon Arabella, whom he'd been prevented from seeing at Brighton, and who was, at that moment, alighting from her carriage in front of his house. But that was merely another detail of which the duke was ignorant.

Arabella ascended Charburn's front steps with great firmness of purpose, and stood impatiently by whilst her footman applied the door knocker.

"Again, Thomas! Harder!"

"I'm knockin' 's loud as I can, miss."

When the creaking old butler or whatever he was finally opened the door, Arabella could not decide whether her wait had been occasioned by the man's infirmities, or by the sheer arrogance and condescension for which this household was famous.

"What."

Apparently, it had been too much trouble to add the "do you want?," and the octogenarian servant stood blocking the door, reveling in his power and regarding Arabella with hostile insolence.

She pushed him aside and entered the house. "I must speak with your mistress!" she said, as the duke came down the stairs.

"Why, Sugar Pig!" he cried, "I was just coming to see you!"

"Hello, Puddles. Is your mother at home?"

"My moth . . . oh, I say!" he exclaimed, as it began to dawn upon him where she was, and where he was, and his mother and everything. "What in blazes are you doing here? And what do you want with Mama? Have you lost your mind?"

"No. And I should hope that you realize I should not be here, requesting to see her, except on a matter of the utmost urgency."

"Hmmm. That's true. Well, I shouldn't think she will *want* to see you, but I'll go and ask her."

"No, Henry," said Arabella, placing a hand on his arm. "I should be much obliged if you would shew me into some small parlor or other and bring her to me there, without informing her ladyship of my identity."

"Why? You aren't planning to shoot her, are you?"

"No. But I have brought something with me in which I suspect she will be deeply interested, and if you tell her who I am, she will miss the chance of—"

"Henry? Who is it? Piston said there was someone to see me."

Lady Ribbonhat stood and gaped at her visitor. "You!" she managed, after a moment. "How dare you come here? Take yourself off, baggage! I have dispensed with charitable deeds, and have no intentions of renewing my previous addresses to you *or* your saucy servants!"

Arabella withdrew from her reticule the sealed letter taken from Madame Zhenay's strongbox on that long-ago night of stormy passions.

"I wish to talk to you about this," she said, waving the letter under the dowager's nose, so that the woman might recognize both the addressee and her own script on the envelope. The visible effect on Lady Ribbonhat was everything Arabella might have wished.

"What . . . what is that?"

"I think you know. This letter originates from you, does it not? I found it in Madame Zhenay's blackmail files. Where can we go and be assured of absolute privacy?"

"In here," Lady Ribbonhat replied quickly, opening the door to a kind of study. "Henry, tell Piston that we are not to be disturbed."

All of Charburn's rooms were ostentatious, but this one topped the lot, as it was intended to intimidate visitors whilst they waited . . . and waited . . . and waited for an audience with the dowager duchess. The marble! The ormolu! The overbearing heaviness of the furnishings! The tasteless gaudiness of the paintings! Arabella was not so much overawed as overcome, and she pressed a handkerchief scented with eau de cologne to her nostrils to keep herself from fainting—stupidity and bad taste often took her this way.

"How long have you had my letter?" Lady Ribbonhat demanded.

"We haven't the time for non-essentials. The point is, I am perfectly willing to return it to you, in exchange—"

"Whatever you want," said Lady Ribbonhat quickly, turning her head away.

"'Pon my soul!" said Arabella. "As important as all that?"

The dowager's head did not move, but the eyes slid back to regard her visitor.

"You must not be familiar with the contents, if you have to ask that question!"

"No. As you see, the seal is unbroken. And I am prepared to return it to you in that state, Lady Ribbonhat, provided you give truthful answers to the questions I shall put to you."

"Very well," said the dowager duchess, yanking the bell pull. "What will you have? Tea? Sherry?"

"Tea, I think."

But Henry had told the butler that his mother was not to be disturbed on any account. So the bell was ignored.

"I want you to tell me," said Arabella, "exactly what took place between you and Madame Zhenay on the day she died."

"I did not see her that day. I'd gone to sleep . . ."

"Spare me your circumlocutions, Lady Ribbonhat. The two of you were seen together on Beachy Head early that morning."

The dowager turned the color of clay. "Impossible! And . . . and untrue!"

"There was a certain woman, a widow Greely, who had been tailing Madame Zhenay for some time, intending to kill her when she got the chance. She saw what she saw, but I would rather hear it from your own lips."

"*She* was going to kill Zhenay? You mean, all I had to do was wait, and my problem would have been solved?"

"I have no wish to expose you to the authorities," said Arabella. "You are my own, cherished nemesis, and no one shall take you from me, if I can help it. On the other hand, Constance Worthington is being held for Zhenay's murder. If she pays the penalty, I shall be destitute. (Financially, that is. The loss of Constance herself is of little consequence, either to myself, or to the world.) It would not be fair, though. It would be monstrous unfair. And only you can put things right."

"How, pray?"

"I won't know that until you tell me the truth. Then we may between us concoct a believable lie. Now, I know that Zhenay was your dearest friend, but the facts simply do not add up. Had you quarreled?"

Lady Ribbonhat began to laugh. It started low and slow in her chest, becoming faster and higher in pitch as it moved up her trachea. By the time it reached her head it was a truly horrible sound, like the squealing of an hysterical puppet. Recalling the Punch and Judy show, Arabella gritted her teeth and put her hands over her ears, until at last her hostess subsided, with a kind of sob at the finish.

"My dearest friend!" she spat. "I hated her!"

"You did? But you were always together. Wasn't she going to marry Henry?"

"Yes!" Lady Ribbonhat snarled. "Because I thought she had my letter! But *you* had it! You had it all along! Oh, when I think of how she made me grovel and slave for her, and threatened to expose me! I wish she were still alive, that I might have the pleasure of killing her, again!"

In the sudden silence that followed this statement, Lady Ribbonhat turned toward Arabella, with the stricken gaze that is sometimes seen in the eyes of an animal when it realizes that it is about to be slaughtered.

"That is . . . I didn't kill her, you know," she faltered, "though I often wish I had. But precisely speaking, I suppose I may have manipulated certain circumstances to the point where Zhenay's death was facilitated through actions taken by myself to encourage certain developments."

"I am sorry, Lady Ribbonhat," said Arabella. "Your meaning escapes me."

But the dowager's face wore a closed-up look now. She did not offer to elucidate.

Arabella cleared her throat. "I think we are both agreed that the woman is better dead, and I repeat, I have no wish to see you swing for her murder, as you are far too enjoyable an adversary. Therefore, if you will vouchsafe to tell me what really happened, I shall leave this letter with you. Otherwise, I shall read it, turn it over to my lawyers, and instruct them to denounce you publicly as the principal suspect in this case."

Lady Ribbonhat tugged on the bell pull again. "Where the devil is Piston? I shall require some tea if I am to tell the whole story!"

"Piston!" cried Arabella. "Your butler's name is Piston? What is his Christian name? Don't tell me it's Harry, for I shan't believe you!"

"It *is* hairy, as a matter of fact. But his first name is Richard."

All things considered, it was just as well that tea *hadn't* arrived yet, for Arabella would have choked, had she been swallowing. How the deuce would Lady Ribbonhat have such intimate knowledge of her servant's anatomy? How, indeed?

"No, of course," said Arabella, making a fair recovery. "Harry is your footman's name, is it not?"

"What is that to you?" asked the duchess suspiciously. "Piston!" she bellowed.

Arabella opened the door, that her ladyship's voice might

carry farther. The enjoyable adversary got up from her chair and crossed to the threshold.

"*Piston!!*"

"My Lady?"

"We want some tea! Are you deaf, man? I rang the bell some time ago!"

"His Grace told me—"

"I do not care what His Grace told you! Does he pay your wages? I am mistress here! You will do well to remember that!"

The butler bowed, and Lady Ribbonhat slammed the door before he'd straightened up again.

"Many years ago," she said, returning to her chair, "when Henry was a young man, he struck up an unfortunate liaison with a low type of woman, and the connexion seemed quite serious. I was worried. Any mother would have been. The girl was greedy, spiteful, and determined to marry into my family. So, whilst Henry was away, I arranged to have her deported to France. She was English, as it happened, but according to my research, one of her grandparents had been an Alsatian. On that basis, I represented her to the authorities as an undesirable alien."

"When was this?"

"A while ago."

"No, but *when?*"

"Oh, twenty, twenty-five years."

"You sent her to France during the Terror." Arabella had already known this, of course, via her uncle. But she wanted to stress it to Lady Ribbonhat; to make Lady Ribbonhat say it and feel it, because it had been such a horrible thing to do.

"Yes, I suppose so," said the dowager, with a dismissive wave of her hand, "but she survived, and returned after some years, having re-styled herself 'Madame Zhenay.' You know the rest: She set herself up in business and made a fortune, but having already made her fortune in Paris, she might just as well have stayed over there. Paris is cheaper than London, and her money would have gone further. Do you know why she didn't, though? Because she wanted revenge! All those years, she told me, she had dreamt of only two things: Marrying Henry, and making me suffer!

"Well, she nearly got Henry, and she certainly succeeded in making my life a living hell! I was forced to introduce that . . . that . . . commoner into society, to take her with me everywhere I went; to seem as though I doted upon her! And when we were alone, she forced me to be her slave!"

Lady Ribbonhat poured herself a glass of sherry from a decanter with golden lion's paws. But she didn't offer one to her guest. "I'd taken lodgings at the Tiger, so that Zhenay and I could watch Henry's ship come in."

"There is no dock at Eastbourne."

"No," said Lady Ribbonhat, after a pause. "There isn't. But Zhenay didn't know that. She was ignorant of geography; monstrous ignorant. She was ignorant of everything in the world except business. So I knew I could entice her out there with little trouble, and I promised that she and Henry should be married as soon as his ship docked."

"You planned the whole thing in advance, did you? The murder, I mean?"

"I planned it, yes, but my plan was not realized. The night before she died, Zhenay arrived at my rooms very late. She had come down from town in my private carriage, so I knew that no one had seen her all day except for my coachman.

"Your *private* carriage," murmured Arabella. "I did not think of that. We were only checking commercial concerns."

"And Zhenay told me when she came in that no one at the Tiger could be roused to take the horses, so my coachman had dropped her off and driven on to another inn, where he was personally acquainted with the owners.

"Thus far, everything was going better than I had hoped: no one was aware of Zhenay's arrival but me and my coachman. I had two plans in place, in case the first should fail. The first involved poison, and a glass of poisoned claret stood at the ready. But it was essential that she die in bed, and Zhenay was not in the least bit tired. In fact, she was more animated than I had ever known her. I presume she must have taken something to prevent her from sleeping on the way. (The woman took care never to sleep whilst traveling, for fear she should be robbed unawares.)

"As it was then close to dawn, she said she wouldn't go to bed at all, and she bade me get up and dress myself—for I had not brought my maid. Thus, I resolved to implement Plan B. At first light, we walked out to the cliff."

"However did you get her to do that?" asked Arabella. "Even Zhenay must have known there was no harbor in *that* direction."

"I told her I always waved to Henry's ship from there as it sailed past, and that he would be searching us out with his spyglass."

"Good Lord."

"I don't care whether *you* believe it. The fact is, *she* did. The fog was very thick. There was no one about. At least, I did not see anyone. Zhenay complained that we shouldn't be able to see the ship in such weather, but I told her the fog would soon lift. Then I glanced down and said, 'Your shoe ribbon is untied, madam.' It wasn't true, but the woman can't see a thing without her spectacles, and the vain cow refuses to wear them in public. *Used* to refuse, I mean. She was forever misplacing them, too."

"But in any event, Zhenay could not have worn her spectacles that day, even if she had wanted to," said Arabella. "Because you had hidden them."

Lady Ribbonhat jumped as though bitten.

"What do you mean?"

"You *did* hide them, didn't you? Wasn't that part of your plan?"

"How could you possibly have known that?"

"Because you made such a point of telling everyone how Zhenay was always misplacing her spectacles, and how blind she was without them. You did it again, just now. You were planning to suggest her handicap as the probable cause of her accidental death, were you not?"

"What if I was?" cried Lady Ribbonhat. "Wait till you hear the whole story, before you judge me! 'Your shoe ribbon is untied,' I said. And do you know what answer she made me? 'Tie it up then, you hideous old crone!' The confounded impudence! I planned to push her off the cliff as soon as she bent over to do up her shoe. But she was spoiling my plans! She had no intention of bending over, and her personal insult had enraged me to the point of attacking her with my finger-nails, then and there. Fortunately, I—"

"Well, it's high time you got here!" Lady Ribbonhat broke off, as tea was brought in. The steeping process had been effected during the long journey from the kitchen, but now the business of pouring it out, adding the milk and sugar, and stirring it all up required additional time, during which Arabella was feverishly taking mental notes. Her reluctant hostess would never have permitted her to write things down, of course, so the transcribing would have to wait till she got home.

"I did as I was bid," Lady Ribbonhat continued. "I tied Madame's shoe . . . to the other shoe! Then, happening to glance up, I noticed a flock of low-flying gulls headed our way. I warned her, and she attempted to step aside. But the tethered shoes caused her to lurch forward instead, and she fell over the cliff."

Arabella gazed at the duchess in thoughtful speculation. "Were there actually gulls in the vicinity," she asked, "or did you simply invent them?"

"We were at the seacoast!" cried Lady Ribbonhat. "Of *course* there were gulls in the vicinity!"

Her visitor reflected on the coincidence that both Constance's alibi and Lady Ribbonhat's ruse should involve the ubiquitous sea bird.

"Anyway, that is all there was to it," said Lady Ribbonhat. "But no one else was up there, and no one saw us. Of that, I am certain."

"You may be right," said Arabella. "At least, *I* never found any witnesses. You see, you are not the only person to use your imagination in a tight spot."

"Hmm! I thought as much," said the dowager grimly. "I might have known better than to trust you!"

"I feel the same way about trusting you, dear enemy."

"Well. If you've quite finished your tea, I must attend to other matters. My letter, please." The dowager held out an imperious hand.

"But I have *not* finished," said Arabella, taking the envelope from underneath her saucer and holding it back out of reach. "How did this come to be in Zhenay's possession?"

"I refuse to discuss that subject!" said her hostess. "I agreed only to speak with you about the circumstances pertaining to the death of a parasite!"

"Very well," said Arabella, drinking down the last of her tea and handing the letter over. "I would like to both thank you for your help, and offer my congratulations."

"On what cause?"

"Your narrow escape from the gallows."

Chapter 20

For those readers unfamiliar with Rotten Row, the author begs to inform them that there is nothing "rotten" about it. It is a wide bridle path (and for some, I have heard, a *bridal* path) skirting Hyde Park's south side. The path's actual name was "the King's Road," for it was made by order of some monarch or other, and a prevailing fashion for all things French led people to call it *Route du Roi*. But the trouble with fashions is that they don't last long. Before long, England was at war with France again, and some wag coined the nickname "Rotten Row," fancying himself clever, I daresay. But it's really rather feeble, if you think about it.

Anyway, the name caught on, despite everything, and the place *itself* was all the rage, because rich and famous persons, along with the merely well-bred, rode there twice a day in their carriages or on horseback. It was *the* place to show off one's riding habit, or seat on a horse, or new barouche, or simply oneself. Naturally, it was popular with London's courtesans—Arabella simply doted on the place.

"So, what I am going to do," she told Belinda, as they cantered side by side, superbly mounted on two of Arabella's parchment ponies*, "is to instruct counsel to tell the story as it was told to me, as a reasonable hypothesis, omitting all mention of Lady Ribbonhat. Let's walk them for a bit, Bunny."

"Were you finding it hard to talk and canter at the same time?" Belinda asked, once the pace had slackened.

"Somewhat," her sister replied, "but chiefly, I wanted to see who that lady is in Cecil Elliot's curricle . . . hmm, Caroline Lamb. I should have thought he'd have better taste.

"Anyway, Corydon-Figge will posit that Madame Zhenay was alone when, having lost her spectacles (which she was always doing), she mistakenly tied her own shoe ribbons together, whilst wearing the shoes. Then she may have been startled by a gull, tried to step back, started to lose her balance, tried to step forward to prevent herself from falling, and gone over the cliff, where, once in the turbulent sea, her shoes came off and wrapped themselves around her forearm, seaweed fashion. Then the body was borne off to Brighton by the current."

Belinda was horrified. "But that is twisting the truth!" she protested. "Why not say it was Lady Ribbonhat?"

"Bunny, don't be tiresome. It is not 'twisting the truth,' as you call it, to state a hypothesis."

"It is if you know the truth, and withhold it."

"But this *is* the truth, essentially, and I am determined to leave Lady Ribbonhat out of it. Besides, we should never be able to *prove* any of this. The important thing is to win an acquittal. Zhenay was a vicious, vengeful woman, who must not be allowed to claim this last victim from beyond the grave."

"Lady Ribbonhat, do you mean? For she killed Zhenay. The detail about not having pushed her is unimportant."

---

*Namely, Sippet and Miss Ferguson. The former had been named after a kind of crouton of roughly the same color as its hide; the latter for a horse-faced governess the sisters had shared as children.

"I know that. No, I was not referring to Lady Ribbonhat."

"Oh. I suppose you meant Constance."

"Well, Constance, also, but I was mainly referring to myself. And yet, for all Zhenay's wickedness, I freely acknowledge that I am indebted to the woman for one truly excellent idea. Oh, look! It is Egerton, the publisher! Scrope Davies suggested I speak to him with regard to publishing my Palomina adventures!"

"Oh, but not *here*, Bell, surely! Call upon him at his place of business!"

"I suppose you are right."

"Perhaps I should speak with him, also, about publishing my play. Anyway, what is this excellent idea you had from Madame Zhenay?"

"You will hear all about it at the Cyprian Society meeting tomorrow."

"Very well," said Belinda. "But I thought you said the House of Lords would condemn Constance no matter what. Why have you changed your mind?"

"I haven't. I expect her to be acquitted before she ever gets to the House of Lords, by the grand jury, which will hear the evidence in order to determine whether there will even *be* a trial. I don't think there will be, now."

"Good!" said Belinda, with satisfaction. "Because the sooner this is put in motion, the sooner poor Constance can be released from prison!"

"I think 'poor Constance' is better off where she is," said Arabella. "After all, she's quite safe in the Brighton lockup, where Mr. Pollard and our Cyprian sisters are kindly seeing to all her creature comforts."

Belinda was dumbfounded. "But, Bell! Surely you cannot mean to keep her in gaol, when she might be free to come home?"

"Yes, I can," replied her sister. "Constance cannot possibly get into any more trouble as long as she remains behind bars, and the silly chit is perfectly happy where she is. Besides, the woman has turned my life upside down! Can you really blame me, Bunny, for finding myself in need of a breather? At least now I shall be able to sleep soundly, knowing that I won't have to run all over town attending to Constance's problems!"

The Cyprian Society's first general members' meeting was a great success. Unlike gentlemen's clubs, which rarely or never hold meetings, CS members were rather keen on gathering all together and having discussions. Evidently. For with the exception of Constance, who was still in gaol, all of them had come.

The new lecture saloon was roomy, yet intimate, painted robin's egg blue and punctuated with comfortable chairs and intimate little divans. Many of the members had brought their pets with them, chiefly lapdogs, but Polonia Snow had brought a rabbit, and Alouette L'Etoille was accompanied by what she insisted on referring to as *le furet du bois jolie,* a red-eyed, ermine-furred, sharp-fanged little beast, which, despite being attached via a ribbon to the wrist of its owner, nevertheless contrived to escape, and attacked the rabbit. The lapdogs all went wild at this, except for Cara, and the ensuing pandemonium was greater than that produced from construction, by virtue of its closer proximity to the ears of its listeners.

Arabella made a rule right then and there that pets should henceforth be banned from the premises. The other pet owners glared at Miss L'Etoille, who was not really French at all, and whom most of the members presumed was a traitor.

"Have you no sense?" cried Miss Le Marchand. "Whoever heard of bringing a ferret to a meeting? You've spoilt it for the rest of us, now, you and your ferret 'Napoleon'!"

"Her name is 'Neigeux,'" said Miss L'Etoille loftily. And after handing her pet to a servant, to be kept until called for, she ostentatiously moved her chair as far as possible from Miss Le Marchand's.

"Ribbons are such pretty things," said Arabella, addressing her sister. "Yet they have been responsible for nearly two deaths in as many weeks. I think I shall avoid ribbons in the future." But, of course, she did not mean that.

When everyone had settled down once again, soothed with wonderfully strong coffee, which was served in tiny-hand-painted-sky-blue-and-gold-Spode-demitasse-cups-decorated-with-the-double-bird-of-paradise-crest-on-one-side-and-the-CS-motto-on-the-other-and-a-single-bird-of-paradise-inside below-the-rim, along with little sesame biscuits (because luncheon was still two hours away), Arabella formally addressed the gathering. In the interests of brevity, we shall skip over the welcoming speech and agenda items of lesser import, and go straight away to the object of this meeting.

"I don't know whether many of you have considered it," she began, "but, collectively, we have captured the attentions and affections of the most influential men in the most important city of the most powerful nation on Earth."

Here the courtesans would have applauded, but their president checked them with an upraised hand.

"I mention this, not merely as an item of passing interest, nor a detail upon which we may preen ourselves: Consider, ladies, what it actually *means*."

She paused, significantly, and surveyed the company with a bold, challenging look. "The twenty-eight of us—and I say twenty-eight with the tacit understanding that one of our number, who is not here today, is by nature incapable—can, if we choose, bring about the necessary changes to make this country, nay, to make the entire *world* a better place. Let us, then, in the months to come, decide how we can best use our power to promote the greatest good!"

Amidst thunderous applause, with Cyprians rising on every side to cheer Arabella and her great idea, she smiled and modestly made her way to a chair, where a freshly-poured-tiny-hand-painted-sky-blue-and-gold-Spode-demitasse-cup-decorated-with-the-double-bird-of-paradise-crest-on-one-sid e-and-the-CS-motto-on-the-other-and-a-single-bird-of-paradise-inside-below-the-rim awaited her.

By the time the Beaumonts got home, the sunlight had mellowed to a rich apricot, and the shadows had grown to ridiculous lengths. The sisters changed from their club clothes into much more comfortable chemises and dressing gowns, and dined alfresco, in the loggia, where they ate with their fingers. Bumper after bumper of sparkling wine was lifted high . . . laughed over . . . quaffed . . . to celebrate the very successful outcome of all their adventures.

"Bell," said Belinda, sitting sideways in her chair and draping one lovely bare leg over the arm, "aren't you simply aching to know what was in that letter you returned to Lady Ribbonhat?"

"No," Arabella replied, with a smile. "Because I *do* know. And therefore have no need of aching."

"You *do?* How? Did Lady Ribbonhat shew it to you at Charburn?"

"Good heavens," said Arabella, carefully snipping a small cluster of grapes from a larger bunch in the bowl upon the table. "Lady Ribbonhat may be a clown, Belinda, but she's no fool. Unless I miss my guess, she ordered a fire lit the instant I was out the door, and burnt that letter to cinders!"

"Then how can you be familiar with the contents?"

"Well, as you know, Lustings was formerly in the possession of the Seaholme family, to which Lady Ribbonhat belongs by marriage."

"Yes?"

"The duke still uses my library from time to time, to write the sort of letters he does not wish his mother to know about."

"But I still don't . . ."

"He keeps his family seal in a drawer of my desk for that purpose. So, I simply broke the seal on Lady Ribbonhat's envelope, removed the letter and perused the contents, re-folded it, dripped a new puddle of wax on the outside, and stamped it with the family crest again."

"Oh, I say!" cried Belinda. "How *fiendishly* clever! And what did the letter reveal?"

"Only this," replied Arabella gravely. "Lady Ribbonhat provided the financial backing for the prime minister's assassination."

Belinda recoiled, nearly toppling from her chair. "What?! She—how *could* she? And . . . you have known about it all this while . . . and kept it to yourself?"

"Quite. Just as *you* will keep it to *yourself.*"

"Oh, no, Bell," said Belinda, emphatically shaking her head. "We must go to the authorities at once!"

"And tell them what, exactly? That I am the only witness to a letter, now destroyed, that proves my enemy's involvement in the Perceval affair? They would lock me up in the madhouse, but not before the duke and his mother sued me for every penny I have or ever shall have. There is not a single shred of evidence, now, that Lady Ribbonhat has ever done any such thing. And even if there were, I should never act against her on this. Because I respect her reasons."

Belinda stared at her. "What do you mean? No one can have a good reason for murder! I feel as though I have never known you, Bell; that I am only now beginning to see who you really are!"

"Perhaps I expressed myself badly. I don't approve of murder, Bunny, any more than you do. But under certain circumstances, I can sympathize with, or . . . let us say, *comprehend* someone's state of mind, which causes that person to act out of character in a fit of outrage against an evil-doer.

"Lady Ribbonhat expressed her reasons in that letter:

Spencer Perceval's anti-Luddite, anti-Catholic policies had laid waste to her family. Her brother blew his brains out. Her nephews were hanged ("as an example") after the Luddite riots. The wives and children of those nephews scattered in panic over the countryside, and Lady Ribbonhat was unable to discover where they'd gone, in order to send them financial assistance. At the time of her letter, she reported that she had been unable to locate a single relation."

"How horrible!" said Belinda. "I never thought I should feel sorry for Lady Ribbonhat. I do, though."

"As do I."

"This letter she wrote, to whom was it addressed?"

"I did not recognize the name, and I have forgotten it now. Probably some Irish fomenter who had requested her assistance."

"But, Bell; it's important! The government will want to know!"

"I am not so certain that they will. They were in an awful hurry to hang Bellingham and close the book." (She was not going to tell Belinda about Cecil Elliot's investigation, for she had given her word that she wouldn't.) "You see, Bunny? This is why I hate politics! Everything's done below board. No one ever knows what is really going on! And the names of persons who planned the elimination of a smug, superior little second rater, a so-called gentleman who professed himself a great family man whilst he murdered the families of others, is of no interest to me. I am a great respecter of justified revenge. Poor Lady Ribbonhat has no one now, other than Puddles, and I cannot find it in my heart to blame her for having sought vengeance upon a man who was perfectly comfortable with causing such misery."

"I never knew she was Irish," said Belinda thoughtfully.

"And you still don't," said Arabella. "This conversation has not taken place."

The sky was turning lavender now, and a couple of bats

flittered across what promised to be a magnificent summer evening.

"Bunny," said Arabella, "how would you like to sleep in the pergola tonight, and watch the moonrise from the moon window?"

"That sounds heavenly," Belinda replied. "Pun very much intended! But I shouldn't like to be inconsiderate of the servants. It will take hours to set up beds for us in the dark."

"Yes," said Arabella. "I suppose you're right. That's why I took the precaution of ordering the pergola beds this morning . . ."

Belinda gave a squeal of delight.

". . . And seeing that we are already in our night things, I suggest we repair to the garden forthwith."

A short time later, the sisters were snuggled into their cots and gazing, with the dreamy introspection that comes only from still summer nights and too much wine, at the cosmos.

"Wouldn't it be wonderful to remain awake all night, and watch the stars wink out, one after another, when dawn steals across the heavens?"

"Yes! Let's do that," said Belinda.

"Oh, no; I didn't mean tonight. I have a very busy day tomorrow."

"Really? Now that you're assured of your money, I should think you would want to amuse yourself!"

"That is exactly what I intend to do," said Arabella. "I am having breakfast with Garth. Elliot is coming for dinner in the afternoon and then I'm going out to a late supper with the duke, just like the sphinx."

Realizing that her sister was indulging in artistic metaphor again, Belinda decided to needle her a little.

"You're so learned, Bell," she said. "I never knew that the sphinx had even met those gentlemen."

Arabella was unperturbed.

"I shall begin my day with the fiery passion of youth, then

progress, in the afternoon, to experience and finesse, and finally end with comfort and security," she said. "Thus, I shall experience all the phases of adult life in a single day!"

"Four legs, two legs, three legs? But, surely . . ."

"I wasn't being literal, Bunny. Garth is somewhat younger than I, Mr. Elliot is roughly my own age, and the duke is somewhat older. Three generations, more or less; each with its own advantages. That is all I meant."

"I see," Belinda said, smiling in the darkness. "The sphinx metaphor doesn't quite apply, then, does it? Because they've *all* got three legs."

"Yes, indeed!" said Arabella happily. "Especially Garth."

GLOSSARY

A–E

arsy-varsey: arse over ears. To tumble backward.

chuffed: flattered

cove: a man

crack salesman: a pimp, or brothel keeper

dolly shop: pawnbroker's

F–J

fart catcher: a footman

four-legged frolic: sexual intercourse

gasser: a humorous situation

give the crows a pudding: to have crows feasting on one's corpse

gnarler: a snarling lap dog

goggles: eyes

hide the bone: sexual intercourse

K–O

Marshalsea, the: a private prison, run for profit, containing mostly debtors

mattress jig: sexual intercourse

moon-eyed hen: a woman with a squint

morris off: leave

mort: a woman

muffin man: a pimp

nanny house: a brothel

P–T

peckish: hungry

pugilist: boxer

rhino: money

round heels: one who is easily tipped over onto her back

row: fight

shit sack: a dastardly fellow

sprats: children

stale: a prostitute

tinsel weeks: the first few weeks of a honeymoon

THE CYPRIAN SOCIETY
CLUB ROSTER

The twenty-nine members include:

1. **Almond, Idina**—A small, pointed chin, unruly curls, and enormous eyes. A regular kitten.

2. **Beaumont, Arabella**—You already know her, of course, but what you don't know is that, since there are so many members by that name, *our* Arabella is going to elect, for club purposes, to be known as "Thetis."

3. **Beaumont, Belinda**—When she hears that her sister will be taking a more exotic name, Belinda will decide to have one, too. Because two siblings named Thetis and Belinda seems ridiculous. Belinda's club name will be "Semele."

4. Birdwood, Cecily—Her miniature portraits would never have brought in much income on their own. But people found it thrilling to have their portraits painted, and be able to say, "It was done by a courtesan," which resulted in a windfall for the artist.

5. **Carnac, Kitty**—Plump, sweet, and delectable. A kind of blond version of Belinda.

6. **Chandler, Rosabel**—A redhead, famous for her eccentric habit of fashioning jewelry out of food.

7. **Cobb, Victorine**—Possessed of such a lovely face that she might have married a sovereign, had she had a fortune to go with it. As it was, her face earned the fortune for her.

8. **Denbigh, Louisa**—She had a most fetching gap between her front teeth. And you know what they say about gap-toothed women.

9. **Desta, Feben**—Style. My God, she had style! This woman not only knew how to dress, but how to set a table, throw a party, drive through town, behave in public when encountering an enemy. Arabella was quite envious of her.

10. **Entwistle, Isabella**—A terrifying, icy blonde, known in some circles as the Viking Princess, Isabella was born without emotions. But this stood her in good stead when it came to negotiating, passing judgments, or dealing with the suddenly dead.

11. **Farrell, Olympia**—A voice like an angel's, speaking and singing. An accomplished musician, too. She was one of those people who could pick up any instrument and play as though she'd been practicing for years.

12. **Fortescue, Amber**—First cousin to Arabella and Belinda Beaumont.

13. **Fortescue, Claire**—Amber's sister.

14. **Fortescue, Ivy**—Amber's other sister.

The Fortescues must be credited with saving their Beaumont cousins from starvation after Charles lost the house, but they are also responsible for Arabella and Belinda's entry into a life of shame and ignominy. Judge them how you will. (Perhaps it should be mentioned that Ivy cheated Arabella out of the price of her maidenhead, promising her fifty percent and giving her ten pounds when Ivy had actually charged the customer one hundred pounds. But that is all water under the bridge. Probably.

15. **Fox, Arabella**—Like her name, red-haired and sly. Also a fabulous storyteller—could keep a roomful of people enthralled for hours.

16. **Golder-Green, Amy**—Dressed, acted, rode, shot, fenced, climbed, threw, and ran like a man, but looked, smelt, and tasted exactly like a woman.

17. **Grant, Frances**—Wonderfully observant. Wrote for the newspapers under the initials "F.G."

18. **Hearn, Philomela**—Six feet tall, and fond of fancy dress. But like Thetis, she was always recognized, no matter what disguise she attempted.

19. Imbrey, Arabella—Unbelievable stamina. When not working, she loved best to walk, and was rumored to have trudged the length of Britain four times.

20. **Laithwaite, Dido (aka the Clap Trap)**—Her nickname was undeserved. The man who gave it to her—both the nickname, and the reason for it—had also enjoyed the favors of his wife on the same evening. It was actually *she* who had given him the pox. Dido, fortunately,

escaped infection. Nevertheless, the nickname followed her everywhere. Eventually, she got used to it.

21. **Le Marchand, Marguerite**—A handsome Jewess. Sharp-tongued, shrewd at business, and extremely amusing company.

22. **L'Etoille, Alouette**—From Bigasse, France. And the reader can well imagine the jests that were made of *that*. Her Frenchness was suspect. She frequently forgot to have an accent, and didn't know the meaning of many French words and phrases. She looked French, though.

23. **Moon, Fanny**—Sweet-faced, kindhearted, self-effacing, and loyal. If one didn't know better, one would have taken her for an upstanding, decent young woman.

24. **Savory, Pearl**—Tiny—only four feet, eleven inches! Her hair was so long she could sit upon it, although Marguerite observed that if Philomela had Pearl's hair, it would barely reach her shoulders.

25. **Snow, Polonia**—She had the whitest of white skin, with the blackest of black hair, and red lips. Like the fairy-tale princess, without the dwarf entourage.

26. **Terhune, Arabella**—A keen legal mind. Had she been a man, she would have given legendary barrister Henry Brougham a run for his money. As things stood, she gave him something quite different.

27. **Tilden, May**—A buxom brunette whose large, cowlike eyes had a bovine expression, even when closed. Men

obsessed with their own mothers found her fatally attractive.

28. **Twist, Calypso**—This was not her real name. It *couldn't* have been!

29. **Worthington, Constance**—Should be familiar enough to readers by now to require no introduction. Besides, were I to give her one, it could not help but be uncomplimentary.